THE DAUGHTER'S TALE

Also by Armando Lucas Correa
The German Girl

THE
DAUGHTER'S
TALE

A NOVEL

ARMANDO LUCAS
CORREA

Translated by Nick Caistor

ATRIA BOOKS

New York   London   Toronto   Sydney   New Delhi

ATRIA
BOOKS

An Imprint of Simon & Schuster, Inc.
1230 Avenue of the Americas
New York, NY 10020

ATRIA BOOKS and colophon are trademarks of Simon & Schuster, Inc.

Manufactured in the United States of America

ISBN 978-1-5011-8793-3

To Judith, the lost girl on the Saint Louis.

To my mother, my first reader.

To my children, Emma, Anna, and Lucas, yet again.

To Gonzalo, always.

Contents

The goal is oblivion. I have arrived first.

—JORGE LUIS BORGES

ONE

The Visit

New York, April 2015

1

"*I*s this Ms. Duval? Elise Duval?" The voice on the phone repeated her name while she remained silent. "We were in Cuba recently. My daughter and I have some letters in German that belong to you."

Elise had always been able to foresee the future. But not today. Today, she could never have predicted.

For an instant, she thought the call must be a mistake. After all, she was French, and had been living in New York for the last seventy years, ever since an uncle on her mother's side had adopted her at the end of the war. Now, her only living relatives were her daughter, Adele, and her grandson, Etienne. They were her entire world, and everything that came before was shrouded in darkness.

"Ms. Duval?" the woman's voice said again, gentle but insistent. Fraught with terror, Elise groped for some support, afraid she might faint.

"You can come see me this afternoon," was all she managed to say before hanging up, neglecting to check first whether she had any appointments, or if she should consult her daughter. She heard the woman's name,

Ida Rosen, and her daughter's, Anna, but her memory was a blank, closed to the past. She was certain only that she had no wish to verify the credentials of the stranger and her daughter. There was no need to give them her address, because they already had it. The call had not been a mistake. That much she knew.

Elise spent the next few hours trying to imagine what might lie behind their brief conversation. *Rosen*, she repeated to herself as she searched among the dim shadows of those who had crossed the Atlantic with her after the war.

Only a few hours had passed, and already the call was beginning to fade in her limited, selective memory. "There's no time to remember," she used to tell her husband, then her daughter, and now her grandson.

She felt vaguely guilty at having agreed so readily to receive this stranger. She should have asked who had written the letters, why they had ended up in Cuba, what Mrs. Rosen and her daughter were doing there. Instead, she had said nothing.

When the doorbell finally rang, her heart leapt out of her chest. She tried to shut her eyes and prepare herself, taking a deep breath and counting the heartbeats: one, two, three, four, five, six—a trick learned from childhood, one of her only clear memories. She had no idea how long she had spent in her bedroom, dressed in her navy-blue suit, waiting.

It was as if her senses had suddenly been heightened at the sound of the bell. Her hearing became sharper. Now, she could just make out the breathing of the two strangers outside the door waiting to see a weary old widow. But why? She paused with her hand on the lock, hoping against hope this visit was no more than an illusion, something she had dreamed, one of the many crazy notions brought on by the years. She closed her eyes and tried to visualize what would happen, but nothing came.

It was becoming clear to Elise that this meeting wasn't about the future. Instead, it signified the return of a past she could no longer keep out, a constant shadow ever since the day she had disembarked in the port of New York, when the hand of an uncle who was to become a father rescued her from her oblivion. But he could never bring back her memories, removed by necessity, for the sake of her survival.

She opened the door resolutely. A shaft of light blinded her. The noise of the elevator, a neighbor going downstairs, a dog barking, and the wail of an ambulance siren distracted her for a second. The woman's smile brought her back to reality.

Elise motioned for them to come in. Without yet saying a word, she avoided making the slightest gesture that might betray her terror. The girl, Anna, who looked to be twelve years old, came over and hugged her round the waist. She had no idea how to respond. Maybe she should have let her hands drop onto the little girl's shoulders, or stroked her hair the way she used to do when her own daughter was the same age.

"You've got blue eyes," she said timidly.

What a ridiculous thing to say! I should have said she had beautiful *eyes,* thought Elise, trying not to notice that they were the same blue, almond-shaped, and hooded eyes as hers, that her profile . . . *No,* she told herself fearfully, because it was her own reflection she saw in the face of this strange little girl.

Making an effort, Elise led the pair of them into the living room. Just as she was asking them to sit down, Anna handed her a small, lusterless, ebony box.

Elise carefully opened the box. By the time she finished unfolding the first letter, written in faded ink on a page from a botanical album, her eyes were brimming with tears.

"Does this belong to me?" she whispered, clasping the crucifix around her neck, a charm that had accompanied her ever since she could remember.

"Your eyes," she repeated, staring at Anna with anguish.

Elise tried to stand up, but could feel her heart failing her. She was losing control over herself, over the life she had so carefully constructed. She could see her own face at a distance, staring at the scene from afar like another witness in the room.

Her palms grew sweaty, the box fell from her grasp, the letters spilling out onto the carpet. A photograph of a family with two little girls with a frightened gaze lay buried among yellowing sheets of paper. Elise saw herself closing her eyes and a stabbing pain in her chest took away her balance. Collapsing onto the faded carpet, she knew it was happening, at last: the final act of forgetting.

Silence, walls of silence all around her. She tried to recall how many times a heart could stop and then start beating again. One . . . silence. Two . . . another, even longer pause. Three . . . the void. The silence between one heartbeat and the next cut her off from the world. She wanted to hear one more. Four. And another. She breathed in as deeply as she could. Five . . . just one more and she would be safe. Silence. Six!

"Elise!" The shout made her stir. "Elise!"

That name, that name. Elise. It wasn't her, for she was no one. She did not exist, she had never existed. She had lived a life that didn't belong to her, had created a family she had deceived, spoke a language that wasn't hers. All these years spent fleeing from who she truly was. To what end? She was a survivor, and that was not a mistake, nor a misunderstanding.

By the time the paramedics lifted her onto the gurney, she had already forgotten the other woman and her blue-eyed daughter, forgotten the letters written in a strange language, the photograph.

But in the space of forgetting, a memory emerged. Herself, as a little girl, trying to find her way through a thick forest, surrounded by enormous trees that prevented her from seeing the sky. How could she know where she was going, if she couldn't see the stars? Blood on her cheek, hands, her dress, but not hers. A body lying lifeless on the ground in a gory mess. No helping hand to support her. She could feel the thick, damp air, hear her childish voice stammer: "Mama! Mama!" She was lost, abandoned in the darkness.

In the fog of jumbled memories, she saw it all: the letters, the ebony box, the purple jewel case, a threadbare soccer ball, a wounded soldier. Withered flowers and blurred lines.

It had taken this little girl, Anna, for Elise to discover who she really was, stripping off the mask she had been wearing for seven decades. The past was now rewarding her with this final, unexpected visit, with the image of handwriting on the pages of a familiar book, a book not important because of what it said, but for the hours she had spent tracing the letters and flowers that had been with her every day of her childhood.

"*Hydrocharis morsus-ranae*," she whispered.

She felt herself floating freely like one of those aquatic plants, its flowers tinged with yellow. She was delirious, but if she could remember, that meant she was still alive. It was time to allow herself to die, but first she had to do something with the pages torn from the mutilated book.

Yet the damage was done; she had no right to ask for forgiveness. She shut her eyes and counted her heartbeats. The silences between them helped drive away the fear. *Who had taught her to do that?*

"Ready!" she heard.

She felt a weight on her crushed chest. The first electric shock produced palpitations of a kind she had never experienced. She told herself she wasn't going to let them revive her. She didn't want to live. As a child, she had been put on an enormous ocean liner, and had never dared to look back. She wasn't going to look back now.

The second shock brought new warmth, forced her to open her eyes. Tears began to flow, beyond her control. She couldn't tell if she was alive or not, and that made her weep. Someone took her by the hand and gently stroked her brow.

"Mama!" She heard her daughter's tearful voice. She was so close that Elise could not distinguish her features.

Would she be able to find the words to explain to Adele, her only daughter, that she had brought her up with a lie?

"Elise, how do you feel? I'm so sorry . . ." Ida was there as well, clearly distressed by the effect of her visit.

Adele stood silent. She couldn't understand what this stranger and her daughter were doing here in the hospital with her mother, a dying old woman.

In a language she no longer recognized, Elise heard herself muttering a phrase that came from somewhere beyond: "*Mama, verlass mich nicht.*" *Don't leave me.*

One . . . silence, two . . . silence, three . . . silence, four, five . . . She took a deep breath, waiting for the next heartbeat.

My little Viera,

 It's only been a few hours, but your mama misses you terribly. The hours are days, weeks, months to me, but I take comfort in knowing that you will still hear me at night, your nights, which for me are early mornings, when I sing in your ear and read you the pages of your favorite botanical album.

 You are like those flowers that have to learn to survive on an island, in damp earth and with a scorching sun. You need light to thrive, and there will be plenty of that over there. It will be piercing, but don't be afraid of it, because I'm sure you will grow and become stronger all the time.

 Your sister misses you. When we go to bed, she asks me to tell her stories about you and those happy days when we were a family. Be strong, stay in the sunshine and grow, so that when we meet again, because we will meet again, you can run to us and hug us, just like we did in the port at the foot of that enormous ship.

 My Viera, remember that your mother, although so far away, is watching over you. When you're afraid, count your heartbeats to calm down, the way Papa taught you to do. Your sister is an expert at that as well now. Remember, at first they are rapid, but as soon as you start to number them, you'll discover the silence between each one. Fear goes away as the space between them grows. Don't forget that, little one.

Every Friday, light two candles, close your eyes, and think of us. We are with you.

All my love,
Mama

TWO

The Escape

Berlin, 1933–1939

2

$\mathscr{A}$manda Sternberg had always been terrified that she'd meet her end by fire, so somehow it wasn't all that surprising to her that her books would soon meet the same fate.

The student union had already left her a warning pamphlet with their *Twelve Theses* at her small bookshop in Charlottenburg, and so she had to begin the cleanup, from the front window to the deepest recesses of the storage room. She was supposed to get rid of all books that could be considered offensive, unpatriotic, or not sufficiently German. This parody of Luther's theses was intended to eliminate all Jewishness from the printed universe, and had reached every book owner in the country. Amanda was certain that only a small number of her volumes would survive. She had spent so many years among parchments, manuscripts, volumes with calfskin covers and hand-drawn illustrations, tales of duels, furtive lovers, diabolical pacts, deranged madmen. They constituted her own past and that of her family, her father's love, the art of ancient scribes: all of it would now be reduced to ashes. *A truly Wagnerian act of purification*, she told herself.

She still clung to the desperate hope that a storefront with the sign GARDEN OF LETTERS might escape notice. If she showed German purity in the window display, and hid the books she loved most in the back room, perhaps they would leave her in peace. The clouds too were on her side: several weeks of rain had slowed down the advance of the bonfires.

Despite her shred of hope, she could not put her family at risk and so had decided finally to begin the cruel task. But first she lay down beside one of the bookcases, resting her head against the warm floorboards. Gazing up at the cobwebbed ceiling, she allowed her mind to drift among the cracks and damp patches above, each with its tale to tell, like the volumes of a book. Who had brought it, why they acquired it, how hard it had been for the shipment to be accepted in that city obsessed with judging every idea, every metaphor, every simile, and the need to find one culprit to toss into the fire in the middle of a plaza trembling with applause and cantatas. In the infinite bonfire she foresaw, not a single book would survive, because in even the most German, the most nationalist, the purest of them, countless ambiguities could be found. She knew well that no matter how the author fashions his characters, no matter which words he chooses, it is always the reader who holds the power of interpretation. "In the end, the scent of books, even of autumn, depends on our sense of smell," she murmured to herself, trying to swim among possible solutions, none of which proved to be viable.

She sighed and placed her hands on her abdomen, which would soon begin to swell. The tinkle of the door-chime roused her from her lethargy. Tilting her head backward, she recognized the silhouette: only Julius came into the bookshop at this time of day.

The man knelt behind her resting head. His large, warm hands covered her ears as he kissed her first on the forehead, then on the tip of her nose, and finally on her warm lips. She was always overjoyed at the sight of Julius crossing the threshold of the store in his charcoal gray overcoat, cracked leather briefcase in hand.

"How have my darlings been?" came Julius Sternberg's deep gentle voice. "What were you dreaming of?"

Amanda wanted to tell him she was fantasizing about her shop swarming with customers eager to buy the latest books, about a city without soldiers, with only the distant rumble of automobiles and streetcars, but he spoke again before she could say anything.

"We're running out of time," he said. "You have to get rid of the books."

His tone made her shudder, and she responded with pleading eyes.

"Let's go upstairs, now, darling. Your baby and I are hungry," was all he said.

⌒⌒

Their living room was a kind of garden bordered by a wall of literature. Brocade curtains with floral patterns, tapestries showing bucolic scenes, carpets as thick as newly mown grass, and every spare surface occupied by books.

Over dinner, Amanda made polite conversation so that Julius wouldn't return to the most pressing topic. She told him she had sold an encyclopedia, that someone had ordered a collection of Greek classics, that Fräulein Hilde Krahmer, her favorite customer, had not been by the bookstore for a week now, whereas previously she would come after teaching her classes and spend hours browsing the shelves, without ever buying anything.

"First thing tomorrow, clear out the shopwindow," Julius demanded. When he saw how his stern voice made Amanda recoil, he went over and pulled her to him for an instant. He leaned his head against her chest and breathed in the perfume of his wife's freshly washed hair.

"Don't you get tired of listening to hearts?" asked Amanda with a smile.

Gesturing for her to be silent, Julius knelt down to put his ear to her stomach and replied, "I can hear hers too. We'll have a daughter, I'm sure of it, with a heart as beautiful as her mother's."

Since his schooldays in Leipzig, Julius had been fascinated by the heart—its irregular rhythms, its electrical impulses, its alternating beats and silences. "There's nothing stronger," he told her when they were newlyweds and he was still at the university, always adding the caveat: "The heart can resist all kinds of physical trauma, but sadness can destroy it in a second. So no sadness in this house!"

They waited until he had his practice established before having their first child. Amanda would go with him to his office to try out the electrocardiogram recently acquired during a trip to Paris. It was a great novelty in Charlottenburg, and looked to Amanda like a complicated version of the Singer sewing machine that she kept in the attic.

That night in bed, buoyed by the thought of his daughter growing inside Amanda, Julius enthusiastically described to her the phases of the heartbeat. "A heart in diastole," he explained to her as she lay in his arms, "is resting." He went on, and bewildered by his terminology, Amanda soon fell asleep on the chest of the man who had been protecting her and her baby from the horror brewing among their neighbors, the city, the whole country, and apparently the entire continent. She knew he was taking good care of her heart, and that was enough to make her feel safe.

She woke with a start in the middle of the night, and tiptoed out of the room without switching on the light so as not to rouse Julius. A strange feeling led her down to one of the shelves in the back room where the books not for sale were stored.

The shelf was piled high with books by the Russian poet Mayakovsky, the favorite of her brother Abraham, who had left Germany several years earlier for a Caribbean island. There too, with their worn spines, were the storybooks her father had once read to her at bedtime. She paused to consider which she would choose if she could save only one. It didn't take her long: she would protect the French botanical album with its hand-painted illustrations of exotic plants and flowers that her father had brought back from a work trip to the colonies. Picking up the volume whose unique scent reminded her of her father, she observed how the pages were yellowing and how the ink on some of the drawings was fading. She could still recall the exact names of the plants in both Latin and French, because before she fell asleep her father used to speak of them as if they were souls abandoned in distant lands.

Opening a page at random, she paused to look at *Chrysanthemum carinatum*. She closed her eyes and could hear her father's resonant voice describing that *plant originally from Africa, tricolor, with yellow ligules at the base and flower heads so long they filled you with emotion*.

She took the book back up to her bedroom and placed it under her pillow. Only when she had done so was she able to sleep peacefully.

The next morning, Julius woke her with a kiss on the cheek. The aroma of cedar and musk from his shaving cream brought back memories of their honeymoon in the Mediterranean. She hugged him to keep him with her, burying her head against his long, muscular neck, and whispering, "You were right. It's going to be a girl. I dreamed it. And we'll call her Viera."

"Welcome, Viera Sternberg," Julius replied, wrapping Amanda in his powerful arms.

A few minutes later, she ran to the window to wave goodbye and saw he was already at the street corner, surrounded by a gang of youngsters wearing swastika armbands.

But Amanda wasn't worried. She knew that nothing intimidated Julius. No blow or shout, much less an insult. He looked back before turning the corner, and smiled up at her. That was enough. Amanda was ready now to sift through the shelves, having already chosen the book she would save from the bonfire.

∽∾

When she went downstairs to open the front door to the Garden of Letters, Frau Strasser was already standing in the doorway like a brick wall. Amanda didn't know if this impression resulted from the heavy suit she was wearing—a kind of belted military uniform that was the new fashion in a city where femininity and elegance were frowned upon—or because of her threatening demeanor. Frau Strasser was now part of an army of women pretending to be soldiers, although they had never actually been called to arms.

"I am not going to permit noxious books to be sold right under my nose," she thundered. "You were lucky with all that rain, but your grace period is over."

It was true. In May, Amanda's store had survived the burning of more than twenty thousand books in Opernplatz, dragged like corpses on wheelbarrows by spellbound university students who imagined their futures would be made by feeding the biggest bonfire ever seen in Berlin.

That dark evening of May 10, 1933, they had all heard on the radio the speech that would seal the future of what until that moment had been their country: "The era of extreme Jewish intellectualism has come to an end, and the German revolution has again opened the way for the true essence of being German."

How can a country survive without poets and thinkers? Amanda had wondered as she sat lost in thought next to Julius. The radio began broadcasting the youth anthem of the National Socialists boasting of a new era.

Although the rainy days of late spring had prevented them from continuing with their book burnings around the city, now they were ready to renew their efforts and Amanda's collection would not be spared.

Frau Strasser was still standing on the threshold, but Amanda was not intimidated. She stroked her stomach, determined not to let this burly neighbor with her military fantasies ruin her happiness. *I'm going to be a mother*, she told herself under her breath, but Frau Strasser remained there, arms folded, defiant. Observing her more closely, Amanda thought that the only thing human about her were her eyes.

Beyond her harsh exterior, it was evident from her garb that she was not one of the chosen ones: she merely represented the power of the masses, not that of the elite. An elite to which she doubtless paid homage with unfettered adoration and submission.

After holding Amanda's gaze for a few moments, Frau Strasser strode off in silence. Amanda knew that the next time she appeared she would be escorted by members of the National Socialist youth. She was plotting something.

Amanda stood by the shelf in the store window ready to make her verdict, feeling like a mother casting her children into oblivion. The barbarians were destroying centuries of civilization, attacking reason in the name of a supposed ideal of order, for what they claimed was perfection. She was unable to hold back the tears as she recalled her father organizing books by subject, running his hands along their spines, blowing the dust off their tops. She summoned up the scents of ink and glue, of almond and vanilla, of the dry, cracked leather of the antique books. And she could hear her father describing how the paper crumbled, the volatile substances it gave off, about cellulose and lignin, acid hydrolysis.

She tried her best to avoid the names she had to confront. *Why some and not others?* She began with Zweig, went on to Freud, London, Hemingway, Lewis, Keller, Remarque, Hugo, Dostoevsky, Brecht, Dreiser, Werfel, Brod, Joyce, and Heine, her father's favorite poet. She was unable to hold back the tears, as if they could save her from the misfortune of being her own pathetic censor. She began throwing books onto the floor, preparing them for the worst.

The door-chime rang and a freckle-faced university student with rosy cheeks entered. His appearance looked so cheerful, it even made his crisp brown uniform seem friendly. Though she knew better, she nodded at him as if he were a frequent visitor, someone who spent hours browsing through book covers, illustrations, and texts.

"Where is the owner?" he asked, stressing each syllable as if to insist on his power and overcome the impression of his small stature.

Amanda remained coolheaded. Smiling, she explained that she was the only one there, that if he wanted to see a man he would have to wait for her husband.

"You have today to clear all that garbage from the shelves!" the young man barked, then left the store, slamming the door to intimidate her further, and saying under his breath "Filthy worms."

What was the point of her selecting books if they had already made up their minds? The moment had come to allow her Garden of Letters to wither and die. There was nothing she could do: her bookstore would be abandoned to the mercy of the executioners.

The sun was at the zenith when she left the bookshelves behind, locked up the store, and made her way across a neighborhood that she already had trouble recognizing. *Today is the summer solstice, the longest day of the year,* she thought. *Summer is about to start.*

❧

As she walked along, she noticed her neighbors avoiding one another. Everyone seemed to be surreptitiously whispering and eavesdropping. The chaos of doubt was gripping the German capital: it was safer to listen, for speaking carried risks. From house to house, window to window, the news on the radio, those harangues in praise of purity, had become the city's daily soundtrack: "Germany for the Germans."

Am I not German, too? she wanted to ask.

Eventually she found herself in Fasanenstrasse. Realizing she was close to the synagogue, she crossed to the opposite side of the street. On the next corner, she was surprised to see dahlias outside a flower shop. She rejoiced in this shock of color amid the gray, drab city that had become devoid of life.

She went inside and asked for the flowers with the most blooms, deciding to take them to her husband's office and surprise him. The florist, a stooped woman with hands like claws, began to prepare the bouquet.

"I only want ones in different shades of pink," Amanda interrupted her.

"They're all the same. They're red dahlias," the florist grumbled. "What's the matter with you? Are you blind? If you don't like the way I'm doing this, you can do it yourself!"

After selecting a few French, Persian, and Mexican pink dahlias, Amanda quickly paid the florist and left the store. Cradling her bouquet, she left Sybelstrasse and walked down the busy Kurfürstendamm, and then went to Pariser Strasse, which would take her to Julius's office. With every minute the colors of the dahlias became more intense. The vulnerable pink hues defended themselves from the hurtful atmosphere.

Although she was tempted to lose herself in the dahlias' frail beauty or in the faces of the children she passed, Amanda was shaken back to reality by the realization that she and her husband were the only ones who hadn't yet fled. Her cousins were in Poland. Her parents were dead, and so were his. What was left for them here?

She and Julius had friends in France: they could get secure safe passage and leave everything behind, starting afresh in Paris or some small town. Her husband even had patients who only needed to be asked in order to recommend them at the Office for Palestine on Meinekestrasse. But Julius felt he could not abandon his cardiac patients. Nowadays, they arrived for their appointments with a swastika in their lapel or on an armband. Julius turned a blind eye to these symbols that tormented Amanda so much.

"Nothing has changed," he would tell her. "They're still my patients. I see only their hearts, I don't read their minds."

When Amanda entered the office, Fräulein Zimmer looked up from behind the giant mahogany desk stacked with thick medical files. Her expression was far from welcoming, for she knew that whenever Amanda interrupted the doctor with one of her surprise visits, he would cancel his appointments or postpone those that weren't urgent.

Amanda sat in the gloomy waiting room as close as possible to the office door, hoping it would open at any moment. First she heard voices and laughter; then out came a tall, gray-haired man in a dark brown suit with a swastika glinting in his lapel. As he entered the room, he noticed Amanda, who rose to her feet. He stared at her as though wondering why a beautiful young German woman would be in need of a heart consultation.

Whenever she felt she was being examined in this way, Amanda lowered her eyes, in a gesture that some might have interpreted as submission. Following behind this imposing man was a youngster in his image, with the same blunt features: widely spaced eyes, snub-nosed, thick eyebrows, and almost nonexistent lips. His suit hung so loose on him it was impossible to tell if there were muscles or merely bones beneath the huge shoulder pads. His eyes looked as if they were about to pop out of their sockets, and his lips were a sickly purple.

When Julius saw her, he stepped past them, gave her a kiss, and put his arm around her.

"Your wife?" asked the stocky old man with an air of surprise. "She doesn't seem . . ." His voice trailed off.

The younger man fixed his eyes on her with an expression that seemed to say, *Why me, and not her?* He belonged to a superior race; she was trying to hide behind an Aryan facade, but was obviously only an inferior, contemptible being. Why did he have to be the one, just when the nation most needed him, who had a heart so weak it could not even pump enough blood for him to breathe properly?

Father and son departed hastily, bidding goodbye to Fräulein Zimmer.

As soon as Amanda left the office on Julius's arm, she felt invincible. The two of them were together; they needed nothing more. Julius gazed at her and she smiled. *What would my life be without you?* he thought. They made their way to Olivaer Platz in silence and sought refuge on a terrace overlooking the trees in the park, waiting for the sun to set. Julius ordered wine and something to eat.

"Today is the longest day of the year," Amanda told him.

Life was going well for them. They were soon to be parents, and his medical practice was growing. Although the year had turned ominous with the rise of National Socialism, they had no thought of leaving behind everything they had built up. *Why flee and start all over again?* Julius thought. *Where to?*

They set out for home before having coffee, just as the sun was setting. Amanda's steps slowed as they drew near, as if she was reluctant to arrive. *Let's take longer, let's stay here, stop,* she wanted to say. Julius fell in step with her silently, sensing what was troubling his wife. Gangs of youths were running in all directions in the encroaching gloom; no soldiers or police were anywhere to be seen.

Turning the corner, they spotted a disturbance outside the Garden of Letters. From afar, they could see Frau Strasser surrounded by neighbors and curious onlookers. Students came hurtling toward them pushing wheelbarrows overflowing with books. They were singing some kind of anthem, but Amanda couldn't catch the words.

She saw her favorite customer, Fräulein Hilde Krahmer, running toward her.

"Hilde!" she cried out when she was a few feet away, her voice cracking. Julius squeezed his wife's hand hard, as though begging her not to let fear engulf her.

The young woman, with cropped chestnut hair and a white blouse buttoned up to the neck, rushed up to them.

"They smashed the door in and took away all the books," Hilde shouted.

All of them. Amanda's only hope was that her most precious volume, the one that woke her from her dreams to go and save it, was still under her pillow. Hilde was still talking nervously, obviously distraught.

"I thought that after the big bonfire in May, the students would have calmed down, but instead . . . What has become of us, Amanda?"

When Amanda saw the orange glow emerge from behind Hilde, she knew this was the sign. A part of her life was going to perish in the flames together with those books.

As the three of them approached the Garden of Letters, they saw

Frau Strasser standing outside with what looked like a hoe in her hand. She seemed pleased at having fulfilled her mission.

There were only a few young people watching the blaze. They were the sole onlookers; no one else seemed interested. Amanda wanted to scream, but instead she closed her eyes as she breathed in the smoky air, picturing all the leather, the paper, the glue succumbing to the heat of the fire. Tears streamed down Hilde's cheeks and Julius's eyes bore a dark gleam of sadness. Amanda's face, however, was now frozen in a strange smile.

"They're only burning paper. The books are still here," she said, raising her first finger to her temple, all her anguish captured in a gesture. "If they really want them to disappear, they will have to burn all of us," she declared. "Do they think they can incinerate everything I learned from my father? They can never do that, Hilde. My father's voice will always be with me . . ."

She was unable to continue.

"There are still some good Germans left," Hilde said, trying to console her.

"I'm German too. This is my country, no matter what they say."

"A poet predicted this a century ago: 'Where they burn books, they will also end up burning people.' The chancellor has hypnotized everyone, especially the young people, who act on impulse."

In her dreams, Amanda had already seen the bonfire. The flames reached right up to the clouds; the pile of books was higher than any building in Opernplatz. In the real world, it was no more than twenty or so students emboldened by their swastikas and the National Socialist youth anthem, taking revenge on a handful of books. There would be others, she knew. This was just the beginning.

There was nothing more they could do. As she said good night and hugged Hilde, Amanda sensed that a long, close friendship would unite them. Together they would recite phrases from their favorite authors in secret, and in doing so, keep them alive. She took Julius's hand as they climbed the stairs to their apartment. They had survived the bonfire, at least this time, and Amanda had the satisfaction of having saved at least one book from the flames. It would remain with her until the day of her death.

"Let's count the days until winter," she murmured as they climbed the stairs back to their apartment. "When our daughter will be born."

"But it's only June, my darling," Julius pointed out serenely. "We've a long way to go."

3

*V*iera Sternberg was born one cold morning in January 1934. She arrived at the dawn of a new year, with the first rays of sunshine struggling to pierce the thick Berlin clouds, heavy with snow and icy rain.

Winter was Amanda's favorite season. During the months when the days were short, the calm of rainy evenings soothed her troubled mind. She took refuge in watching over her tiny daughter, who soon began following Amanda with her eyes when she heard her voice.

Amanda often read to the baby in French or Latin, from the botanical album she had saved from the bonfire. Viera would fall asleep lulled by languages that little by little became familiar sounds to her.

"Your grandfather adored Bourbon roses. You had to start them off in February, covered in dead leaves. He preferred roses that could withstand low temperatures, the strongest ones like Souvenir de la Malmaison and Madame Pierre Oger—they also had softer thorns."

And as she breastfed her, Amanda would quote from the album, sometimes improvising comments about the flowers the way her father had done when he read to her as a child.

Ever since that summer solstice night, Amanda's eyes wore a permanently doleful look. She struggled to smile as she breastfed a daughter who would grow up without books. She couldn't help gazing at her with pity. *Why bring a child into such a hostile world?* she repeated to herself without feeling guilty that her daughter would suffer for her mistake and the hatred of others. In her waking hours, she waited anxiously for night, so that time would go by more quickly, but in her dreams she saw a desolate future in which she was just another book, destined for the bonfire. One day she too would die in agony amid the flames.

Now, when Julius arrived home his first kiss was for Viera. He appeared later and later each night, because since the birth of their child his patients had almost doubled in number.

"My little Viera has brought us good luck," he would say, referring to the cardiac problems that were proliferating in the German capital. *This National Socialist euphoria has shrunk many people's hearts,* thought Amanda.

When Julius moved away from her, Viera's lips trembled; she screwed up her dark eyes and began to wail, her whole body turning bright red. He would pick her up, almost asleep, and rock her to the rhythm of her pulse, his movements echoing the beats of this tiny heart that had come into the world with the force of a tornado.

"My little Viera," Julius whispered to her, though she could not yet understand. "Whenever you're afraid and can feel your heart racing, start counting its beats. Count them and think of each one, because you're the only person who can control them. As the silence between one beat and the next grows, your fear will start to disappear. We need those silences to exist, to think."

The child's wails grew less frequent, and Amanda also felt at peace with the sound of Julius's voice.

"In summer we'll rent a house at Wannsee, next to the lake," he suggested before going to bed. Amanda hugged him with all her remaining strength.

In the darkness, Julius lay gazing at the delicate lines of his sleeping wife's face, which seemed to be withering with each passing day.

❧

On Friday afternoons, though, despite the cold and rain, Amanda blossomed. Hilde came to visit her after midday, when her classes finished in the eastern part of the city. If the weather was bad, they would settle by the window and drink exotic herbal teas that Hilde brought back from her trips to Paris, and watch people scurrying by in the rain. If it was sunny, they would stroll down the avenues pushing Viera's baby carriage. A thick mop of reddish hair was already growing on her head, and the first freckles had sprouted on her cheeks. The baby enjoyed these walks, and the bouncing of the carriage on the cobbles sent her gently to sleep. They would stop off at Georg's café near Olivaer Platz and beneath the dim amber light of lamps that had once been gas-lit, warm themselves in the hope that the spring would quickly give way to summer.

If Viera became anxious, Amanda would take her in her arms, cradle her, and whisper in her ear, "One day we'll go to Greece and live on one of the islands, far from all of this. Papa will open his practice with views over the sea . . ."

"Viera is the spitting image of her father," Hilde would comment, which made Amanda swell with pride.

Hilde wasn't very maternal, but she loved to be included in her friend's fantasies. Her family lived in the south of Germany, but she had come to Berlin to study. When she qualified as an elementary school teacher, her parents bought her a small apartment in Mitte and she gave classes on Greek mythology at a nearby private girls' school she loathed. She was fascinated by French literature, and although she had only a basic knowledge of the language, she read the German translations she used to find in the Garden of Letters.

From behind, she looked like an adolescent. She went to the hairdresser every week to keep her hair cropped to show her neck and the angular line of her chin. Her thick, dark eyebrows and black eyes contrasted with her lips, which were always a bright crimson. When she was emotional or frightened, red blotches would appear on her throat and chest, as if blood were seeping through her pores.

Whenever she had some free days from teaching, she would travel to Paris by train to meet her girlfriends in the capital of leisure and celebration. "Life is more lighthearted in Paris," she told Amanda.

She was the black sheep of the family, Hilde explained, because she had made it very clear she would never get married, much less bring children into a world she was ashamed of. Since her ideas were anathema to the new Germany and could cause her problems, her family attempted to keep her safe by helping her financially so that she could travel and continue to live in the capital where they, conservatives from the south, hoped there would be greater tolerance for her rebellious ideas.

"I'm going to Paris next Friday to see some of my friends. I need a bit of fresh air; this city is choking me. I can only breathe easily when I'm with you."

Amanda imagined Hilde and her friends all dressed in baggy pants and with modern haircuts, perfumed with herbal and wood essences, as they strolled down the narrow streets leading to the Seine, visiting the bookshops in Le Marais or searching in the bouquiniste stalls for a lost edition of a classic.

Every Friday when she and Hilde returned home before sunset, Hilde helped her cook dinner for Julius, they put Viera to bed, and lit two small candles in the dining room lined with empty bookshelves.

One day after her Paris trip, Hilde appeared with handfuls of Swiss chocolates and bags of aromatic teas.

"You have to convince Julius to move to Paris," she told Amanda. "If you could see the streets in Le Marais . . . You'd be free there, you might even be able to open your bookstore again. Though sometimes I wonder if I should continue going there. They don't like Germans. They all say that Germany's warlike attitude could start another conflict like in nineteen-fourteen. God help us . . ."

Amanda was overwhelmed by her friend's insistence that they should pack their bags and leave the city they had always considered theirs, yet she felt it was inevitable.

"Lots of families like yours have moved from here to Le Marais. You both speak French, so what more do you need?"

Yes, everyone was fleeing, and according to the newspapers the stories of those who were leaving were increasingly sordid. Amanda had decided to cut herself off from the slander on the radio and in the press. They kept repeating over and over that the emigrants had stolen their family fortunes and abandoned their old folk in run-down apartments with no electricity or hot water. That they left their children, with a star of David around their necks, in church doorways.

"This summer we're going to the lake," Amanda responded calmly, to put a stop to any thought of exile. Her husband wasn't yet ready for it. But she was.

4

During their stay that summer in the house by the lake at Wannsee, Amanda told her husband she was pregnant again. Neither of them greeted this news with great enthusiasm: they found it hard to imagine raising another child in this environment of fear and darkness.

One morning, a moving shadow appeared on the path to the house. Julius went to the front door, and Amanda glimpsed him talking, crestfallen, with the owner, while she kept her eye on Viera, who by now could crawl and hide in corners. When Julius came back, he stood in silence for a few seconds, and Amanda immediately understood. She picked up her daughter and turned to him.

"I'm ready for anything. Tell me what it is," she said, trying to show her husband she was stronger now, that he should trust her and rely on her.

"We have to return to the city," Julius said, and slumped into the armchair facing the garden. "He can't rent the house to us any longer. The new racial laws don't permit it. He wouldn't take the rent for next week. If we stay, the police will come and make a complaint."

"Well then, there's nothing left to say. Come on, Viera, it's time to go home."

Later that day, the three of them sat in the back of the car as the driver silently returned them to Berlin. Entering the city, Amanda found that every corner looked the same, every building like the next one. A stifling monotony. The soldiers multiplied like flies, all of them identical: lined up with a sickly perfection and stuffed into stiff uniforms, they looked like toy soldiers, each one with the same outline. Their driver was one of them. Everything seemed identical until they came to the yellowing building that had once been moss green, and on whose ground floor a beautiful bookstore had once proudly stood.

The spring had been a hope; the summer, a waste. By the time the harsh winter arrived, catching Amanda by surprise and forcing her indoors during her late pregnancy, Viera was becoming increasingly active around their apartment. In the early months Amanda had suffered badly from morning sickness, and during the last trimester she could feel the baby in constant movement, above all at bedtime. It would be a daughter, she was certain of that, and her name would be Lina. Sometimes the baby's kicks startled Amanda, and her groans woke Julius and alarmed him. She knew she ought to eat, but the price of even staple foods had reached exorbitant levels, and she wanted to make sure that Viera, who had a voracious appetite, stayed healthy.

Lina Sternberg was born in the middle of the night a few days before the arrival of spring in 1935. Amanda was happy, because now she would be able to go out with the baby and Viera to enjoy the sunshine, and because the rainy, cloudy days were coming to an end in a Berlin that seemed to her increasingly alien. Sometimes she would turn a corner and not recognize where she was, feeling like a dissonant note drowning in an unvarying city.

This daughter who had been so active in the last part of the pregnancy turned out to be a serene baby who slept all the time. The hardest thing proved to be breastfeeding her, because soon after drinking some of her mother's warm breast milk she would fall fast asleep. Julius was worried that she wasn't putting on weight as she should, and thought she was too small for a baby of her age.

"She'll grow; she's a healthy child," Amanda reassured him. "Give her time. We're all different. You can't expect her to be like Viera."

By the time Lina was a few months old, her most prominent feature was a pair of deep blue eyes. When she was awake, she observed everything that came within her sight so intensely it was disturbing. She never smiled.

She began to walk before her first birthday, and would follow her sister everywhere. They were inseparable: one of them with reddish hair and honey-colored eyes, the other with shiny golden curls and an intense blue gaze. They were so happy playing together that Amanda had more time for her chores and could enjoy her Friday afternoon meetings with Hilde more fully.

It was Lina who gave their home its rhythm and who led the games with her sister. When he came home from work, Julius would hold her in his arms; she would lean her head against her father's chest and imitate the pumping of his heart, moving her head as if the force of the heartbeats were making it bounce. Julius would smile and call her "my little one."

He was only concerned that she was still tiny and weak. That fall, whenever there was a cold spell, she caught a fever and a cough and refused to eat. Eating was a nuisance for her: the world was much more fascinating than a colorless plate of food, exploring it much preferred to sitting at table for an hour raising one boring spoonful of food after another to her mouth.

By the time she was eighteen months old, Lina had already learned to speak and was very advanced for a girl of her age. Sometimes she even seemed more mature than her sister; to listen to them you would have thought she was older than Viera. It was only her size that gave the game away.

Before their bedtime, Julius would pick them both up in his arms and rush around the apartment like a whirlwind, telling them stories about the Egyptians, the Greeks, and the Romans, about sacred scarabs, pitched battles, wide oceans, nomadic tribes, slaves. Sometimes he would talk to them about crazy philosophers, or experts who studied the heart, inventions that would save humanity in the next hundred years, as though he were speaking in a university lecture hall. To please their father, the girls would open their eyes wide in alarm, and then burst out laughing in a way that made him the happiest man on earth.

"Is that how you put them to sleep?" Amanda would interrupt them, colluding in a game that she secretly prayed would never end.

5

One night in early November 1938, Amanda woke with a start. She went to the window and saw some of their neighbors out in the street, staring up at the sky. One of them noticed her and shouted with a dismay that had become all too familiar:

"The synagogue on Fasanenstrasse is on fire!"

Amanda closed the window and, with the resignation of the condemned, went back to bed in a useless attempt to get back to sleep.

The next morning, Julius found the windows of his practice smashed, a shaky star daubed by enraged fingers on the front wall, and next to it a word that had become hateful and was now to be found all over the city: *Jude*. When he stepped inside, Julius found stones everywhere. Shortly afterward, his secretary arrived. Without the slightest hint of sympathy, she told him she would have to quit.

Julius sat on the sofa in the waiting room to see who would be the first heroic patient to defy the orders of this supposedly perfect race. But not a single one came, that day or the next; no one even called to cancel their appointments. Taking from his pocket two gold chains from which hung tiny six-pointed stars, he gloomily read the inscriptions bearing the name of his daughters.

"What's the sense of the girls wearing these now," he murmured to himself. "What protections would they offer?"

That Friday, Amanda went for her usual walk through the neighborhood with Hilde and the girls. The smell of fire and ashes still hung in the air; the sidewalks were strewn with broken glass. In the distance, a thin spiral of smoke rose from the ruins of what had been Berlin's most beautiful synagogue. They reached Georg's café, which was a little emptier than on previous Fridays, and were ordering their tea when a policeman came in. He silently scrutinized all the customers' faces.

"Yet another toy soldier," Amanda said. "They could change them every day and I'm sure their families wouldn't notice. They all think the same, have the same voice, the same face, the same look. Even their souls have been diluted into the same terrifying uniformity. We are the others. But do you know something, Hilde? I'm growing tired of being the other . . ."

The policeman left the café and, with the help of a group of youngsters, clumsily drew a six-pointed star on the front of the building. They, the others, the different ones, simply remained in their seats. They were used to the insult: What could they do?

That night, Amanda waited until Julius was asleep to get up and go to sit alone in the living room, close by the window. She needed some time to herself, without Hilde, the girls, without her husband. She had to order her thoughts, although she had no clear idea why. *It was already too late. The damage was done.* She sometimes thought that it was for the best that her parents had died and her brother Abraham had gone off to Cuba, leaving just in time to escape the barbarism engulfing her and her family, drowning them minute by minute without any hope of a rescuing hand. Their two daughters were all that she and Julius had.

She knew now was the moment to leave, but there was no welcoming shore. The larvae had been laid in every corner of a rotting Berlin and were reproducing with a terrifying hatred to devour everything that was not like them or prevented them from spreading everywhere. They had infected the whole city, the whole country, and now they aimed to contaminate the entire continent, perhaps even the entire world. Their goal had no bounds: the universe itself was to be perfectly Aryan.

∽⦚∾

The following Friday somebody knocked at the front door with disturbing insistence. Amanda went downstairs while Hilde and the girls were drinking hot chocolate and eating fruit preserves, behaving as if life were still normal. A patient, his face distorted with anguish and fear, had brought a message from Julius.

"They've taken him away," cried the old man, who was obviously ill. "They're closing all the doors on us, Frau Sternberg."

Amanda spoke before she could react. "Where did they take him?"

"To the gestapo office on Oranienburger Strasse. At least that's what they said; who knows if it's true. They have the power to do whatever they like."

Amanda grabbed her coat and handbag, and left the girls with Hilde. Without any questions, or explanations, or saying thank you or goodbye.

The city was in tumult. Everybody was rushing aimlessly from north to south, east to west, bumping into one another with no gesture of compassion or apology. She tried to hail a taxi, but they all shot past without stopping, and so she decided the only possibility was to take the S-Bahn to Mitte: What did she care now for any disapproving looks?

When she reached the gestapo office she saw several women inquiring about their relatives, but no one was giving any answers. There was nothing to be done until they had an up-to-date list of those arrested.

Someone suggested they might be in the former old people's home on Grosse Hamburger Strasse.

There were still traces of the great synagogue near the gestapo office. The wind blew a scrap of parchment into Amanda's face. On it was written a phrase in Hebrew that she avoided deciphering. Perhaps her destiny was written there, and she wasn't yet ready to confront it. At her feet were bits of wood reduced to embers; all around her was a permanent column of smoke, as if the fire refused to be extinguished.

She entered the old building, and a young soldier immediately led her up to the office. Maybe he singled her out because unlike the other women who were shouting or sobbing desperately, Amanda remained astonishingly calm. She climbed the stairs resolutely behind the toy soldier.

"Who are you inquiring about?"

"My husband."

"Is your husband a communist?"

Amanda said nothing. She realized that this callow soldier had confused her with one of them. He had not realized she belonged to the others, was another one of those howling for their relatives at the entrance, mingling with the ruins of a place of worship that for him should never have existed.

"Jewish? What are you doing with a Jewish husband?"

Why give any further explanation? Amanda kept silent and quickened her step. Alongside her, he scrutinized her features—the size of her ears, her nose, as though he was an expert in craniometry. If he had with him an instrument to study the facial characteristics that differentiate mortals from immortals, he would have measured her forehead, the distance between her eyes, how far the base of her nose was from her top lip.

The official, shielded behind an enormous mahogany desk that was strewn with lists in immaculate handwriting, organized by alphabetical order and date of arrest, listened to the name Amanda gave in a firm voice and went down the list one by one.

Amanda's heart was pounding. She didn't want to show she was afraid, for the official would be able to sniff it and she'd lose control. She couldn't allow herself to do that. Instead, she counted in silence. *One, two, three, four, five, six—*

"Sternberg. Sternberg, Julius. So you are the doctor's wife. Frau Sternberg, your husband is no longer in this building. He wounded himself on a piece of glass in his office. He made himself a tourniquet on his leg. We can't keep anyone wounded here."

The toy soldier was still standing behind her.

"Which hospital was he transferred to?"

"Frau Sternberg, your husband didn't go to a hospital. The wound will heal. Your husband is in Sachsenhausen."

At first she didn't understand, but repeated the name several times in her head until she recalled what she had heard about it: *A forced labor camp on the outskirts of Berlin. No one came back from Sachsenhausen.*

"But isn't that where they send gypsies, communists, people involved in politics? My husband is a cardiologist. A medical doctor."

"Frau Sternberg, there's no mistake. Your husband has been sent to Sachsenhausen with all the others of his kind," the official said, emphasizing the "of his kind' so there could be no doubt. "They need doctors in Sachsenhausen too. Wait, be patient, and he'll write to you."

These last words pierced her like an arrow. On her way out, she descended the stairs with the gait of a wounded horse about to be put down. She lost all sense of time and space, and it was only when she was out in the street again that the shouts of the helpless women roused her from her stupor.

An old woman held out a scrap of crumpled paper to her. Two names were written on it. Her sons, she sobbed. But Amanda could no longer listen, hear, or see. Bewildered, she made her way through this crowd of phantoms. As she walked away, she could see the evening sky turn purple at the far end of a directionless avenue.

Crossing beneath the railway line, she noticed an elegant, elderly man coming toward her wearing a hat and tie and using a cane. He was walking with a long-acquired dignity, repeating over and over a phrase Amanda only understood when she almost bumped into him: "They took them all away. They took them all away."

She realized that this was the echo of loss: her loss, the old man's, that of the women in Grosse Hamburger Strasse tearing themselves to pieces as they wept, fearing that their loved ones who had been taken away would never return.

6

$\mathcal{T}$he next morning, Amanda went to the abandoned practice to see whether it was true that Julius had wounded himself on one of the shards of glass from the front door. There were traces of blood everywhere, but there were also obvious signs of a struggle. Her husband had fought for his life, fought to escape, not to let himself be defeated. Amanda sat on the sofa as she used to do on those sunny afternoons that were already slipping from her memory. She remained for a while staring at the door with the somber hope for a miracle, but she didn't believe in miracles.

She tried to recall the last time she had seen him, the last words, the last embrace, the last kiss. Nothing. She couldn't even remember Julius's tone of voice when he said goodbye to her every morning. She had wiped away all those happy moments, and now was face-to-face with the dried, lifeless blood of the only man she had ever loved.

Hilde decided to move in with them until Julius was released. Lina studied their faces closely; her solemn look seemed to express the conviction that her father would never return. Amanda smiled at her and prepared herself to receive the fateful news her daughter seemed able to predict. She sensed that, with Lina at her side, the future would never come as a surprise.

Three weeks later, Julius's letter arrived. With no indication of where it had come from, only her name on it. Amanda stood in the doorway to the bookstore, letter in hand. At first she was disconcerted, because it appeared to be full of instructions. She didn't recognize the shaky, scrawled handwriting with some incomplete words. That yellowing, stained, and crumpled piece of paper was the last thing her husband had touched.

December 2, 1938

Amanda:

You are to go to police headquarters in Alexanderplatz. In reception ask for Herr Christmann and identify yourself. From there go to the Office for Palestine at number ten Meinekestrasse and ask for Mr. Donovan. Register as the doctor's wife, you won't have to tell him anything apart from that.

The suitcases are on the only shelf with doors in the back room.

I can't control the infection in my leg. It keeps spreading, and here, as you can imagine, there are no medicines. I can no longer walk, but I have at least one piece of good news: it doesn't hurt.

How are my little girls? Tell Viera she should always look after her sister. All three of you, remember that fear leads nowhere. Fear only ends up taking away what little lucidity we have left. Count every heartbeat; you can be sure that from here I will count with you all.

What would my life have been if I hadn't met you? You came to me when I most needed you. You are my light. Once in Leipzig we had a dream together. We imagined getting married, starting a family, opening a practice, and for you to reopen your father's old, abandoned bookstore. We would have two, perhaps three children.

*We would spend summers at Wannsee and one day climb the
Acropolis together. We have achieved our most important dreams.
Now help me build the finale for us.*

*From this dark, cold place I can hear your heart. I know from
memory all its movements. When you are asleep or awake, happy or
sad, like today.*

*My Amanda, I want you never to forget that we were happy
once.*

Your Julius

When she finished reading his words, Amanda realized this was her
husband's farewell. She allowed a cry to emerge from deep down inside
her, and collapsed onto the sidewalk, in full view of everyone. Yes, she
wanted them to see her weep, to see what they had done to her family.
She wanted each and every one of the perfect race to recognize the horror and feel the guilt they would have to bear and one day, yes, one day
in the not too distant future, would have to pay for.

Leaving the girls with Hilde, she wandered wild-eyed and coatless
across the city, as if it would take only seconds from her home to Alexanderplatz. She didn't feel the cold. She clutched her stiff brown leather
bag to her. She had slipped Julius's letter in it, and other than that it
was almost empty, with only a few banknotes and coins inside, as well
as the last photo of the four of them together, when Lina was born. A
family with solemn eyes, even though the photographer insisted on an
impossible smile. A dark photo, where the only light was in their faces;
the rest of the image was blurred, out of focus. Remembering that she
had it with her gave Amanda a tenuous sense of happiness, a fleeting
emotion that was already foreign to her but which she could recognize
and smile at.

It was a weekday—she didn't know which, but that didn't matter.
She took the first train and was jostled by the passersby, swept along
like an already lifeless body. She made her way down impeccably clean

streets where there was no broken glass, no charred remains, no traces of the horror. Who were the phantoms? Them or her? She couldn't work it out.

She entered the police headquarters without anyone seeming to notice or care; she felt like she was already dead. She followed Julius's instructions and was given an envelope that she put unopened in her stiff handbag. She was trembling, but not from fear. She was sure of that, because her heart had stopped the moment she received the message from Julius. Where had she left his letter? There it was, in her hand.

She again got on and off a train; traveled from Mitte to Charlottenburg without being aware of it. Now she was outside the building bearing the huge sign PALESTINE & ORIENT LLOYD. There were no long lines of desperate people, now there was nobody. Everyone had left. The windows were smashed, the offices abandoned, a single curious onlooker lurked in the entrance.

She continued walking distractedly. She had no idea where to go now, because the letter did not say what she should do if the Office for Palestine was shut or if Mr. Donovan had gone, been arrested, or killed. Searching for somewhere she knew, she walked on to Olivaer Platz: the windowpanes of Georg's café were also smashed, the door torn off its hinges, the tables and chairs overturned. It seemed there were no places she knew left in Berlin.

She found herself beneath an illuminated marquee and a few minutes later, inside the building, engulfed in the choking smoke from the cigarettes of souls lost to the shadows. To her and Julius there had been nothing more mysterious or awe-inspiring than to sit in this sacred arena invaded by luminous ghosts on the enormous screen where even the darkest corners came to life in black and white. Among the credits she saw the name of a childhood friend she used to call by her first name, Helene. They had both gone to classes at the Grimm-Reiter Dance School, at a time when she dreamed of becoming a dancer and Helene an actress. They went swimming together and competed until they were panting for breath.

Now, led on the screen by Helene, she allowed herself to be taken through the countless columns of Greek temples, then she rises to the skies, where a goddess of Olympia opens her arms to her. She sees perspiring faces, ready to compete and shouting at the tops of their voices, as if they have been thrown to hungry lions in the arena. Someone must always win: this is the hour of victory, the moment for flight, when the fastest man in the world strides out and wins, to the dismay of the perfect race. If he can do it, so can she. If he surpasses human limits, nothing will stop her.

The masses howl, thirsty for blood, shouting for the downfall of the other. She is the other. The Olympic flame is about to be extinguished when someone launches a discus to the most distant clouds and the faces blur in a salute to the void. The men smoking in the orchestra, soldiers in an invisible army, stand when they see the man controlling their destinies appear on the screen. They respond as one to an impulse, a force outside them, and raise their right arm to the infinite . . .

One of the soldiers in front of her rebukes her:

"How can a perfect German woman stay seated, and not respond to the triumph of the superior race?" he says, trying to encourage her with a triumphal gesture.

I wonder if Helene remembers what we dreamed? thinks Amanda, ignoring the man. Helene has become a star in the service of Nazi power.

When Amanda closes her eyes, the dark auditorium vanishes. Now she is dreaming with Julius at her side, as on those evenings when they used to lose themselves in the Palast, smiling at men in white ties and tails and shiny pumps as they danced down marble stairs by the light of a silver moon and crystal stars, and she followed their rhythm in the silk gown molded to her as if it were an extension of her ethereal body.

A man whistling makes her shiver in the dense fog of the forgotten. She huddles in Julius's arms, asking, *Why do you bring me here?* but he only smiles.

She is still shivering at the whistling that terrifies her whenever it fills the auditorium, before the man with the anguished face reappears out of the shadows. A chorus of girls sing a song about a murderer: *In the hall of the mountain king . . .*

Amanda closes her eyes again and tries to forget that image on the screen at the Palast.

Why remember Julius through a movie that makes me shudder? she wonders. Bewildered, she sees the story being repeated and knows she must flee. Her daughters are at the mercy of a serial killer hidden behind the victors' spotless uniforms.

Leaving the cinema, she opens her bag to retrieve Julius's letter. All she reads is the date, which she repeats to herself.

December 2, 1938. Was that a Saturday?

7

*W*hile Amanda was searching for a way to escape from the city, Viera and Lina amused themselves by playing with their father's old stethoscope, listening through walls and windows. To Lina, every inanimate object was alive, and she was there to demonstrate it. Before raising a piece of fruit to her mouth, she examined it to see whether it was breathing or not. Every night, before her mother read to her in French from the botanical album, she would listen for its heartbeat, and wouldn't allow Amanda to open it to the page they had reached the night before until she said she had detected it. Viera would smell the faded pages and sigh.

From having been read to so much in French, Lina could recite whole paragraphs from the book fluently. When they went out with Hilde on the way to a café or a park, they spoke in the language that Amanda herself had learned from her father as a child.

Every so often, Amanda would wander among the empty bookshelves of the old store with Lina at her tail, recalling where the novels of chivalry and romance used to be, the first editions, French translations, botanical books, atlases, and popular encyclopedias, dictionaries. With her eyes shut, she could recall exactly where *Madame Bovary, Crime and Punishment,* or *Les Misérables* had once been. In her dreams she sometimes imagined that one of her literary treasures, that had been a favorite of hers or her father's, would return as if by magic and surprise her.

Hilde entertained the girls by pulling out of the wardrobe silk dresses that were no longer worn, shawls embroidered with gold thread, or fans made with Bruges lace. She would put lipstick on their mouths, cheeks, and the tips of their noses, and use her eyebrow pencil to create beauty spots in their dimples. They roared with laughter as though they were happy, as though Julius had never left and still put them to sleep on hot nights.

"Mama is sad," Lina said one day, and the happy moment was gone in an instant. "I know Papa is never coming back."

Leaning back in her armchair, Hilde invented stories to shield them as best she could.

"One day when you're least expecting it, that door will open to let the doctor in. Herr Sternberg is going to come back, and do you know why? Because if he is capable of saving someone with a weak heart, the most important organ in the body, he must know how to recover from any wound, however serious. He will get better and return to you. Let's see, what would you like to do tomorrow afternoon?"

The girls did not respond. They preferred not to go out, feeling protected in the apartment above what had once been a bookstore, far from the street and neighbors who did not like them.

One afternoon, when they were singing an old lullaby that Lina insisted on even though it wasn't bedtime, they were startled by a thunderous knocking on the street door. Hilde went down, determined to find out who was trying to invade their precious home; Amanda followed her. The first thing she saw was the swastika in the man's lapel; then she recognized the face of the patient she had exchanged a few words with in her husband's office. She had an even more vivid memory of his skinny son, the boy with the purple lips. She asked Hilde to go upstairs to the girls, and, refusing to greet her enemy, waited for him to come out with another insult like the one she had received when they met the first time.

"Frau Sternberg, I've brought a message from your husband. May I come in?" he said, glancing all around as if to make sure no one had seen him enter this building marked with the sign of shame.

Amanda stepped aside. The stocky man was still looking around nervously. He did not know how to begin or how to explain himself. Without saying anything he took a bulky envelope out of his raincoat pocket and held it out to her.

Amanda couldn't understand what he was doing there, if he had come to pay a debt that with the new racial laws would not be valid anyway, or if these documents were announcing that she was to be arrested as well.

She confronted the man with her most defiant look.

"What do you want from us?" she snapped, ignoring the envelope.

"I've come to help," the man said hesitantly.

"We don't need your help. You know very well that my husband will be back any time now."

"Frau Sternberg, I'm afraid to say that your husband will not be coming back."

They stood in silence for a few moments, until the composure that Amanda had carefully maintained since his arrival began to dissolve. Tears welled up in her eyes, and she made a huge effort for them not to roll down her cheeks.

The man still had his hand extended, as if to insist that this stubborn woman should trust him despite the distance between them as far as race and even more importantly, ideology, were concerned. He was a militant of the party in power; she was a Jewish woman with the looks of a German.

"It's the least I can do for your husband. Please take it."

"I don't need your money," Amanda told him.

"My son is alive thanks to your husband," the man insisted.

"And how is your son?" she asked, her voice growing ever fainter. She couldn't meet his gaze anymore without bursting into tears.

"He won't be able to serve the Führer, but at least he is with us," the man replied with a smile he immediately stifled, unsure if he had said the wrong thing.

Amanda took the envelope. She was about to check what was in it when the man interrupted her.

"You already have your passports. I know you couldn't get visas for Palestine, but I managed to obtain permits to disembark in Cuba. They're first-class tickets on a German ocean liner. The tickets are in the envelope. I made sure everything is in order. With your husband's help I was able to locate your brother in Havana, and he has sent word that he is willing to receive all of you."

"We're not leaving without my husband," Amanda protested, realizing at that moment that Julius had been plotting his family's escape for weeks, if not months.

"Herr Sternberg died six days ago," the man interrupted her, lowering his gaze and clasping his now empty hands in front of him.

Without raising his head, he tried to see how Amanda would react. Still silent, she smiled faintly. She had been prepared for this; it was nothing new. From the day Julius had been arrested, she had known he would not return. Lina too had foreseen it. The only letter she had received had been his farewell, and she needed nothing more. Much less any compassion from this man, who was as guilty as those who had let the father of her children die. All she wanted was for him to go, to leave her alone with this fresh, lacerating sorrow she would have to learn to live with.

"Herr Sternberg was a great man. He asked to see me, and I managed to visit him before the end. The infection was consuming him, but he had enough strength left to beg me to help you and your daughters."

Hearing this stranger talk about her husband in the past tense, Amanda's lips began to quiver. She bit them as hard as she could: there was no way she was going to share her suffering with him. Her eyes too refused to express any thanks: she was just counting the minutes to be on her own with her daughters, her friend, and to read Julius's last letter again, as often as she could.

"I could only obtain two landing permits. Herr Sternberg insisted you should send the girls. The *Saint-Louis* sails at nightfall on May thirteenth from the port of Hamburg. You'll find all the instructions in the envelope." He paused and drew in a nervous breath, then went on slowly. "It's the only way to save them . . ."

He left the last phrase unfinished, torn between what he saw as his duty as a citizen and the debt he owed to the man who had saved his son's life. He was the one who had to protect beings from an inferior race that his country intended to wipe from the face of the earth. The scum, the worms, the lumpen, those who were rifling the coffers of Germany, stealing their jobs, humiliating the purest race God had created.

There was another lengthy silence. When he saw that Amanda was not reacting, he took a step toward her. She pulled away, her whole body shaking.

"Frau Sternberg, do as your husband says. From Hamburg you are to travel to Paris by the first train the next morning, and from there to Limoges. You are to head for a small village in Haute-Vienne, where Claire Duval will be expecting you. She has already been paid for a year, until you can rejoin your daughters. It's also a way of helping Frau Duval: as you know, she is a widow living on her own with her daughter."

It had been a year since Amanda had been in touch with Claire. Claire's husband, who was much older than she was, had been a great lover of botany, and had shared this passion with Amanda's father since they had met in the colonies. He had died several years earlier.

What Amanda couldn't understand was why Julius had kept her in the dark about all these escape plans, this possibility of salvation of which, apparently, he had never envisaged being a part.

"It's the best thing you can do for your daughters," the man concluded somberly. "The only thing." Giving her one last glance, he turned to the door and disappeared.

For several seconds Amanda did not move, as she rapidly went over in her mind the panorama opening up before her. She was condemned to bury herself in a tiny village in the southwest of France, while her daughters did the same on an insignificant island on the far side of the Atlantic. At a loss, she went straight to the back room and for the first time looked for the suitcases her husband had referred to in his farewell letter. All she could find was his doctor's bag. Opening it, she discovered it was stuffed full of reichsmarks. She left it where it was, and paced around the room, deep in thought.

"Julius, Julius, what have we done . . . ?" she cried out bitterly, and the tears began to flow, heartbroken over her loss and the idea she would have to cast her daughters into an abyss. *I know you meant to look after us, but how do you expect me to part from my daughters, our treasures, our little stars? Viera is older, but Lina . . .*

She spent a long while in the back room of the bookstore, with the bag crammed with a fortune that could not buy freedom for her or her daughters. Time was against her. She had to prepare them for a crossing into the unknown, to an island lost in the middle of the sea, far from this dark world. *Yes, on that island there will be sunshine, lots of light, and no one will dare look down on them. My brother will protect them,* she told herself over and over.

She tried to imagine the future her daughters would have on a Caribbean island with an uncle with communist ideas, who confronted the world angrily, always ready to take up arms; all she could see was a thick, black cloud.

Oh, Abraham, I'll have to have blind faith in you, from such a distance . . . what other choice do I have?

She remembered Abraham as a young warrior ready to combat the established order. From childhood, he had challenged his parents, religion, politics. In history classes he'd often ended in fistfights with his schoolmates, forcing his mother to intervene to save him from being severely punished. Her brother had been obsessed with the Russian communist writer Mayakovsky, and made his father buy all his poetry. The books arrived in Germany with their red covers hidden under brown paper. *What is Abraham like now?* she wondered. The last time she had seen him had been a long while ago, before her marriage to Julius.

Pondering this, Amanda finally went back upstairs. The girls were already asleep, and Hilde was waiting for her at the table with a cup of tea that gradually calmed her.

"They're leaving," she said, taking a sip. "Viera and Lina are leaving on a ship. It's the only way they can survive."

In that moment with Hilde, it felt as if someone else were speaking for her. These were not her words, or her thoughts. She slowly breathed in the tea's aroma and repeated what she had just heard herself say.

"Let's run away to Paris," said Hilde, awaking from her initial stupor.

"They're to set sail at night, in mid-May, from Hamburg."

Seeing tears falling from Hilde's tightly closed eyes, Amanda smiled at her friend. Hilde could let her emotions out, could weep, shout, be comforted in her place while she remained stoic.

Amanda told her they were leaving the Garden of Letters and Berlin behind, but did not mention where they were headed, apart from insinuating that it would be a one-way journey. Hilde understood. Amanda did not embrace her, nor allow a single sob to escape her.

"I have to pack the suitcases. Three of them: one for each of the girls and one for me. We won't need anything more."

In her bedroom, she looked for the small ebony box that her father had given her, pausing to stare at the delicate mother-of-pearl inlay.

"*Diospyros ebenum,*" she whispered, tucking the box in the suitcase along with the precious botanical album.

Stripped of its books, the room was nothing more than an empty, lifeless space. There was nothing more to be saved, no reason to stay there, no possibility for nostalgia.

"The girls are going to Cuba," she explained to Hilde when she returned to the dining room. "At least there they will be able to go to school. They're not allowed to do so here. And with no books . . ."

What most disturbed her was being at the mercy of the unknown, of distance, of time. She stood up to comfort her dearest friend. Hugging her, relieving someone else's pain, she found the strength to say it:

"They let Julius die six days ago."

Six days: an eternity. She tried to reconstruct in memory what she had done that day: *Was it raining? Was it cold? No, it was sunny, and she had gone out with the girls.* Yes, now she remembered. *It was a beautiful day. Did he die at dawn or in the middle of the night? Who could have held his hand, or closed his eyes? Who said goodbye to him, who listened to his last words?*

"We're going to be all right. Julius arranged everything. The girls will be with my brother in Cuba, and I'll be in the south of France, on a small farm, with my friend Claire, far from the savage hordes. You see? Julius has saved us. He'll always be looking after us. I married an angel."

The two women smiled. The image of Julius watching over them gave them a false but consoling sense of peace. Now they had to plan how they would keep in touch, and when Hilde could visit her.

"Ah, Hilde, we still have time to say goodbye. This won't be forever." She paused painfully. "We'll meet again, when Germany has come to its senses. We live in darkness, but you can be sure the light will triumph in the end. No one can live forever in the dark."

Hilde retired to her bedroom, leaving Amanda alone, something she had needed ever since she had begun to accept that she must be parted from her daughters.

Alone. With nobody to judge her or feel sorry for her when she cursed the air she breathed and put the blame on her ancestors, the parents of the parents of her parents, for having made Germany the promised land and given up their nomadic life—the one, when it came down to it, for which they had been born. She had no right to put down roots. Now she, with her two daughters, was responsible for closing the door on a century of illusory permanence. It was up to her to set out and conquer a new world that would be just as hostile, she was certain, as the one they were being forced to abandon.

8

*F*riendly greetings disappeared from everyday speech, substituted by an impetuous raising of the right arm to the skies, accompanied by the howl of *Heil Hitler!* Amanda was completely cut off: she was not permitted to use the telephone, buy a newspaper, or board a streetcar.

Each day after Hilde had gone to her classes, she went out with the girls to search for bread, cheese, meat, potatoes, down streets where they were constantly fighting against the tide. *No one walks anymore,* thought Amanda, *they all either march or run. We go at our own pace.*

One morning from the doorway of the butcher's shop, she saw a gang of them beating the owner, who was trying desperately to shield his head. His yarmulke had fallen off a few feet from him. A young boy started kicking it as if it were a football, jumping up and down and crying victory.

"What are they doing to Herr Ross?" Lina asked tremulously. Viera started to cry.

A man wearing a hat and a swastika armband on his right jacket sleeve bumped into Amanda.

"Get out of here, it's not safe for you. Take the girls home at once," he ordered in a low voice, casting her a complicit glance before joining the group assaulting the butcher.

Amanda dragged the girls away, and this time they did run as quickly as the barbarians, trampling on everything they met, until they finally sought shelter in an entryway on a street leading to Grolmanstrasse. Pushing open a rusty iron gate that creaked jarringly, they entered the courtyard of a large tenement building whose bricks were covered with mold. Her face lifted to the skies, Amanda begged for a beam of light to guide her out of this humiliation. *Only a few more weeks and the girls at least will be safe*, she told herself in what was all at once a prayer, a profession of faith, and a request for forgiveness for having brought two beings into this turmoil. It was too late, there was no going back, Julius had understood that, and devoted his final days to protecting them.

She closed her eyes and gave thanks. She wondered who that man could have been who gave her the warning at the butcher's. He must have been another angel sent by Julius, a barbarian whose heart he had rescued. She was convinced Julius had filled the city with angels.

After supper, while Hilde was clearing the plates, Amanda took hold of Viera and Lina's hands and asked them to pay attention. All that could be heard was the clatter of dishes.

"Girls, your papa managed to arrange for you to go and spend some time with my brother, Abraham," she said, not giving them time to complain, protest, or reject the idea. "We have to do what Papa has organized for us. First you two go, and then we'll all meet up again there."

Lina turned around, hoping Hilde would intervene to help them convince their mother not to send them so far away, to an uncle they didn't know, and who must be taking them in because he had no choice. But Hilde kept her back to them.

"When are we going?" asked Viera.

"Soon. In a matter of a couple of weeks."

"I'm afraid, Mama." Viera began to tremble, her eyes reddening.

"What do we do when we're afraid?"

"We count our heartbeats one by one," Lina answered instead and began to count them slowly under her breath. *One, two, three, four, five, six . . .*

She smiled, hoping to be rewarded for having answered her mother's question correctly.

"Very good. We need to start packing. We'll only take what we absolutely need."

Hilde tried to determine what lay behind that face giving instructions as if someone in another dimension were controlling all her words, obliging her to inform her daughters that she was sending them to a distant island, possibly forever. She dropped a plate, and was startled when she heard the sound of the china smashing against the kitchen floor tiles. But none of the others noticed. None of them turned to see what Hilde had broken. They didn't care. They were leaving.

Amanda went to her bedroom with her daughters. They got into bed together, the three of them hugging one another as if this was their last night. What they needed was time.

"One day we'll visit the Acropolis . . ." Amanda whispered to her daughters, giving them a beautiful fantasy to hold onto as they drifted off to sleep.

❧

As night fell that Friday, while they were lighting the candles in the dining room and their supper was almost ready, they heard a loud knocking at the front door. By now, nothing could alarm them. In a week, on Saturday, May 13, they would be apart. Nothing could be worse than that. Hilde went to open the door and returned to tell them that two women, each with a clipboard full of lists, were downstairs.

Amanda went down with the girls to the Garden that had no books.

"They've come to do our *Vermögenserklärung*," Hilde told her, deliberately including herself in this inventory of possessions that everyone leaving the country had to complete.

One of the women gazed contemptuously at Hilde.

"How does she dare get mixed up with this garbage?" she said to the other woman, who burst into a coarse laugh. "To sink to their level . . ."

Hilde ignored them, and Amanda did not react either. She felt protected by the emptiness around her: there was nothing of value for them to put in their inventory, nothing she wanted to save from their search. Sheltered with her daughters and her friend amid the empty shelves of what had once been the Garden of Letters, they would be safe while these women plundered a past she no longer had any wish to protect.

The timid spring had finally reached Berlin, and the billboards with the grandiloquent ode to perfection had cast their shadow over the pale flowers. To Amanda, who walked around bidding goodbye to the city she had once believed was hers, the seasons had vanished. She wondered why the lime trees on Unter den Linden were still not in bloom.

On the last night, they ate in silence by the tremulous amber light of the candles. At the foot of the stairs stood their three light suitcases. Hilde brought some labels from her last trip to Paris and, with the girls, attached them to the luggage.

"Hotel Bellevue," Lina read. "Is it a palace?"

"A small palace in the center of the most beautiful city in Europe that is full of palaces with no princesses. You can be the first."

The car was due to arrive very early the next morning to take them to the port of Hamburg. Hilde made sure that their documents were in order, that they didn't forget the landing permits, the first-class tickets, the passports with the proud eagle darkened by a swastika. Amanda on the other hand was hoping there was some mistake, something they had forgotten, a slipup that would save her from the guilt she was going to have to carry with her for the rest of her life.

That night, the girls rested peacefully, anticipating their journey. Amanda and Hilde remained awake, listening closely to the precarious sleep of those innocent creatures.

9

$\mathcal{A}$s the sun rose that Saturday morning, the last they would see in Berlin, they prepared their escape. There was no going back. Amanda clasped Hilde's hands and smiled her most radiant smile. Tilting her head to one side, she gazed into her friend's eyes and embraced her.

"You'll always be with me, my beloved friend," she murmured. "Thank you."

"Are you sure you don't want to take the girls with you to Paris?"

"I have to protect them, Hilde. We must escape from here. Even an ocean may not be enough to save them from this barbarism."

"Will I be able to write to you?"

"Better not, Hilde, better not. This is our goodbye."

"What's become of us, Amanda?" said Hilde, her voice starting to crack.

"They will pay for it, Hilde. We all will. As you once said: 'They start with books and finish with people.' Germany is not what it used to be. My parents were proud to belong to the most civilized, the most cultured and creative country in the world . . . what are we now? Even worse is that the years will go by and we will still be paying for other people's guilt. They have led the nation into an abyss it will be impossible to climb out of. Who will want to have a German child? We'll grow old, we'll be shunned by the whole world, and generation after generation will try to wipe clean this baseness, but they won't be able to. It's the end, Hilde. It's the beginning of the end."

Amanda moved away from her friend, and watched as Hilde turned her back and covered her face in despair. She walked out of the Garden of Letters, eyes downcast, staring at the ground. The girls kissed Hilde lovingly. Lina was carrying her stiff rag doll, arms outstretched. Viera had a flowery head scarf on, tied at the neck. Eager to embark on their new odyssey, they threw themselves onto the backseat of the car.

Amanda gave her friend one last look of pity. She was fleeing the terror, but Hilde would have to bear the shameful weight of the nation she belonged to. She couldn't help feeling sorry for her.

Hilde in turn saw in Amanda a terrifying, emotionless calm; she seemed as light as someone who no longer existed or has departed heaven knows where.

"How do you feel?" Hilde's voice was soft and sad.

Hearing her friend, Amanda returned to the present.

"As though they had lined us up in the darkness in front of a firing squad. You can't see who is shooting, who is attacking you. You hear the sharp, penetrating whine of bullets, but you're still standing. It doesn't matter how often the bullets have pierced you. You stand there until gravity overcomes you. On the ground, all of us are in a straight line, riddled with bullets, eyes wide open. They can't kill you. And you're still there, because nothing and nobody can distance you from your suffering. How do I feel, Hilde? I don't feel."

They embraced silently, without tears. An embrace like an island. An embrace no one saw apart from the neighbor lurking at her second-floor window.

Up in the sky, the full moon refused to disappear with the dawn. Amanda stared up at it, her eyes brimming with tears.

"What a stubborn moon." She sighed.

She clutched her throat as if it were a wound. She had died when they took Julius, yet now she continued to wither away. *How many more deaths await me?* she wondered.

As Amanda was climbing into the car, she stumbled against a soldier marching by. What did she care? The girls were already in the backseat, and Hilde was double-locking the Garden of Letters, closing the door on a wonderful era. Amanda clambered into the car, which moved off as the girls frantically waved goodbye. Hilde remained standing in the doorway of the bookstore for a few seconds, then headed off in the opposite direction, her eyes filled with a cold fury. They saw her walk slowly away but not turn the corner, as if both she and the car were suspended in time. Then Amanda watched as Hilde became a dark shape that gradually faded. She took a deep breath so that in the vertigo of their flight she could retain the essence of her friend in her memory.

"In Havana we won't have to wear coats," Lina whispered. "There's so much sun that sometimes night never arrives. Can you imagine that?"

Viera smiled, her gaze fixed on her mother's tear-filled eyes.

"We're going to an island where it's always daylight, always summer," Lina continued excitedly.

"Why hasn't Uncle Abraham had any children? Perhaps he doesn't like them . . ." Viera interrupted her.

"Uncle Abraham doesn't have children because he works so hard."

"Then he won't have time for us," said Viera, still staring at her mother's absent eyes, her agitated breathing, trembling lips, and drooping eyelids, the way she was opening and closing her fists, containing her despair. "Mama," was all she said, trying to rouse her from her lethargy.

Amanda was wracked with doubts. She should have never followed the instructions of that barbarian who had belittled her in her husband's office. He had done all he could to save his son, even handing him over to a doctor from an inferior race so that his heart would keep pumping, and now she had to leave with her daughters. What kind of a mother was she, to let herself be duped by a man whose only aim was to remove her and her daughters from his absurd idea of a nation?

"Mama!" shouted Viera.

"What are we doing here?" Amanda finally reacted. "Where are we going?"

"To Cuba, Mama. Uncle Abraham is waiting for us," Lina told her, not very convinced.

At that instant, Amanda's face cleared and she smiled at them. The girls breathed a sigh of relief, but Lina was still unsure. She sensed that her mother had made a decision that would change them forever, a decision she could not yet define. Maybe she had decided it was too risky to send them on their own to an island where the summer was scorching hot; or possibly it was her mother who would leave on the boat to see if Uncle Abraham really was happy to receive them. Maybe it would be her and Viera who ended up on the farm in France, surrounded by sheep as they waited for the rescue signal from their mother. Lina had her suspicions, but the immediate future was cloudy, she wasn't able to decipher it.

Lina tried to count her heartbeats, Viera's, and her mother's, to synchronize those silences that were needed to repel fear, as her father had taught her. *If only we could go together . . .* she fantasized. *When the captain sees we are two little girls on our own, he'll ask Mama to travel with us. He'll find a cabin for the three of us, with an enormous porthole. How could you abandon them, Madam? Can't you see they're just little girls? There's no way I'm going to allow it. Look, here's your landing permit, and you can have the best cabin on board. See how happy your girls are. Ready to disembark in Havana. You'll see what a beautiful city it is.*

10

$\mathscr{T}$he port at Hamburg was chaos, in the midst of which rose the enormous black, white, and red ocean liner like a huge mass of floating iron. They got out of the car with their suitcases and made their way through the crowd. Amanda tried to get her bearings among all the people rushing in different directions. A band was playing a discordant farewell song; orders were being shouted, goodbyes called out. Viera and Lina gazed in wonder at the size of the boat that was to take them to their uncle's island.

Amanda was struggling to identify those in the crowd who were leaving, and those who like her were staying behind. She joined a line that led the chosen ones to a checkpoint before they could climb the swaying, slippery gangway.

At the end, three soldiers were slowly scrutinizing documents and stamping them. Yes, all her papers were in order, she had the girls' passports . . . She knew something was missing, but couldn't pinpoint what it was.

In front of her stood a man and a woman aged about fifty who had no luggage and were dressed in dark suits. They turned and smiled.

"We're the Meyers," the woman introduced herself, noticing Amanda staring at her.

"Frau Meyer, my older daughter is traveling alone," said Amanda, without either Viera or Lina hearing her. "I am Amanda Sternberg," she said after a pause, forcing a smile.

The woman drew back and looked at her severely.

"We have no choice."

The woman still didn't understand. The man ignored their conversation.

"Frau Meyer, please, please look after my daughter," Amanda went on. "There's no one else I can entrust her to. My brother will be waiting for her in Havana."

As the line edged forward, Frau Meyer glanced down at the child, who was still enthralled by the band playing muffled military marches.

"Her name is Viera," said Amanda, pointing to her. "She is older, she'll be able to manage it, she's going to be six. Lina is still very small; she's only four."

The woman nodded silently. A gentler light had come into her eyes. Amanda understood her earlier rejection. Frau Meyer must have silently questioned her as a mother: how could she bring herself to abandon her daughter to two strangers? But she herself was boarding the ship out of despair, and Amanda's situation was doubtless even more desperate.

"I don't think you're doing the right thing," she said, "but I'll do all I can to make sure your child doesn't feel completely alone." Her tone of voice was firm; it was as if she wanted to rebuke Amanda, but felt unable to do so when, like everyone else in the port, she and her husband were fleeing the ravaging barbarism, leaving behind all that they knew.

The officer took the Meyers' documents and stamped a red "J" on their passports. Next to him, another officer asked Amanda for her papers. She handed him Viera's passport and landing permit. With the "J" stamped on it, they headed for the gangway. The Meyers stepped to one side, making room for Amanda to say goodbye. They had no one in Hamburg to bid farewell to.

Viera and Lina couldn't understand what was going on. Their mother had made her decision at the last minute; they still thought they were leaving Germany together to begin their island adventure.

Amanda bent down to her elder daughter. She wanted her to listen, to understand, to at least forgive her. Taking a small purple jewel case from her handbag, she lifted out two gold chains bearing the Star of David. She picked out the one with Viera's name, put Lina's back in the case, and dropped it in her bag once more.

"Viera, you're older." She looked her daughter in the eye as she hung the chain around her neck. "I don't think Lina would survive the trip."

Viera's lips began to tremble. Her eyes filled with thick tears.

"Mama!" she begged.

Lina was still staring fascinated at everything going on around her in the port: the waves breaking against the liner's prow, the swaying gangway, and the out-of-tune band that was still drowning out the shouts of goodbye.

"I'll always be with you, day and night, from afar," said Amanda, taking out the botanical album and tearing from it a handful of yellowing pages. "Listen to me, Viera. I'll keep these sheets. I'll write to you every morning on them while we're apart. The day the pages are finished, we'll meet again. I promise."

The three of them hugged and kissed each other.

"Mama loves you. We'll always be together. Your chain and mine will unite us. It's a gift from your papa," she said, touching the Star of David. "Look, Viera, Frau Meyer is waiting for you."

The little girl turned away from her mother, walked to the bottom of the gangway, gritting her teeth and making her way up the ramp, eyes downcast. Her heart was not pounding; she wasn't afraid. There was no need to count the absurd heartbeats.

Amanda looked for the ebony box in her suitcase, folded up the pages from the botanical album, and put them inside.

Lina stared at her mother despairingly. There were no questions she could ask: for the first time ever, she did not know what to say. Frau

Meyer turned, her eyes now filled with compassion, and gave them a compassionate smile. She had understood.

What have I done! Amanda screamed silently, her face contorted but without sighs or tears. As she watched her elder daughter disappear into the void, giving her the chance to be saved, she was suddenly filled with doubts. She was condemning her younger daughter. Although she was protecting her from the unknown, she was exposing her to the torments that were bound to come. Opening her eyes, she etched the details on her memory. It was May 13, 1939. Eight o'clock at night. Lina clung to her mother, unable to comprehend why she had been forced to remain on dry land.

What did I put in Viera's suitcase? What was the last thing she ate? Will she be cold? She could catch a fever in the high seas. Yes, there were several dresses, two pairs of shoes, but her clothes will soon be too small for her. My God! She wanted to stop time, to shout for her daughter to be brought back to her—but the ship's horn made her realize it was too late. The liner began to pull away from the quay; on the main deck she could make out the anxious faces of those who were fleeing. She couldn't see Viera or the Meyers. She imagined Viera alone in her first-class cabin, unpacking her small leather suitcase, smiling. *Yes, she was smiling*, Amanda told herself.

Taking hold of Lina's frozen hand, she turned her back on the boat, the Meyers, and her daughter.

My little Viera:

The days here grow grayer and grayer. Every morning the sun struggles to rise: sometimes it succeeds, and other times it fails, staying hidden in the clouds.

I have had no news from Uncle Abraham, but these days the mail is not a priority. I'll have to be patient a while longer.

I was waiting anxiously to hear from you, and checked the mailbox every evening until a few days ago the first letter I sent you was returned to me. I'll include it with this one, and this one with all the others they send back, because Mama will never give up, you can be sure of that.

We are at war. The world is at war, but fortunately we are protected in this village, on a farm, far from any big city. I don't think we will be found.

Your sister Lina is growing, and her French is more fluent by the day. You should hear her, she sounds just like one of the locals.

We've started attending a church, although I want you to know that I light a candle for you every night and clasp my Star of David as if it was yours. I can feel you on every one of its points in the palm of my hand.

By now you must be speaking Spanish, or at least a few words of it. I want you to write to me in your new language. I'm writing to you early in the morning, because I know that is when you would be going to bed. Get some rest, my little Viera, and every morning let the sun be your guide.

We will never stop thinking of you, even if on this side of the world day never dawns.

All my love,
Mama

THREE

The Refuge

Haute-Vienne, France, 1939–1942

11

Claire Duval feared oblivion. First her mother, then her father, and finally her husband had all disappeared into a thick fog of confusion, closing the door on their past. Eventually all three of them failed to recognize her, lost the ability to speak, spent their time gesturing blankly; in the end they gave up moving and curled up like newborn babies, returning to the seed.

She cherished the image of her husband, Jerome Oliver, a noble man with kind eyes who loved exotic plants and had dedicated his life to the study of botany. But he became irascible and violent, devoured by the most desolate old age, bedridden, his body full of sores, decaying by the minute. Jerome responded to the pain with a fixed, icy smile that made Claire shudder even to recall it. Yet she forced herself to do so, to remember every detail, to relive both radiant and bitter times, to find her way through labyrinths, in hopes that these memories would not haunt her dreams. Claire was afraid of dreams. They were the only thing she permitted herself to forget.

Recently she had been having recurring nightmares. She would wake up in a sweat, and try to erase the cloudy messages that told her she was putting her daughter's life in danger. She would open her eyes and wake up shivering, in the grip of fear. It had all started the day she received the letter from Julius Sternberg asking a favor she felt obliged to grant. She had agreed to take in his wife, the daughter of one of her husband's best and oldest friends.

It was her Christian duty, she thought, and repeated it to herself until she was weary, trying to convince herself she was not making a great mistake. She could not abandon Amanda, and yet she also had to protect her own daughter. She could still remember her husband sending antique French botanical albums to the Garden of Letters in Berlin. The two plant-loving men had enjoyed a long correspondence. Following the death of Amanda's father, Jerome became overwhelmed with sadness, and gradually succumbed to a loss of memory. Dementia took its toll, and after his death Claire devoted herself entirely to raising her young daughter. Now, by helping Amanda, she felt that she in turn was repaying a debt she owed her husband.

She got out of bed that May morning and breathed in the warm air, a sign that summer was not far off. After praying silently, she filled the window box by the front door with violets and gathered a bouquet of wildflowers: baby's breath, stems of early wheat, astilbes, gorse, dried lavender. These she placed in a bouquet on the table as a welcome for Amanda, whom she knew only through short letters and friendly references. She would try to help her recover from the anguish of being abandoned, from the pain of having sent her two daughters in a ship filled with tormented souls to an island lost in the ocean.

Peering out from the front door moments later, she could see a wavering shadow in the distance.

"Danielle!" she called out loudly. Alarmed, her daughter ran to her.

"*Maman*, you never told me Madame Sternberg was coming with someone else."

Putting her arm around her daughter's shoulders without saying anything, Claire began to stroke her hair.

Spring was at its height. Reds, oranges, yellows, and greens were winning out over the retreating gray. The woman and child coming toward them in heavy overcoats seemed to be dragging along an unseasonable winter.

Danielle clung to her mother as they both stood on the threshold, waiting. Amanda stepped forward, smiling timidly, and Claire helped her take off her dusty coat. When they embraced, she could feel the frail, emaciated body of this woman who breathed so slowly.

"Danielle, this is Madame Sternberg, Amanda. And . . ." she hesitated, as though waiting for confirmation: ". . . and this is her daughter."

"Lina," the newcomer clarified, looking down at the ground. "Viera traveled alone on the boat."

For a few seconds, the two girls peered curiously at each other, exchanging shy smiles. In a matter of seconds, they hugged, and Danielle took Lina by the hand and disappeared into the house with her.

Amanda turned and looked back, as if wondering if anyone could have followed her. A fleeting fantasy went through her mind: her daughter had escaped from the boat, jumping into the cold waters of the river in Hamburg, and swimming to the shore, determined not to be separated from them.

"But Viera can't swim," she said to herself.

"Time goes by quickly, you'll see," said Claire soothingly. She led Amanda into the dining room, filled with the sweet smell of cream and cinnamon from the welcome cake she had baked.

"All I can do is wait," said Amanda, spreading the loose pages of the botanical album on the table. "Viera is older. I gave her the book, but tore out these pages when we said goodbye. I'll use them to keep in touch with her. When they're finished, we'll meet again." She smiled ironically. "That's what I promised her. Have you ever heard of a mother who didn't keep the promises she made to her daughter?"

"Viera will be fine," Claire replied. She got up and came back with a cup of chamomile tea with a star anise clove floating in it. "What you did was for the best."

They sat in silence for a few minutes. Claire patiently observed the vague gestures, lost look, and constant sighing of this stranger to whom she had offered refuge.

Amanda already found it hard to recall the journey from Hamburg to Haute-Vienne, the long wait on the railway platform. Whether or not she had fed her daughter, or even if they had drunk any water. Her most recent memory was of the conductor's whistle as he called out the name of the village they had reached.

Claire led her to what would be her bedroom, behind the living room. Amanda had arrived in a temporary shelter with rickety wooden beams, peeling walls, unhinged doors and windows. A house full of shadows and glints of sunlight filtering in through cracks and holes. Her room had green, flaking walls, but the freshly pressed sheets shone impeccably white.

She tried to smile, but her face wouldn't obey her. Alone in her room, unable to weep, Amanda was engulfed by her pain: a physical, palpable pain like that of a missing arm haunted by the memory of its absent hand. Picking up one of the sheets from the botanical album without looking at the flower illustration, she tried to write a random sentence in the empty space, feeling as though at that moment her soul was parting from her body. It rose and bumped against the wooden ceiling beams: she could see her inert body below, facing the blank paper, pen in hand, waiting for inspiration as to what she could say to her abandoned daughter.

My little Viera, she wrote in German, the language she had sworn never to speak again. *Maybe it would be better to write in French?* she thought. Her writing was shaky, with looping letters, heavy and uneven. Fear was obvious there too. *It's only been a few hours, and yet your mama misses you . . .* She had to give Viera a sign, some indication they would meet once again. *Summer of 1939*, she managed to write, a date as vague as her thoughts. She had no idea when she would be able to finish the letter, which would cross part of France and an entire ocean before reaching the torrid streets of Havana. She fell asleep still holding the pen, her head only a few inches from the sheet of paper.

〰

Shortly after midnight, Claire heard some muffled sounds. She crossed the darkened living room silently, reached Amanda's room, and put her ear to the door. She realized Amanda was singing what to her sounded like a lullaby. *Guten Abend, gut Nacht, mit Rosen bedacht, mit Näglein besteckt, schlupf unter die Deck: Morgen früh, wenn Gott will, wirst du wieder geweckt.* With the little German she knew, Claire made out: "roses and carnations under the bedcover" and "God willing, you'll wake again in the morning."

It would take Amanda six weeks to complete that first letter. She could not allow herself any mistakes: the precious sheets from the book she had mutilated couldn't be wasted. Every word, every sentence, had to be carefully weighed. It was vital to sense how it would sound to her daughter, all alone and lost on the far side of the world. She had repeated doubts about what she had written: she wanted to avoid Viera thinking she was weak and grief-stricken. She had to convey the impression that she was happy in order to raise her spirits.

One damp summer's night, she sealed the envelope and put it into the red mailbox up by the town's main street. Three days and two storms went by before the mailman collected it. From there maybe he would take it to Limoges, where it would be processed and sent on to its destination. Who knew whether letters destined for the far side of the Atlantic had to go through Paris? Amanda discussed this endlessly as she helped Claire in the kitchen or the two of them sat together to knit scarves for the winter while the girls ran about, climbed on branches, or collapsed into the already withered flowers along the path.

Some nights, Amanda read them the text accompanying the illustrations in the botanical album. Danielle was enchanted by the French and Latin spoken by this German lady. Before their goodnight kiss, she always told the two girls about Viera, how mischievous she was, and how she would listen with the stethoscope to books before she read them, or sniffed at them to try to guess what story they told.

"We should have brought Papa's stethoscope," Lina commented one night. "Danielle and I could have played with it like Viera and I used to."

After switching off their light, Amanda withdrew slowly to her own room. She was surprised that in the house there were only recipe books, ones about medicinal plants, and a Bible; all of them hidden away on the top shelves in the kitchen.

On Sundays, all four of them went to Father Marcel's mass in the village church, where Amanda learned about Christian views on guilt, punishment, and forgiveness. Although she had no intention of changing her religion, she simply let herself be carried along by a liturgy that soothed her, and felt moved at seeing Lina kneeling down, hands clasped, eyes shut, and head bowed as she prayed with childish fervor to a foreign god.

Danielle amused herself trying to get rid of all traces of German in Lina's accent. Sometimes she put a pencil in her mouth, at others a bread crumb under her tongue. Or she made her say the words as if she were about to blow a kiss, which left them both roaring with laughter. To the village children though, no matter how much Lina tried, she was still the German girl, or the girl from Alsace, or even Danielle's refugee friend. Amanda worried less when she realized no one rejected her for being "the Jewish girl."

At sunset every Friday, Amanda lit candles in the window, waiting until the stars appeared in the sky the following day to write unfinished sentences to Viera. Fridays were also the night they welcomed Father Marcel at home. They had supper together, which always included an intense discussion about the terrible shadow hanging over Europe.

Father Marcel was tall and full of life. His hair was cut so short around the ears and the nape of his neck that they could see his veins bulge whenever he became agitated. His kind gray eyes contrasted with the vehement way he challenged the world, although he never raised his voice and spoke with a gentle cadence that delighted Claire and confused Amanda. His fervor, the bitterness of his words, his pessimism about the dark days approaching sounded old-fashioned and strange to someone who did not understand his precise French. It was only when he was in the pulpit that his tone of voice became harsher and flooded the entire church.

"I sometimes think the world is coming to an end," he said slowly one evening. "Is praying all we have left? War is imminent."

For Amanda, the war had already started. Father Marcel's words did not trouble her as much as they did Claire, for whom the priest was the only person she felt she could trust and turn to for protection after her husband's death.

"I don't think the Germans will dare invade France," she ventured.

"They've already done so once, and were on the losing side. But now they have the military might and the support of an entire blinkered nation," Father Marcel said in a low voice. "We're talking about Hitler, not some ordinary military man."

"Are the Nazis going to reach us here?" asked Lina, terrified.

"We'll never let them in," Danielle encouraged her.

"War hasn't been declared yet," Claire interrupted them, "so let's not worry about it. Finish up your soup, that's what's important now!" She had seen terror flash in the girls' eyes.

"All I'm saying is that we have to be prepared," the priest insisted, before continuing with his meal.

Amanda listened to their talk without joining in. The Nazis had already destroyed her family, and she was almost certain there was no safe haven for her daughter.

"He's an orphan who was raised by nuns. That's why he's such a 'rebel,'" Claire whispered to Amanda so that Father Marcel would not hear. "He gets hot under the collar about everything. He's as wise as an old man, but the vigor of youth makes him impetuous."

"What are we doing while the world goes to ruin? Nothing. I can't believe what I've turned into," the priest went on passionately, shaking his head. "I no longer know who I am." He sighed and dropped his spoon on the table, shutting his eyes as if in the midst of an epic battle with himself.

"We're all facing the same dilemma," Amanda dared to comment, then instantly lowered her head, afraid she had been indiscreet.

The priest paused, and realized he was upsetting his hosts.

"There won't be a war," he said. "At least, let's pray there won't be," he said, rounding off his heated speech with a spoonful of soup. He stared down at the flowery tablecloth.

Claire got up to clear the table. Before taking his plate, she extended her hand to him in a consoling gesture. Father Marcel was still looking down at the tablecloth.

"I'll make sure Lina is enrolled in the girls' school in the village," he said eventually, glancing across at Amanda. She thanked him with a smile.

The evening ended without goodbyes. Amanda took the girls to their room and put the chair between their two beds, next to the small light.

"Mama's going to read the pages of the torn-up book for us," said Lina, stressing "torn-up" in a mysterious fashion. "She's going to tell us about flowers and the roots of legumes and the phlox family . . ."

Claire accompanied the priest to the road, and stood beside him. They didn't look up at the moon, which was hidden behind clouds; there were no stars either. They gazed at the dark night sky. Father Marcel took Claire's warm, familiar hand, and she dared to rest her head on his friendly shoulder. They remained like that for several minutes, until he moved silently away from their tranquil closeness. Almost as if he was escaping, he strode off into the darkness.

12

$\mathscr{L}$ina was overjoyed at the possibility of going to school with Danielle. She promised herself she would practice her French until there was no trace of an accent left. She wanted to be more French than the French girls, she told herself, endlessly spelling out the most difficult words.

"We won't be in the same class," Danielle, who was eight years old but mature for her age, warned her as they sat on the step at the back of Claire's house.

"But we can go and come back together, and that's the most important thing."

One afternoon, their conversation was interrupted by a whirlwind of leaves on the dusty path. Out of it emerged a young boy.

"That's Remi," explained Danielle. "You'll see, he spends his time making mischief."

"So this is the foreign girl," said the boy. He approached Lina, studying her intently, trying to figure out where exactly she came from. Realizing he was intimidating her, he backed off a little and dropped the threadbare ball he had been carrying under his arm, as if to protect it. "Don't be scared, little girl. We don't eat anyone here."

"Are you sure?" said Danielle. "As far as I can tell, you're always hungry." Danielle took Lina's hand and the two of them set off on a shortcut toward the village.

"I hope this *Elise* speaks some French," Remi continued as he followed them, running in front and around in circles.

"*Elise*? Her name is Lina, and she can speak French better than you. Don't forget your family came from the north, so you're more of a foreigner than she is . . ."

"She looks more like an *Elise*, doesn't she?"

"Don't listen to him," Danielle told Lina. "He spends all his time inventing words for everything he comes across."

"Let's go to the river!" shouted Remi, and raced off, adjusting the white belt with its metal buckle holding up a pair of pants that were already too small. He was wearing shoes, but no socks. The girls ran after him. The whole way to the village, Lina didn't dare utter a single word.

The boy took them to the train tracks by the village entrance. Just where the rails rounded a bend, right before the bridge, there was an enormous boulder. They rested in its shadow.

"The train should go by in half an hour," said Remi. His cheeks were flushed from the run, his shirt collar soaked with sweat. "This is a good place to sit."

Lina studied him in silence, trying to follow the avalanche of words and jokes that poured out of him.

"That's how Giampiero Combi wore them in the World Cup, and that's how I'll always wear them," he explained proudly when he saw that his new friend was curious about his white belt.

His family was from Rheims, although his mother came from Emilia-Romagna. She fell in love with a Frenchman and left her family and country behind, fleeing the inanity breeding in the heart of her city. At least, that was the story that Danielle had heard during one of the

Friday suppers with Father Marcel. Remi had never learned his mother's language, but was passionate about the soccer team of a country he didn't know "and had no intention of visiting while Il Duce was in power," he would say, in a phrase repeated from his mother. Whenever they listened to a game on the radio, his father would say jokingly: "So you're a Juventus fan? That makes us mortal enemies." His mother would wink at him, while Remi would reply proudly that he would never support a losing team, and that France would never win a World Cup if members of the Juventus team were playing. Italy had won it the previous year, and he would support them "to the death." "Fascist! My only son has turned out a Fascist!" His father would moan, head in hands. "We will no longer eat pasta in this house," he ordered his wife, who laughed while her son wondered why his father called him that.

"My dad says there'll soon be a war. If war does break out and the Germans invade France, instead of heading north we'll cross the Pyrenees and go as far south as we can, into Spain. We already have a plan. What about you?"

"If there's a war and the Germans enter Paris, I don't think there will be many places left to escape to," Danielle insisted.

"We escaped once, but if every time the Nazis get near we all run away, what will become of us?" said Lina, who up to that moment had not said a word. She spoke very slowly, trying to pronounce every word exactly, so as to seem older and give herself an air of childish superiority.

Slightly taken aback, Remi ran to the rail tracks.

"The train's coming! We have to cross to the other side."

In the distance they could see the locomotive about to enter the bend. Remi took Danielle by the hand and they crossed the tracks. Lina was left behind.

"Lina!" shouted Danielle. "You won't have time to cross. Stay where you are!"

Remi buried his face in his hands. Lina climbed onto the rail, hesitated for a moment, staring at the onrushing locomotive, and sprang forward, falling headfirst onto the stones in the center of the tracks. The vibration from the rails shook her whole body, but she lay still until the train had disappeared. Danielle thought she saw beneath the train the feet of the girl she was meant to protect, but she was blinded by the dust and her scream made no sound. Remi ran over to Lina, helped her to her feet, and gave her a hug.

"Are you all right?"

Lina didn't reply. She jumped up; a trickle of blood ran from the cuts on her knees.

"She's a brave one, your little German girl," said Remi, while Danielle ran over to them, still recovering from the shock.

Lina set off, stiff and erect, trying to ignore the burning sensation on her knees. She knew that to win the respect of Remi and the girls at the school she mustn't cry. She was determined not to let anyone intimidate her: her accent would disappear and she would be ready to take on the world, even the Germans if they dared invade. Over time, the traces of her past would be erased from her memory.

From that moment on, Remi became their inseparable companion. They often played soccer, each of them fighting to gain control of the old ball. It was Remi's pet; he even took it to bed with him. He called it Combi, after the legendary Juventus player.

13

The world was at war. Eyes downcast, the schoolteacher gave her pupils the news, which was a surprise to no one. Lina and Danielle weren't too worried. They lived in a tiny village deep in the French countryside; it was impossible that the German army would want to cross meadows, mountains, and rivers just to reach such an insignificant spot with only two or three stores and an austere church.

Despite this, the dynamics in the village changed. During their Friday suppers with Father Marcel, long silences replaced their formerly animated discussions. Lina and Danielle left early in the mornings, came back home for lunch, and then returned for their afternoon classes. After school, they played with Remi in an abandoned orchard behind the church.

Some days Father Marcel joined them in kicking the increasingly tattered ball. On Fridays they all went back together for supper at Claire's house. Remi was a new guest, and Father Marcel found it strange that he had succeeded in converting Lina and Danielle into fans of that foreign team that had won the World Cup a second time in France the previous year.

Thanks to Remi and the start of the school year, life in the village had become easier for Lina. She spent more time outside the house, and liked to think that the worst had already passed, that she could grow up in a family at peace, even though her teachers occasionally spoke of a Nazi occupation, which frightened her. But she had Danielle and Remi, and this made her feel like the luckiest girl in the world. Still, when she went to bed each night she always missed Viera. What more could she ask for? They had come to a new country; she had found two new friends, and felt protected. Alongside them she was capable of facing even the most powerful enemy.

One Friday, after their soccer game with Father Marcel, they saw the taciturn, bulky figure of the mailman coming out of Madame Beauchêne's café. He was obviously heading for Claire's house.

"The letter!" Danielle shouted to Lina. "News from Viera!"

Lina frowned, came to a halt, and then lagged behind the other two. She sensed that this letter would not be bringing good news, and was sure her mother would once again become despondent. Her father had explained to them that life was like the peaks and valleys of an electrocardiogram, an endless roller coaster. For the first time since they arrived in France, Lina began to count her heart's rapid beats to try to measure the silences: *one, two, three . . .*

Amanda was standing beside the red mailbox. Every evening, like a sentinel, she waited for some sign from the distant island, and wrote meaningless phrases on the sheets from the botanical album. She could not help feeling punished whenever Viera's face became blurred in her memory. Only six months after her departure, she could no longer picture her daughter clearly, recall the exact color of her eyes, or remember what clothes she had been wearing when she left. *We distance ourselves from the past far too quickly*, she told herself.

The mailman was panting. He opened the enormous bag that contained nothing more than a small, yellowing envelope covered with red and black stamps. Amanda took it without a word. The mailman looked at the ground, but she gazed up at the cloud-filled sky.

"It's getting darker earlier. I must light candles," she said, and hurried back to the house.

Perhaps she ought to try to understand better the Christian idea of trespasses and forgiveness. Perhaps she should confess all her sins and try to redeem them. Perhaps she should forget who she was, put herself in the hands of a merciful god and worship the cross. But she could not, she must not. For her own sake and that of her dead family, and for her daughters.

Amanda searched in the wardrobe for a perfectly ironed dress and changed into it, avoiding the sight of herself in the mirror. She put her hair up and fastened her pearl earrings. Switching off the light in her room, she lit two small candles, rubbing her icy hands above the flames to warm them. Weeping in a jagged silence, she glanced at the envelope by the candles' meager light. They had returned the letter after it had crossed France, the Atlantic, and the streets of Havana, without finding her daughter.

She put the envelope away in the ebony box. Leaning on the windowsill, she watched the sun begin to set and prayed for some respite from her pain. When she heard Lina come into the room, she bent toward her and greeted her with a smile. She blessed her with a kiss on the forehead, then told her to wash her hands before supper.

Amanda prayed for strength on the path she still had to follow and decided to start another letter as soon as she could see three stars come out on Saturday night. She could not give in. She was sure her daughter was well, and so at dawn she would sing silently just for her at that special moment when they could communicate even though the letters never reached their destination.

14

$\mathcal{A}$t school they had begun air-raid drills. France had declared war on Germany, and Lina was afraid she would once more be seen as the enemy. That was what she had been in Berlin, and now they might regard her as the invader. She was only comforted by the fact that this time she was part of the majority. Shutting her eyes, she begged all the gods in the universe to leave her in peace, to let her be just another little French girl in her class.

The teacher explained that they all had to be prepared for the first bomb to fall, unable to avoid sounding terrified, not because of the imminent attack, but rather due to the fear she could be instilling among her students. When they heard the siren go off, the girls were to hide under their desks until they were told they could go out into the yard. They had to respond quickly to orders, without thinking or hesitating.

For the girls, the enemy was still invisible. Lina thought they would come out of the sky, hidden among the clouds, and crush them all. This time there would be no chosen ones, no religion. All of them, no matter which god they worshipped, would fall in the clutches of the same power, and no one in the world would be able to withstand it.

"We're in the *drôle de guerre,*" Father Marcel told Claire as he stood in the doorway after supper. Amanda was watching the two girls dig a grave for a baby bird that had fallen from its nest.

"I bet it was shot down by a German plane," whispered Lina.

"The first victim of this phony war," Danielle agreed.

"If we go on like this, the Germans will swat us like flies," the priest went on. "We have an old man commanding our army, and the British aren't going to cross the Channel to defend us. Why would they?"

"The Germans won't dare invade. It won't be easy for them to take Paris," Claire repeated, trying to sound convinced simply to calm her friend's suppressed anger. In fact, she was far from sure of what she was saying; an obscure fear kept her awake most nights now.

For Amanda, the future was veiled. Her mind fixed on her reunion with Viera, she was no longer able to see what lay ahead. At dawn one Saturday she picked up another sheet from the book and began to write. The war she had left behind in Berlin, as well as this one pursuing her even in the fields of Haute-Vienne, made no sense to her. But she also knew that however much she hid, she would be found out and humiliated time and again before eventually being annihilated. To her that war, the only war that mattered, was not in any way phony.

Fall of 1939. My little Viera . . . The days here grow grayer and grayer. The sun struggles to come out every morning: sometimes it succeeds, and other times it fails, and stays hidden in the clouds. I'm sure that on your island it always shines, and lights up every morning . . .

With the November rain the sky came crashing down on the roads. The Vienne River seemed to spread everywhere. Stones, tree trunks, house facades, and even windows became covered in moss. Lina would spend hours fascinated by this green carpet clinging to every surface and growing with each passing day. *One day, the light will no longer enter the house,* she thought, trying unsuccessfully to scrape the dark wet velvet from the walls.

One morning, Claire didn't appear from her bedroom. The rain had left them all disoriented, walking around in an endless dusk. Amanda knocked gently on her door. Nobody answered, but she could hear Claire's labored breathing in the dark. When she went in and pulled back the curtains, the reluctant daylight revealed Claire bathed in sweat, with cracked lips and half-closed eyes. She was shivering with fever.

Amanda sent the girls to soak some towels in cold water, then gently pressed them against the back of Claire's neck and on her forehead.

"You're going to be all right," she whispered. "It's impossible not to get ill with weather like this. Are fall and winter always the same here?"

Lina and Danielle hung in the doorway, not daring to come into the room.

"We must let her rest," said Amanda, and went to make an herbal tea.

When he heard from the girls that Claire was ill in bed, Father Marcel came running back to the house with them. He was overwhelmed by the smell of eucalyptus and the calendula, mallow, and celandine infusion when he entered his friend's private chamber for the first time.

"This rain is getting to us all," he said, sitting down at her bedside.

He took Claire's hands in his, and kissed them timorously. She smiled and tried to sleep: that was all she had the strength to do. Father Marcel scanned every corner of the dimly lit room. He recognized Claire dressed in white in a faded photograph, alongside a man in a jacket and straw hat. They were both staring out with startled eyes. The priest picked up his wooden rosary and concentrated on his prayers.

The next morning, Claire was worse. The fever had not come down, her breathing was increasingly irregular. Amanda thought they should send for a doctor.

"No," protested Claire. "I'll be better tomorrow."

For six nights, Father Marcel prayed and kept vigil beside Claire's bed. He would leave in the rain at midnight, and return at dusk the next day. He quickly grew accustomed to being alone with her and recounting the details of his life: his childhood with the nuns, the seminary, the early discovery of his destined vocation, when he realized he would never find out who his parents were. Possibly two fearful adolescents who had left him on the convent doorstep. "Too melodramatic to be true," he joked.

"For a long while I felt abandoned and helpless," he went on. "How can anyone leave a child out in the open like that? But I came to understand, and forgot and forgave. Who knows what was going through my mother's mind? And now I have a huge family, don't I?"

One morning color began to seep back into Claire's pallid, feverlined face. Father Marcel was ashamed that this good news didn't fill him with joy. If Claire recovered, his contact with her would once more be limited to the Friday evening suppers and the occasional conversation after mass, or a trip to the abbey with the girls. He knew there would no longer be any reason for his daily visits to the house, still less to remain alone with Claire. She understood his ambivalent feelings.

"This is your home, Father. You'll always be welcome here," she said without looking at him, blushing and grateful.

That night they did not say goodbye with an herbal tea but drank freshly ground coffee outside her bedroom. They sat together in the dining room, staring out at the storm that had kept them happily imprisoned.

15

The second letter was returned as winter arrived. They already knew what it was when they saw the mailman approaching, head down. Amanda took the envelope and stored it away in the ebony box. She was convinced that someday her daughter would read them all and discover she had always been by her side. That was the most important thing. She would wait for the new year; it made no sense to send another letter at a time when it was bound to get lost among all the Christmas cards and packages. She was hopeful that, in the first days of January, the distances would grow shorter when some post office employee on the island would take pity on her for insisting so much, and finally uncover the whereabouts of her daughter, who must by now speak Spanish like a native. Or maybe it would be better to start to write again in spring, when the flowers bloomed once more. Amanda was resigned to the passage of time, but not to oblivion.

At the start of this new decade, the war still seemed like a silent threat. There had not been a single clash on a battlefield, a single explosion, no invaders, no defense maneuvers. War ships against war ships in the mid-Atlantic, far from land. In the city, occasional leaflets fell from the skies onto roofs and squares like delicate snowflakes. Father Marcel lamented that this was the only response that a nation willing to go down on its knees before the enemy was willing to make. For her part, Claire was convinced the German attack was imminent, that the days of peace were slipping away. Amanda also sensed that her place of refuge would soon vanish.

❦

In the middle of spring, with the tulips in full bloom, the Netherlands collapsed like a house of cards. A month later, the Germans crossed the weakest border and entered France. Two months later, on June 14, 1940, Paris, *la grande dame*, surrendered at their feet.

"Nobody can resist the Germans," Amanda told them. "It's dreadful, but that's the reality. They will rule the world."

"I don't think we'll see any Nazis around here. They won't raise their swastika flag over our village," said Claire, although she herself was not entirely convinced.

Amanda shuddered. If she abandoned Claire's house and headed south across the Pyrenees, Viera would not know how to find her. She had to wait a little longer before making a decision.

They listened heavyhearted to the voice of the French general calling from his London exile.

"Whatever happens, the flame of the French Resistance must not be extinguished, and will not be extinguished."

It took Amanda a year to finish her next letter. She was well aware that it would never reach its destination, at least not while she was alive. But she had to write.

> *Winter of 1940. My little Viera: Darkness has come over us. Can you see how right I was to let you go, even though my heart suffers for it every hour of every day? Only God is witness to the strength I had to summon to abandon you. Only He could give me the determination to take your sister by the hand and walk away from you.*

This was the first time Amanda was writing about leaving her daughter, and she did so resolutely. It was also the moment when she had to face up to herself and take responsibility for her possible mistake. And now she needed to be even stronger to save Lina. She began to quietly hatch her plan, studying all the different possibilities. She had a mission, and could not allow herself to be thwarted.

The change in her was obvious to Claire, who could not understand how Amanda could seem so serene, happy even. Her face was lit up. She was more affectionate with the girls, and her silences over supper turned into lively conversation.

She began to call her friend "*Maman* Claire." "Come on, Lina, help *Maman* Claire." "Run along, *Maman* Claire needs you." "Go to the market with *Maman* Claire." In this way she began a kind of transfer. From that moment on for Lina, Claire was *Maman* Claire. Now, whenever her daughter asked if she could go down to the river with Danielle or Remi, or stay in the village after school, she told her to ask *Maman* Claire. Soon, even Father Marcel began to call her that as well.

The following year, 1941, even though they had not seen signs of them anywhere near the village, it was rumored that the Nazis had occupied Limoges, about twenty kilometers away. The newspaper headlines began to publicize the new regulations for Jews, signed by the French government in Vichy. The new laws authorized the "Aryanization" of Jewish businesses and prohibited Jews from working in newspapers, the theater, or radio. For Amanda, history was repeating itself. This time she was indifferent to it. There was nothing to be done.

Claire had taken over reading to the girls at night, and told them fantastic stories to take their minds off the invisible war.

When Lina had fallen asleep, Danielle asked Claire about her father.

"You were the apple of his eye," Claire would tell her nostalgically, glancing at her wedding photograph and sighing. "Thank God your father is no longer with us, Danielle. He wouldn't have been able to bear what France has turned into. He was a man who devoted his entire life to his country . . ."

16

One summer morning in 1942, the mailman knocked on Claire's door. This time he was accompanied by a gendarme and Limoges city hall employee.

Claire's heart sank. She greeted them warily, with Amanda by her side. An icy blast entered the house with them, and the girls ran to hide in the loft. The mailman pointed to one of the two women with a trembling hand. There was fear in his gestures, but his eyes glittered with the relief of being able to denounce someone.

"She is Amanda Sternberg," he said.

"Your papers," the uniformed gendarme demanded. This was the law and it had to be obeyed, even if it came from the enemy. Though when all was said and done, no one was very clear on who exactly the enemy was.

Amanda went to her bedroom, then returned and slowly handed the gendarme her documents and those of her daughter.

The man laboriously jotted down their names and dates of birth. In the margin he wrote the date, July 16, 1942, and the word JEWS in capital letters. Proud of his beautiful handwriting, he checked what he had copied into his notebook, then held it out for the mailman to admire as well.

"It's a mere formality," the city official added uncomfortably. "We have to keep an up-to-date record of all the Jews in the area. That's the law."

Confronted by the two women's forbidding looks, the three men turned and left without saying goodbye.

From that moment on, Amanda and her daughter lacked protection. Their fates would be decided at the whim of the French police who, according to Father Marcel, were becoming more cowardly and submissive by the day.

The letters. The letters gave us away. The thought hammered at Amanda's temples. Her determination to find Viera had put Lina at risk. She and Claire sat silently over a cup of tea while they tried to find some consoling idea, some words to offer them hope. Claire's eyes flashed with anger and terror: Amanda and Lina's lives were in the hands of a law signed by the French to please the Germans—a provision that allowed them to carry on in return for denouncing the undesirables.

There's no way out. No one can rewrite their fate, Amanda told herself. She was protected by a village priest and a woman who had endangered her own daughter's life by taking her and Lina in.

Father Marcel arrived in a state of alarm. The few Spaniards living in the village, the Gaullists, and the "undesirables" had just been rounded up and taken away to a forced labor camp.

"I can prepare a baptismal certificate for Lina and send her to the convent I grew up in," he said, stumbling over his words. "Neither of you is safe here, but we can at least make sure they don't take Lina. There is talk of people being rounded up in Paris. With the help of the Vichy government, the Germans have filled France with forced labor camps."

Amanda listened to him eyes half closed, showing no emotion. Outside, the girls were chasing happily after Remi's ball.

"The best thing would be to talk to Father Auguste at the abbey.

I'm sure he'll help us. This isn't a safe place for you anymore," the priest insisted.

"No place is safe. We can't spend all our lives running."

"Amanda, with the abbot's help we can save Lina," said Claire. "He's an old man, but I'm sure that if Father Marcel asks him, he won't refuse. With the baptismal certificate . . ."

"I'm not going to abandon my daughter," Amanda interrupted her sternly. "I did that once, and I'm not going to do it again. She is only seven years old."

They sipped wine as they sat around the table. Claire grasped Amanda's hands; her friend allowed herself to be comforted, while Father Marcel drank in silence until he suddenly thumped the tabletop twice and stood up with a sigh.

"We'll find a solution. For now, I think it's wiser if Lina doesn't go to school."

17

$\mathcal{S}$hielded by the light of a candle in the small loft, the girls hid behind some wooden barrels. They had built a den with discarded blankets and rusty pieces of junk.

"They won't find us here," Danielle said. "From today on you will be Elise, so everyone will think you're French like us. Maybe *Maman* can adopt you, then we would officially be sisters. Who would doubt it? You look more like her than I do."

Lina said nothing, staring at the candle's wavering light. When it went out, the two girls fell asleep in each other's arms.

Amanda had difficulty convincing Lina, but decided they shouldn't go with Danielle and Claire to mass that Sunday. Father Marcel's homily began with references to princes, Philistines, surrendered daughters, and betrayals. None of the congregation understood quite what he was trying to say with these biblical references. There was no mention of the war, of Paris handed over to the Germans. Everything revolved around guilt and betrayal, shame and duty. At the end, staring hard at the faithful, Father Marcel slowly read them a psalm: "For it was not an enemy that reproached me; then I could have borne it. Neither was it he that hated me that did magnify himself against me; then I would have hid myself from him. But it was thou, a man mine equal, my guide, and mine acquaintance . . ."

An uneasy murmur filled the church. Tears ran down some of the congregation's cheeks. Claire fell to her knees and began to pray, while Danielle and Remi ran off to find Lina.

The priest shut himself in the sacristy. For a long while he paced up and down, hands clasped behind his back, deep in troubled thoughts. When he emerged, he bumped into the mailman who had apparently been waiting for him. The priest walked straight past him: he had no intention of stopping. He could not improvise another sermon, and had no wish to punish this fellow who was consumed by his own cowardice. He had to concentrate on something far more important: finding a new refuge for Amanda and Lina.

"I was only following orders," the mailman burst out, running after him. "I couldn't ignore them."

"What do you want me to say? That you should recite ten Our Fathers? Go on then, if you think that will clear your conscience."

"There were instructions from city hall that the register had to be updated. All I said was that there was a foreigner living there. I had no idea she was Jewish. We were ordered to locate all *étrangers indésirables.*"

"And what's the difference?"

"You know, Father, that we cannot hide Jews. They are acting against us."

"They are?" Father Marcel was about to add something else, but there was no point. "I think it's better if you leave now. I've got important matters to attend to."

"The thing is, if we don't get rid of them, if we don't collaborate, the Germans will unleash all their fury against us, Father. I have a family . . ."

"They've already unleashed that fury on us. We are on our knees." Father Marcel sighed. "Well, each of us must decide for himself." He turned on his heel and strode off across the village square, heading for the abbey.

The mailman did not move. He thought about returning to the altar, genuflecting, and asking forgiveness, but in the end preferred to reassure himself that he had done the right thing. "We have to carry out the laws," he told himself as he confronted the image of the crucified Jesus. "That's the only thing we can do. You know that even better than us. You were betrayed as well, and what did you do? Nothing." He dipped his finger in the font and crossed himself with a shrug of the shoulders. "No priest is going to come and tell me what's right and what's wrong. Neither he nor anyone else is above the law."

As he crossed the square, Father Marcel was thinking about the incident with the mailman. *The stench of fear contaminates: everything that comes into contact with it becomes vulnerable, and once someone has started down that path, it's impossible to get off it. The stench of disgrace is even more disgusting: nobody thinks, nobody reacts. And God simply looks on,* the priest mused, analyzing his own refusal to argue with the informer.

This episode amplified his vigilance. He was alert to any activity in the village, aware that anybody could follow the mailman's example. All those who had taken communion from him could become informers, because the moment had arrived to betray one's neighbor to save one's own skin. He went into the Hotel Beaubreuil to buy a newspaper. He read the headlines and tried to keep himself informed, but only had access to news that he mistrusted. He had no doubt that soon all the "undesirables" would be rounded up. He spent sleepless nights trying to find excuses for his congregation by dwelling on the smallest act of kindness. He even came to question his own vocation, and his doubts caused him physical pain. It would be more useful if he joined the Resistance, he thought, if he went into the maquis. But he was nothing more than a priest, who could only speak out and forgive in the name of God.

"First they'll take away the undesirables. When not a single one of them is left in France, it'll be our turn," he told himself under his breath.

18

$\mathcal{T}$he presence of the Germans in Limoges meant the nearby towns and villages felt exposed. The time to begin the exodus had arrived. However small their farms and village squares, however distant they might be from the big cities, the Nazi occupation was a fact, and everyone feared the outcome.

Those who had arrived from the north or from Paris set off again southward in search of refuge. The villages emptied; the roads became crammed with people. For Claire, the war was just beginning. For Amanda, it was coming to an end; it was impossible to keep up a fight for more than three years. Her only hope lay with time, the cure to all her ailments. But how long would she have to wait?

The days seemed longer to Lina since she had been prevented from going to school. Danielle and Remi told her that a bomb could fall on them at any moment, and that the protective measures the teachers demonstrated were a farce that the children took part in gleefully as they would a game.

The days were filled with danger; Lina's aim was to reach nightfall safely. She didn't think the French or German soldiers would come to *remove* them at night—that was the word her mother used whenever Claire or Father Marcel mentioned the roundups in neighboring villages.

"What if they do come to remove us at night . . . ?" Amanda was saying to Claire one afternoon when she saw Lina and Danielle rush in, wild-eyed and with their shoes covered in mud.

"We saw them," cried Lina, trying to catch her breath.

"They crossed the bridge heading for Limoges," Danielle whispered.

"Well, that's where they'll stay. They've got more important things to do there," Claire retorted, trying to play down the significance of what the girls had seen. She went into the kitchen and stood there, head bowed. Amanda followed, and when she reached her, stared at her for a long while. The moment was coming.

At sunset, Amanda lit her Friday candles. She was convinced Father Marcel would bring bad news to the supper table, and her mind was made up. She went back into her room, packed a suitcase for her and Lina, then called Claire in.

They sat for several minutes on the edge of the bed in silence. A shaft of light shining in through the window caught them by surprise. Claire looked down anxiously at the ebony box on Amanda's lap. In the half-light, her friend's face lost its soft outline and looked severe, imposing.

"The only thing that unites me and my daughter is in here, Claire. Can you imagine that something so big could fit into such a small space?"

There was no answer to a question like that. Claire's heart started racing.

"I know they're going to come sooner or later," said Amanda. "They'll take us away, to who knows where. This box contains what's most precious to me. Someday my daughter will hear from us, someday she'll understand that I didn't abandon her."

Her voice cracked, and the last words sounded like a moan. A dry, tearless moan.

"Everything must come to an end, and I know that this war will be over one day and life will go on. But not for me. It's too late for us."

Claire couldn't help feeling guilty, wounded, desperate. She prayed silently to God to help her find a way to save her friend.

"Promise me these letters will reach Viera. Promise me that, Claire. That's all I ask of you."

Claire tried to embrace her, but could feel how stiff Amanda's body was, refusing all compassion. They moved apart, and Amanda went over to the window. Lighting another candle, she picked up one of the pages from the botanical album. She read out aloud the name of the flower illustrated on the faded sheet: *Matthiola incana*, admiring the delicate purple of its petals, its enduring beauty.

All of a sudden, she felt breathless, as though the flower was absorbing all the oxygen in the room. She dropped the sheet, trying to capture a reviving breeze. A letter wasn't going to solve anything; she had to put a stop to this pointless farce.

And yet she began to write, and the words spilled out furiously, unrelenting. When the candle burned down, she snuffed it out with her fingers, and continued writing in the darkness. The light from the window glinted on the mother-of-pearl decoration on the small box that Claire was still holding.

Suddenly, Amanda halted. She took the sheet of paper, crumpled it in her fist, and threw it into a corner of the room. She stood up and, without looking at Claire, made her way into the dining room, as stiffly as a robot.

Alarmed, Claire rushed to retrieve the crumpled sheet of paper. She stroked it smooth against her chest, then opened the box to put it with the other returned letters.

"We have to go. There isn't much time," Father Marcel urged them as he came into the room.

For the first time, he was including himself. And he didn't mention Lina's baptismal certificate, or speak of sending her to a convent, or say Amanda should cross the border into Spain, or that Claire and Danielle should get as far away south as possible. This time, he would be leading their escape. That was the only thing that made Claire feel safe: it was the only way she would run the risk of fleeing.

Amanda didn't get involved in these new escape plans. She thought that she was paying for the guilt of having betrayed her husband by not sending Lina to Cuba with Viera. If she had done so, both would now be safe. But the damage was done, and it was irreparable. There was no way back.

That night, Lina slept with her in the narrow bed. There were no bedtime stories, no readings about exotic plants, no Latin names. Amanda remembered Hilde, and in her mind went over the infinite different paths she could have taken: what if she had sent both girls to Cuba; what if all three of them had gone to Paris? There were too many possibilities.

Her eyes shut, Amanda tried to picture Hilde in her mind. *My dear friend, the Nazis have also reached the most beautiful city in the world, the city you dreamed of living in with the girls. Paris: Can you imagine? We would have been happy . . . but in the end, happiness is only a moment, a mirage. Viera is on a far-off island, Lina and I are helpless . . . and you, where are you? Berlin, Paris, or did you perhaps decide to seek refuge with your parents in the distant south? We don't belong anywhere. We have no roots, and never will. At this moment I need your hand to give me the strength to make a decision. A decision that I'm sure I will also regret. That is my punishment, constant regret.*

Listening to herself, she thought for a moment of writing a letter to her friend. It was never written; instead, she fell fast asleep.

19

*E*ach morning, Amanda got up as though it was her last. She had a hot bath, scrubbed herself, put up her hair. She left the suitcase packed behind the bedroom door and made sure that in their proper place on the table were the pen, ink, a candle, and the sheet of paper from the mutilated book, so that she could write her final letter to Viera. She had already written the date: *Summer of 1942*. She paused for a moment over the illustration, and read as if she was praying the words of the Latin text describing the flower, with its corolla of five blue petals and a center as red as a wound: *Anagallis caerulea*, she spelled out as she sat on the doorstep waiting for them to come for her. Nobody in the house had the heart to change her silent, deliberate routine. Perhaps she would never write that letter, perhaps the page with the flower was her farewell.

With the first rays of sun, Lina heard something strike the windowpane in her room. Looking out, she saw Remi down below. Danielle ran over to the window, wrapped in a blanket. They knew Remi never slept much, but a visit so early was not a good sign.

They opened the window and waited for him to explain. He had on his best clothes beneath his coat: the Juventus shirt and the white belt with its gold buckle.

"Today is my last day," he told them, his lips a taut line and his eyes brimming with tears.

Seeing him cry upset the girls, but they didn't know how to comfort him. They got dressed nervously and met him at the back of the house, then the three of them set off down to the river.

We should have been ready for this, thought Danielle. She knew Remi would leave with his parents when they were least expecting it, to cross the Pyrenees with the aid of a Spanish Republican who might, who knows, have also been a Juventus fan. Remi had promised his parents that not even in his dreams would he reveal that they were fleeing at nightfall that Saturday. "Fascism is a plague, it's contagious," his father would repeat, punching the walls. One more day with the Nazis and he would go mad, if he wasn't already.

On the path to the river, Remi couldn't find the words to say goodbye to them. He paused at every bend to pick up a stone and fling it as far as he could; he tore off a leaf, feeling and smelling it, as if it wasn't the girls and the village he was saying farewell to, but his own childhood.

"Do you know what I'd like to do right now?" he suggested when they reached the river. "I'd like to shout as loud as I can. Shout for the whole world to hear. God as well, if he can hear, if he really does listen to us."

"Shout if it'll do you good," said Danielle.

"I hate the Nazis," said Remi between his teeth.

The girls burst out laughing.

"I hate the Nazis!" said Lina, a little bit louder.

"I hate the Nazis!" shouted Danielle forcefully.

The three of them were repeating the sentence together when they were surprised by a cart, piled high with boxes, suitcases, and two bleating sheep. The man leading the cart joined their protest.

"I hate the Nazis!"

This solidarity restored their spirits. When they saw an eel swimming downstream, they ran after it to the border of Haute-Vienne and La Creuse. They were brought to a halt by the sound of an animal howling. *It's a dog*, thought Lina.

"It's drowning!" she cried.

Remi crouched down. The front half of the dog's body was out of the water. It was plastered with mud, and its two back legs were bloody and still in the water, where they were being nibbled at by any number of tiny fish. Lina warily stared the poor creature in the eye; it no longer reacted to them being there. It was gasping for breath, and its muzzle was covered in a yellowish froth.

"It must have rolled here from the meadow. It's too small to know how to swim, and the water's very cold." Remi was talking softly, trying to calm the dying animal. He reached out toward it, but when he tried to grasp its front legs to drag it out of the water, the dog growled defensively and bared its teeth. "God knows how long it's been here."

Lina began to stroke its head, and the dog relaxed. It gave another, much weaker growl, and Remi managed to pull it out of the water and lay it on the grass. It closed its eyes and went on breathing painfully. Its paws were crushed.

"It'll recover," said Remi, not even convincing himself.

The three of them sat around the dog, stroking it, waiting for it to show signs of recovery or decease. They couldn't leave the poor creature on its own. They said nothing, watching as little by little it stopped breathing, its body twitching in its death throes.

This was the first time they had come face-to-face with death. They stared at the heaving chest as it fought for air. The pauses became longer and longer, until finally the dog stopped moving altogether.

"It was his fate," Remi pronounced, tears in his eyes. Danielle hugged Lina to comfort her, and stroked her hair.

"Everything will be all right," whispered Lina, without knowing why. Who was she to assure them that they wouldn't also end up like the dog, dying in agony on a riverbank?

When he saw how upset Lina was, Remi put his hand on her shoulder.

"Come on, *Elise*, the world's not going to end today. Listen, I'll give you Combi, but you have to look after it!"

This brought a smile to Lina's face. If her friend called her *Elise*, everything would be all right, even though Danielle protested.

"What are you saying, Remi? Combi is yours. And we're not going to play soccer without you . . ."

But Lina was clutching the ball, her eyes tightly shut.

"I don't need it anymore. I'll buy a new one. Take good care of it! It belongs here with you and Danielle . . ."

They climbed back up to the path. From the top, they looked down at the dog's lifeless body, then gave each other a big hug. Remi peered up at the sky.

"The clouds are very low. If it rains, we won't be able to leave, and maybe I'll spend another day with you."

The wind blew in their faces as they walked home. But that night there was no rain.

20

The weather remained damp and misty. The day was drawing to a close, and as before, Amanda was sitting with the blank sheet of paper in front of her. Danielle was in her room, while Lina was helping Claire in the kitchen. There was a knock at the door.

"That must be Remi," said Lina. She was going to open the door, but Claire held her back and went there herself. Lina followed. Before seeing who it was, Claire bent down and said to her: "This entire nightmare will come to an end one day, and we'll forget it." Hugging Lina, who didn't understand what she meant, she added, "Help your mother. Be strong."

Another loud bang on the door forced her to regain her composure. She opened it. On the threshold was Amanda's premonition come true: a German officer in his black uniform, escorted by two French gendarmes. Beyond them, a car and a truck with swastikas painted on the sides, lights extinguished.

"Good evening, Madame Duval," the officer greeted her in French.

His green eyes were studying her closely. He was smiling in a friendly way that made her shudder.

Lina squeezed her hand.

"*Maman*," she said.

The officer bent down to the girl's face.

"You're as beautiful as your mother, aren't you?" He straightened up and spoke again to Claire. "Frau Sternberg and her daughter are to come with us."

Amanda came into the living room carrying her suitcase. Danielle was behind her.

"Where are you taking them at this time of night?"

"Don't worry, Madame Duval," said the French gendarme, stepping aside for Amanda. "They're going where they belong."

"Follow me," the German officer ordered Amanda in German.

Amanda hugged Danielle, who burst into tears and refused to let her go.

"Lina!" shouted Danielle. The officer looked down at her in surprise.

"We can't waste any more time. Both of you, into the truck," he added in German.

Amanda took Claire's hands and smiled. Danielle stood paralyzed, staring at Lina.

"I've been ready for some time," Amanda said. "Don't cry," she told Claire, moving closer to her and whispering something in her ear so that the others wouldn't hear. The officer grew even more impatient. Amanda took Lina by the hand and the two of them went out through the doorway. Confused, the soldier realized he had made a mistake. He looked scornfully at Danielle, as if she was to blame for it.

Lina accompanied her mother without asking any questions, without saying goodbye, or looking back. Her heart began to thump uncontrollably, making it almost impossible for her to breathe. She had no time to count her heartbeats, she might get them mixed up. Besides, she had to concentrate to understand how they were going to escape, what the plan was that her mother had formed.

Maybe Claire would run over and prevent them from taking her. She was listening for a cry from Danielle for the two of them to run and hide in their perfect hiding place, where no one, not the German officer, nor the French gendarmes, nor the mailman, nor anyone else would be able to find them.

God is a shadow. God is asleep. God can't see us. God has abandoned us. God doesn't love us, she repeated to herself in a senseless litany.

Silence. The roar of the truck engine shattered the calm. She was blinded by the headlights. Still holding on to her mother's hand, not knowing where she was putting her feet or where she was going, she stumbled along blindly, her throat parched, along a path she knew stone by stone but that now was alien to her.

Oh, Remi, why didn't I go with you, why didn't you take me to cross the Pyrenees together? Oh, Mama, everything would be different if I had boarded that ship with Viera. Oh, Mama, why didn't we go to Paris with Hilde . . .

She began to shiver with fear. It felt as if her heart was pumping too much blood for her tiny body to bear. She wasn't cold now, just the opposite, enveloped in a hot cushion of air. *Papa?* She shouted noiselessly.

What if she prayed? Maybe the other God, the one who promised salvation, would hear her. *Our Father, who art in Heaven, hallowed be thy name . . . You see? Nobody hears us. God doesn't exist. He never did. At least not for us. Where is Father Marcel? At the abbey! Let's run to the abbey!*

The sky was so low it seemed ready to crush them at any moment. The leaves by the roadside were swept up in a sudden gust, and then Lina heard the wind begin to howl.

It's a sign, we have to escape. Nobody will find us. Let's go, Mama. This storm is our sign!

"Frau Sternberg, may I see your documents and your daughter's?"

You see, Mama? He's going to let us stay. It wasn't us they were after. It was a mistake. What have we done wrong? Why do we have to flee from everywhere?

The officer was still unsure about the girl's identity. How could he have made such a mistake? He leafed through the documents mistrustfully. Lina lowered her head: she didn't want him to see her crying. She felt she was floating in the air, leaving them all far below. Shutting her eyes as tightly as she could, she saw beside her both her parents, Hilde, and Viera, even Remi with his pet ball.

"I'm not going to hurt you, let me help you," the officer said, but the little girl still seemed in her own world.

Papa, we'll soon be with you. Don't go, wait for us. Mama needs you, and so do I. Now we really are alone.

The wind blew a cloud of dust against the truck's headlights. The driver pressed down on the accelerator to keep the engine going. The officer walked alongside the girl in the hope of hearing her say something that would confirm she was a German Jew. But Lina still did not react, wandering along aimlessly until she stumbled against a stone and fell. She curled up like a newborn baby in the wet grass, waiting for someone strong and brave to come to protect her.

In the darkness, amid the mist and swirling dust, Lina could feel how a giant with warm, muscular arms lifted her so high she touched the clouds with her face. *I'm safe.* She hugged the giant, nestling against his chest as she felt with one hand for his heartbeats. She recognized her father's cologne and smiled contentedly. *My Lina*, she heard, and regained hope.

"I knew you wouldn't abandon me," she said, under her breath, in German, and slumped against him.

The officer smiled with satisfaction: he had got what he wanted. He passed her up into the truck.

"Mama!" she shouted, as a baby began to cry. She had no idea where the noise was coming from. She couldn't tell how many other people were in the back of the truck.

Amanda lifted the suitcase and dropped it inside. The officer helped her clamber into the truck, then used his flashlight to help them find a place to sit.

"Up at the front, you can sit next to the old woman," he said, dropping the canvas flap.

Amanda and Lina found a spot and the truck set off. Suddenly, they heard a shout:

"*Elise!*" it was the voice of Danielle in the distance.

21

They slowly became accustomed to the gloom, and faces began to stand out. Lina smelled something akin to the stench of the dying dog; it occurred to her that all those in the truck were also waiting for someone to save them from being devoured by the Nazis. *Better to die alone than be eaten by the fish.*

Amanda began to weep. The woman next to her took her by the hand to comfort her, and whispered in her ear:

"You saved your daughter."

Amanda rolled up her eyes at this bitter irony: *How can she tell me I saved her, when I've condemned her to death?*

"Your daughter was one of those who could disembark," the woman went on. She stank of dried urine.

As Amanda shifted her foot in the darkness, she felt a pool of urine on the floor of the truck. The old woman had been sitting there for hours. Amanda still didn't understand what she was talking about. Closing her eyes, she listened as the woman continued to speak above the sound of the crying baby.

"Your daughter disembarked in Havana. You saved her."

After a long silence, Amanda reacted. *Was this the voice of an angel? Was she dreaming?*

"Frau Meyer?"

The other woman nodded, ashamed of the desperate state she was in.

"When we reached the port they wouldn't allow us off the boat. We tried for a week. We were all deceived. When we sailed from Hamburg they already knew our visas weren't valid for entry into Cuba. Just when Amanda was starting to forget her Viera's face, a German officer had to come and take her away in order for her to hear news of her daughter. Three years and three letters into the void had been her sentence. But now she realized that writing on the sheets from the mutilated book had been necessary for the meeting with Frau Meyer to happen. If the mailman hadn't taken and returned the letters bearing her real name, and hadn't given her away to the Germans, they would never have met again. Knowing that she had confirmed the safe passage of her forgotten daughter—that Viera was safe on an island lost in the ocean, far from the savage hordes, hatred, the stench of death—she felt more strongly than ever her single remaining aim: to save Lina as well. Only then, knowing her two girls were safe, could she die in peace.

"Forgive me for having judged you," said Frau Meyer.

Amanda embraced her joyfully. For a fleeting moment she relived that May night in Hamburg, at the foot of the ship's gangway. In her mind she saw the huge ocean liner and her daughter disappearing hand in hand with a stranger into a crowd of people who were escaping to the promised land.

"I've lived three years with the guilt of having abandoned my daughter, and now here you are to calm my fears. Thank you for looking after her."

"Viera is a very strong girl."

Hearing her daughter being talked of in the present tense, Amanda smiled with a serenity she was no longer accustomed to. And seeing her mother smile, Lina's confidence was restored. They were going to be all right.

"Her uncle was allowed to come on deck, then they took a small boat to the port," Frau Meyer continued. "We weren't allowed anywhere near the coast."

"Luckily you didn't have to go back to Germany."

"My husband and I were sent here to France, but when war broke out and the Nazis invaded, it was too much for him. He couldn't take any more. Where could we flee to, if nobody wanted us? So here I am, all on my own. I wonder why we didn't choose Great Britain when we were brought back to Europe. It's far harder for the Nazis to reach there, but who knows . . . ?"

Feeling that her fate was already preordained, that she was being guided by a higher force, an angel watching over her, Amanda studied the faces of the condemned in the truck. For the first time since she had left Berlin, she felt fortunate. Even Frau Meyer's calamities made her feel grateful, for an inexplicable chain of events had combined for her to have news of Viera. Her daughter had been chosen to disembark.

Lina was bemused by her mother's attitude. She did not remember Frau Meyer, and even thought she might be an impostor.

An old man collapsed and fell to the truck's uneven floor, banging his head on an enormous iron bolt. No one reacted; no one tried to help him. The thud woke the baby, who started to howl once more.

"He's dead, like the dog," Lina said.

The blood pouring from the man's forehead mixed with the pool of urine at Frau Meyer's feet. Lina lifted her feet to keep them dry. She stared in terror at the old man, and saw the vein pulsing on his wrinkled, grimy neck.

Amanda was sleeping peacefully. She had found Viera.

Winter of 1940

My little Viera:

Darkness has come over us.

Can you see how right I was to let you go, even though my heart suffers for it every hour of every day? Only God is witness to the strength I had to summon to abandon you. Only he could give me the determination to take your sister by the hand and walk away from you.

I would give everything to be able to hear you, to read your words. I know these letters that go back and forth across the Atlantic will reach you someday. Who knows when, who knows whether I'll be there that day, but I'm convinced they will end up in your hands, because they will be the only thing I can bequeath you, because I have written every word to the rhythm of our heartbeats. Yours, mine, Lina's, and your father's, the man who left angels for us. Whenever you receive them, you'll know I never abandoned you, that we never forgot you, my sweet Viera.

The world grows darker with each passing day, but I know that where you're living the sun will always shine for you, and your life will be an endless summer.

Now I have to protect Lina from the night.

Even though by now your Spanish must be perfect, I'll go on writing to you in German, because that way you'll remember my voice and my lullabies.

I read these few pages from the botanical album over and over, because I know that before you fall asleep you will read them too. In them you'll see the flowers and plants of the tropics surrounding you. Take deep breaths, grow, become strong, and think of us. We'll always be here, however far away, to protect you.

Even if you forget us, that doesn't matter, I'll understand. All I ask is that you don't forget your name. You are a Sternberg. Viera Sternberg. That's the only way, for as long as the darkness allows, that I'll be able to sleep in peace.

All my love,
Mama

FOUR

The Return

Haute-Vienne, August 1942

22

A shriek woke Amanda: the dream was over.

The bloody body of the old man rolled violently out of the back of the truck. As it fell, it hit the rocky ground covered in withered leaves with a loud thud.

"He's alive," Lina said to her mother, still bewildered.

It was not yet day: it seemed as though it was still the middle of a spring night, although for Amanda the seasons had lost all meaning. She was immune to cold and heat, day or night. She thought she should have stayed awake, to try to work out which direction they were being taken in, if they were headed north or south, if they had crossed a border or were still in occupied France. She also needed to know which day of the week it was: time had acquired a new dimension in which every second counted.

Clinging to her suitcase as if it was an extension of her body, she jumped down from the truck and turned to help Lina and Frau Meyer.

Haggard-looking, with cracked lips and swollen legs, Frau Meyer twisted her ankle as she clambered down, trying to hide the stains of urine on her coat. Amanda breathed in gulps of the fresh air, attempting to rid herself of the rotten stench that seemed to have stuck to her skin and her impeccably clean and ironed dress. She looked around to get her bearings, to make out the boundaries of this bare field they were to be confined in.

The men were pushed toward one end of the fenced area. The women and children were herded into a hut with a half-open door, near the entrance to the camp. Beyond the barbed-wire fences Amanda could make out a gray forest, and in the distance several tiled roofs, with scattered chimneys and a church spire. Yes, she was sure they were still in Haute-Vienne, and felt protected knowing that Claire remained close by.

Apparently, there was only one hut for the women and children. The rest of the internment camp, flanked by four watchtowers, was filled with men. She heard some of them speaking Spanish, arguing. They were barking like dogs, trying to mark their territory with an illusion of freedom. They were dressed in civilian clothes, seemed to have a supply of cigarettes, and defiantly passed from hand to hand tattered pages from newspapers, their only source of information from the outside. The French guards ignored them and tried to stay as far away as possible, or at least at a safe distance.

Amanda calculated there were only about ten guards patrolling the camp. The ones who had accompanied them in the truck were there, and she could remember the face of the gendarme who had held out his hand to help her. In the darkness, his face had seemed stern, and she had thought he must be at most twenty years old. When the sun came out, she realized he was a regular soldier and was maybe the same age as her. He had thick eyebrows, a dark complexion, and an unruly mane of hair kept in place with brilliantine. Tall and slim, with dark lines under his eyes, he walked stiffly, as though short of breath. When she heard him talk to the other gendarmes, she guessed he must be the same officer who had told Claire where they were being taken.

Lina discovered she was not the only child in the camp. She saw a group next to the hut and went up to them. They surrounded her at once and began to question her with great curiosity: was she on her own or with her parents, was she from the north or the south, had she been tortured, had she ever seen a dead body, had she ever shot a German soldier? Lina responded to all these questions with a loud laugh, the best way to deny them.

"Where did you come from?" asked the tallest boy, who appeared to be the leader.

"I fell from heaven," Lina said without thinking. Her wide-open eyes and smile won them all over.

For Amanda, the plan to save Lina required precision and speed. Every second counted; her daughter's life depended on it. A single mistake could ruin the only chance of escape she had come up with. They would only have to survive the next few days: they could make do without access to drinking water, hot food, or a blanket to sleep under. Lina would be kept amused with her new friends, who it seemed were free to roam around the camp.

Fortunately, Amanda realized, the women's hut was only half full, which meant more would probably be arriving. She looked for a corner on her own away from the windows, because the nights would turn colder.

"If I were you, I'd come down this end, where we all are. If you stay over there where you are, God knows who they might put next to you. The last we heard was that they're going to fill the camp with Jews and Gypsies, and you know what they're like."

Amanda listened to the woman while she was laying the stained mattress on a fragile frame. She smiled timidly at her, and saw her neck was red and raw. As she struggled to turn the mattress over, the woman gave her a hand.

"We all have to help each other in here. That's all we can do." Amanda nodded her gratitude, and the woman continued: "So, is your husband a communist too? I thought only I was unlucky enough to marry a rebel. Now we're all paying for it. We've ended up with husbands who are useless: having a husband who's a prisoner is like being a widow, isn't it?"

Amanda stayed politely silent. She was determined nothing and no none would divert her from her plan. She wasn't interested in becoming friendly with the other women in the hut, and yet she didn't want to create suspicions that could cause problems for her.

The woman turned on her heel and walked down to her end of the hut.

"This newcomer seems to think she's better than the rest of us," she said, obviously intending Amanda to hear.

"Amanda. My name's Amanda," she called after the woman. "I came only with my daughter. They killed my husband, but I prefer not to talk about that. There's nothing to be done now . . ."

"These Boche bastards and the French guards are going to pay dearly for it," said the woman, retracing her steps. "I'm Bérénice. Are you from the north? I bet you're from Alsace, with those blue eyes of yours and that hair . . ."

Amanda realized that her accent still gave her away. Lowering her eyes, she hoped Bérénice would take this as a sign of agreement.

"You can't trust anyone in here. However French those guards seem, they've all sold out to the Germans. They're only interested in getting paid, and it doesn't matter if it's by the Germans or Pétain. They're such cowards they avoid any trouble with the men, because they know that when they get out of here, if they're free one day, they'll immediately want to settle scores." She paused, then added, "And there'll be a high price to pay."

Without realizing it, Bérénice had provided Amanda with valuable information. She realized she would have to use the guards' fear for her own ends. It would only take a friendly gesture that might guarantee a safe-conduct at the conclusion of the war, which, however endless it seemed, was bound to end one day.

Despite the harshness of her gaze and her challenging gestures, Amanda saw a hint of kindness in this small, muscular woman. With Bérénice looking on curiously, she opened her suitcase and put the coat inside. As she was bending down to slide her things under the bed, she saw Frau Meyer sitting bewildered in a corner. She ran to help her up. Completely lost, Frau Meyer began to wander around leaning on the walls, repeatedly bumping her forehead against them. She stumbled from corner to corner, as though trying to find a secret exit.

"A stinking Jew. It's because of her that all us French are suffering," said Bérénice. Amanda frowned at her.

"All right, don't get mad. She may well be a good woman. But you can't deny she stinks."

Amanda led Frau Meyer to a window. Outside they could see Lina with a gaggle of children running after a skinny dog. Amanda tried to take off Frau Meyer's coat, but the old woman clung to it, her terrified eyes begging her not to touch it: the coat was all she had left.

⸙

That night Amanda slept hugging Lina close. She slept so deeply she didn't even notice the arrival of dozens more women and children. Awaking the next morning, she realized that not only had she lost all notion of night and day, but that sounds had also turned into an indistinguishable murmur, that voices were nothing more than noise, that the stench in the hut had become a vague, distant smell, and that colors had become blurred. Nothing was black or white anymore. Brown and gray had faded into a neutral paleness. There was no place for the red, blue, or orange of sunrises. They had started to live in a perpetual night that obliterated any contrasts or shadows. They had learned to breathe just deeply enough to take in the air their lungs needed to expand, but keeping out any overpowering smells. It was the only way to survive. Above all, she needed to learn to rediscover silence. At every moment a groan, a cry, or a blow reminded her she was not alone.

The morning began with the intermittent wailing of a baby who clung to the dry breast of a woman furiously squeezing her withered flesh as if it wasn't part of her body. Apparently whenever she pressed down on the milkless ducts, the baby calmed down briefly, but then his body would begin shaking with involuntary sobs.

Exhausted, utterly dispirited, the mother crawled to a corner of her bed and dropped the trembling baby onto the bare mattress. He fell silent, perhaps stunned by this sudden abandonment.

An old woman from the top bunk came down and sat on the edge of the bed. Pulling on a pair of filthy socks, she completely ignored the baby, who lay there, eyes wide open, possibly because he didn't have the strength to close them.

He won't survive another day, thought Amanda so coldly that for a moment she was horrified at herself. The idea of reaching out her hand flitted through her mind, but she realized at once that this made no sense. The mother had already given up.

"My husband survived malaria, a bullet in the chest, falling down a ravine, and even being crushed by a cart," the woman said to Amanda, her eyes staring into space, anywhere away from the baby lying behind her. "Now, shut in here, he's dying with every second. Each night he shrivels up a little more, and one morning I won't see him come out of his hut. Nothing touches me anymore, nothing can kill me. Why grieve, if we're never free? Neither in here, nor out there."

She rubbed her eyes calmly, a glint of fear shining in the depths of her irises. Trying to hide it with a smile, she lifted her baby, as if he had already abandoned her, and held him out to Amanda.

Lina saw her mother cradling the baby, heard her comfort him with a lullaby that was more like a tuneless humming. Taking a piece of chocolate from her pocket, she bit into it. She pressed the remainder in her hand to soften it, then brushed it across the baby's lips. The child tasted it slowly with a mixture of disapproval and enjoyment as he wriggled awkwardly, trying to settle into this new lap receiving him so warmly.

Amanda looked down at the baby. She was sure he would succumb before nightfall. The tiny sweet scrap of nourishment would only keep him going a few hours, but for the moment at least he had been reinvigorated, and the other women began to take notice of him. Even Frau Meyer came over, took him in her arms, and began to rock him, walking between the beds, raising dust from the floor. Bérénice approached her and she let her take him. Even the woman from the top bunk who had ignored him earlier came over to offer him toothless smiles and caresses. Surrounded by all this unexpected maternal concern, the baby remained silent.

Amanda sent Lina out to play with her friends. She returned to her own bed, did her hair up, smoothed down her dress, and even put some lipstick on her cracked lips. As she headed for the door, Bérénice, still holding the baby, followed her every movement.

"That one is up to something. In a couple of days, she'll be as dirty as the rest of us."

She handed the baby back to his mother and went out to see where Amanda had gone, but couldn't spot her. Thinking she must have been to the men's hut, she looked inside it, but Amanda wasn't there. She went over to the children and grabbed Lina by the arm.

"Where the hell has your mother gone?" she growled.

Slipping easily from her grasp, Lina shrugged and turned her back. Bérénice wouldn't give up, continuing on to the outhouse and then the kitchen. When she finally abandoned her search and was coming back, she caught sight of Amanda's lilac dress behind the women's hut. Bérénice was skirting a group of guards bringing in a group of new arrivals when a swirl of dust blinded her momentarily. When she spotted Amanda again, she was standing by a corner of the hut next to the storage shed for coal and wood. She wasn't alone, but Bérénice couldn't make out who was holding her hand. She went closer stealthily, but could only hear murmurs, meaningless phrases, snatches of words she tried desperately to grasp the meaning of: *my daughter, a friend, Saturday night*. As she drew nearer, she recognized the profile of the man in the shadows.

They were locked in an embrace, and Bérénice saw the man's hand slide down to Amanda's waist. She let him press her to him, apparently unconcerned about being seen, until the sound of footsteps made her react. Freeing herself from the gendarme's arms, she ran back toward the hut.

Her cheeks were flushed with shame, but at least she had managed to slip the letter for Claire and Father Marcel into his hands. At least . . . a thick gobbet of spit brought her back to reality. Taken aback, she shut her eyes to wipe her face, and saw Bérénice standing over her, arms folded and a threatening look on her face.

"So you think that letting Bertrand paw you will help make things better for you in here? What, are you going to give us all away? You make me sick!"

Amanda tried to get past her to the hut entrance, but Bérénice held her back.

"Even though he's French, Bertrand is as disgusting as those Boches, and just as guilty. Don't you get it?"

Amanda stood with head bowed. Deep down, though, she was triumphant: the first part of her plan had been accomplished. Another gobbet of spit wasn't going to deter her.

"You may still have traces of your rose perfume, your hair is shiny, your face still looks fresh and lovely, but in a few days, you'll stink like all the rest of us. We'll see then if he still wants to—"

"It's not what you think," Amanda butted in, without explaining any further. There was a silence as the two women faced each other. Still enraged, Bérénice didn't go on. Amanda replied, "I'm going to do whatever it takes to save my daughter."

As they entered the hut, they saw the mother. Her baby wasn't there. She was smiling crazily, a strange gleam in her eyes. She kept mechanically pushing her hair behind her ears, then went back to her bed and turned the mattress over. Remaining motionless for a minute, she soon began to repeat this absurd routine all over again.

This desolate sight produced panic in Amanda. She suddenly saw herself without Lina, in a hut surrounded by women with no future. Another one just like them, waiting to be thrown into the ditch.

She turned fiercely back to Bérénice, determined not to let her come a step closer.

"I would do anything for my daughter. We don't have much longer here, there's no room for any more prisoners. They're going to start taking us away, and God knows where they'll send us. You don't know what it means to have a child. So get this straight: I don't care if it's a Frenchman, a German, or whoever . . ."

"I managed to save my daughter," Bérénice interrupted her in a whisper, without looking at her. She gathered up her long dark hair and went on: "I sent her to Spain with my sister when I saw they were coming for us."

"So then you have to understand me. We're not here to judge anyone."

Bérénice moved forward, opening her arms wide as if in reconciliation, but Amanda took a step back. She was not looking for pity, and didn't need accomplices. This was her own battle, and she had to study carefully each step she took, as if she were repairing the mechanism of an antique clock.

"You'll have to be quick," Bérénice insisted. "We've been here two weeks now. As soon as the huts are full, they'll move us. Rumor has it that within a month we'll be taken to Drancy. And from there, who knows. They say it's to Poland."

23

*A*manda had studied Bertrand closely: his movements, his dealings with the other guards, how he skillfully managed to keep out of any disturbance, letting someone else intervene. She saw him leaning against the kitchen wall, a cup of coffee in his hand, looking lost, as if asking himself what he, a professional soldier, the son of a military family, was doing guarding prisoners.

Ever since she saw him arriving at Claire's house, Amanda had noticed his voice was distant, reluctant; she could somehow identify with his proud military bearing, ashamed at being reduced to this unpleasant duty.

"What these Spanish swine need first is a good bath; and then a beating that puts them in their proper place," one of the other guards had commented.

"Let them be, they're not much trouble," Bertrand retorted. "Some of them don't even know why they're here."

"Don't give me that. They're all communist garbage."

Whenever he met Amanda, he lowered his eyes in confusion. At those moments, she realized she could trust him, and smiled as she straightened her hair.

She was pleased with what she had achieved so far. Not only had he not rejected her, but he had agreed to pass on the letter. She also felt relieved that she had shared her plan with Bérénice, another mother who had also had to make a drastic decision.

The days were growing shorter; the nights seemed to stretch out endlessly because she could not sleep. Today was Saturday, and although she did not expect any reply from Claire or Father Marcel, she hoped against hope they would appear on the following Saturday night.

Her days had become slightly more tolerable, because Bertrand had assigned her to work in the kitchen. At first she saw this as a punishment, until Bérénice convinced her it was a great privilege, for which she should be grateful. At least she was kept busy, and from time to time could wash up. Sometimes she would leave her hands under the stream of boiling water until her skin almost peeled off. This was her way of getting rid of all the offensive dirt. Another advantage was that she could savor the coffee before it was diluted for the *abandoned ones*, as she preferred to call the prisoners being held against their will in the middle of nowhere.

Working in the kitchen also allowed her to take hard, black bread to Lina, poor Frau Meyer, and Bérénice, who little by little had become a kind of friend and confidant who helped her get a better understanding of the camp's inner workings.

By now, Bérénice was convinced that Amanda was not on the enemy's side, and had no intention of foiling any attempt at resistance, revolt, or escape. On the contrary, thanks to her relationship with Bertrand, she could be very useful to them. She said as much to her husband, who was the leader of a resistance group of men.

Sometimes Bertrand waited for Amanda at nightfall in a corner of the shed. All he had to do was come into the kitchen to inspect how their work was going: she knew this was the signal for them to meet. When they saw him enter, all the women fell silent and lowered their eyes. At that moment, Amanda would smile to herself, although her stomach immediately clenched and she felt a stab of pain in her chest. She was troubled by this fleeting sense of happiness. She couldn't understand how she could experience even a minute's ease with this stranger when the only man she had known was Julius. But now Julius was a phantom; he wasn't there to help her. What most disconcerted her was how safe she felt with Bertrand. Rather than give her a shudder of aversion, their encounters offered her a sense of peace and pleasure that she had long forgotten. Each time he appeared in the kitchen to signal they were to meet, three or four days after their previous encounter, she closed her eyes and buried her head in her hands as if to drive away these sensations that could mean a risk, threatening to distract her from her goal.

Whenever they were to get together, she made sure she was the last to leave the kitchen, and took advantage of the chance to sprinkle hot water on her cheeks and lips. The heat revivified them, and despite the burning sensation, she could feel her old beauty returning. And she smiled.

That night as Amanda walked silently to their meeting place, she looked up in search of the moon. As she did so, a huge shadow loomed in front of her, stretching out a strong hand. She allowed herself to be led along by this hot hand gripping her, attracting her. Bertrand bent toward her, the enemy. He was the one who had more to lose: he was risking his rank, his security, his honor. They were both engaged in a battle against the tyranny of desire. In the darkness, the limits became blurred, their faces indistinct.

"Everything will be all right," he whispered in her ear like a caress, though he knew that for her the only caresses that meant anything were the ones she gave her daughter. "How are they treating you in the kitchen?"

She smiled, at his mercy.

"You'll see, your daughter will get out of here."

Yes, her daughter would, but not her. She was beyond redemption;

she had ceased to exist. She pressed herself against Bertrand's chest, submitting herself to his will, the only one that existed in that dark corner.

She closed her eyes and allowed herself to be taken down unknown, shadowy paths that led nowhere. Like a sorcerer, he had her in his power, he controlled her at his whim. At least she had someone to protect her, she thought, as he quickly sated his rough desire.

He was a French officer, reduced to this after facing defeat by the invaders. An officer who, like a good soldier, simply obeyed orders without stopping to think whether they were directed against his own people. This was what he explained to her whenever they met, as he conquered her with caresses and sweet words.

"You have to understand, I'm only obeying orders," he would tell her, even though she refused to listen, as he did up his trousers, straightened his uniform, wiped away the cold sweat from his brow, smoothing down his curly oiled hair.

This time, when he had finished, his tone became harsh once more.

"Are you sure they'll bring the jewels?"

She had promised him a diamond bracelet and her wedding ring, with the brightest diamond, a perfect specimen. She assured him that with this trophy he could be free of the ignominy of being an officer in a defeated army; he could escape far from shame and dishonor, lose himself in some small farm deep in a valley the Germans would never reach.

"I promise they'll be yours," she said by way of farewell.

She was drifting, as though her body had lost all its energy. When she reached the hut entrance, Bérénice was sitting on a rock, waiting for her. Amanda sat next to her, even allowing her head to droop onto her shoulder.

"Oh, Bérénice, what has become of us?" she said. "The worst of it is there's no room for sorrow, repentance, or shame."

"We're being taken out of here in two weeks' time. It's been confirmed. You mustn't wait any longer."

"Everything will be all right." Amanda repeated Bertrand's words with a smile. "Everything will be all right, he's promised me."

"You trust him too much."

The two women always spoke of Bertrand as *him*. It was best not to mention his name, in case it aroused suspicions.

"Do I have a choice?"

"I'd like to believe he's a good-hearted Frenchman . . ."

"He's running the risk for me, for my daughter."

"Why? Have you asked him why?"

"He'll get his reward."

"I suppose it'll be something more than what he is getting now."

"Oh, Bérénice, do you know what hurts the most? The fact that I feel safe with him. Yes, with him. My body ceased to exist a long time ago, and so I'm not concerned about what he does with this lifeless mass, how he satisfies his lust without any shame . . . But whenever he holds me in his arms . . ."

Bérénice would not listen to any more. She leaped up, pulling Amanda with her. She put her hands on her shoulders.

"Just remember, silly girl, that man isn't doing this to help you, he's doing it for what he can get out of you."

Amanda embraced Bérénice, and the two of them stood in silence for several minutes.

"I'm going to save my daughter . . ."

24

The women's hut was packed with new arrivals. They slept two or even three to a bunk bed. At night the inmates left the door open so that fresh air could get in; their breathing lay stagnant in the corners and prevented the scarce oxygen circulating. Amanda had begun her countdown: there were exactly seven days to go before her plan to save her daughter could be put into action. In this vital week she had to calculate every second, every minute, with absolute precision.

On Sunday night, which marked the start of the week that she would save her daughter, everything was quiet. But shortly before dawn, Bérénice shook Amanda out of her drowsy sleep and took her by the arm. Lacking the strength to resist, Amanda allowed herself to be led stumbling out of the hut toward the outhouse. A feeble light at the far end of its solid walls was all they had to guide them.

The outhouse was a kind of fortress. Not even the kitchen or the guards' quarters were as well built, maybe because this was the best way to limit the stench and prevent any spread of disease. In the center, a cement wall with holes and wooden boards across it presided over the place where the abandoned ones could carry out their bodily functions.

For Amanda, the smells no longer registered, whereas for Bérénice, despite her having been far longer in the camp, the stench still made her wince. The outhouse was the only part of the camp the guards didn't dare enter, convinced that just by inhaling that foul air they would become infected.

Bérénice cast her eagle eye over the room to make sure they were alone. In one corner she spied a woman on her knees, lost in the gloom.

"She won't survive another day here," she said.

Amanda waited patiently to hear the secret Bérénice wanted to share. Glancing at the slumped body of the woman in the corner, she knew instinctively that if she were kept behind the fences for another month, she would end up like her.

"This weekend half of the guards will be on leave to visit their families. I heard they've been given two weeks." Bérénice wanted Amanda to pay her full attention, and not go on staring at the dying woman. "You're the only one who can help us."

Amanda could not understand how. She worked in the kitchen and some nights met Bertrand in the storage shed. He never took her to the guards' bunkhouse or a watchtower.

"Bertrand must know who's leaving, and if they're expecting reinforcements."

"But the women cleaners can find that out much more easily than me. How do you think I can get that information?"

"What's most important is to know whether reinforcements are coming or not. What I'm asking of you is very simple."

"Do you really think Bertrand will tell me? What interest could I have in that?"

"You'll find a way to convince him."

"Bérénice, if Bertrand suspects . . ."

"He won't suspect a thing if you don't want him to. Your daughter's life, and that of many men, depends on it. The men who are going to help us get away from the Boches."

Amanda stared at her disconsolately. *The Germans have taken over everywhere, they've eliminated borders, crushed everything and everyone in their way. We'll never be able to get away from them.* That's what she wanted to tell her friend, but in the end, she said nothing. Bérénice possibly understood, but said nothing either.

"I'll see what I can do, but I can't promise anything."

⚭

When they were back inside the hut, Amanda thought she had to try to help the woman abandoned in the outhouse. She would run to her and save her from her humiliation. She was about to go out again when Bérénice stopped her.

"Leave her; if you get too close you'll only end up sick. Remember that many people's lives depend on you, not just your daughter's. Are you going to put Lina's salvation at risk?"

There were only six days left before her daughter would be free. Amanda counted them as she prayed silently, fearful lest a storm, an uprising, or the arrival of the Germans should spoil her plan. Every night she went over in her mind each possible thing that could go wrong and how to avoid it. The transfer to Drancy might be suddenly pushed forward; they might separate the women from their children; they might transfer Bertrand; Bérénice's husband might organize a revolt or a mass escape . . .

She prayed for none of these possibilities to materialize. *Nothing can occur before Saturday. Nothing.*

On Monday night, Lina was waiting restlessly in bed for her when Amanda returned exhausted from her encounter with Bertrand. She avoided her daughter's gaze, as if the girl could perceive her sense of shame.

"Gilberte is convinced they're going to kill us all."

"Don't pay attention to her; what does she know?" Amanda said, sitting beside Lina, but far enough away for her not to notice the traces of her degradation, the smell of Bertrand clinging to her skin.

"Her mother also works in the kitchen."

Amanda reacted as if her daughter were accusing her. *You ought to know it, you work in the kitchen, but instead of finding out what's going on in the camp or what's going to happen to us, you waste your time in the arms of that filthy guard.* Inside her head, she could hear the reproving voices of Lina, Hilde, and Claire.

"Lina, trust me. They're not going to kill anyone."

Her daughter was waiting for an explanation, something more than an empty promise. She refused to believe that the only thing her mother had done since they left Berlin was to weep over Viera's absence and write a few letters on faded sheets of paper.

"Gilberte says . . ."

"That's enough of Gilberte!" Amanda exploded, with controlled fury. Only loud enough for the two of them to hear, Lina jumped regardless, now even more worried about her mother's reaction. This was the first time Lina had noticed so much as a spark of anger in this subdued woman who had always lived beneath the wings of a man who listened to the weak, irregular beats of other people's hearts.

"They're going to make us walk through the night to a train station. Then they'll put us in a cattle truck and we'll travel for days until we reach a concentration camp. And there they'll separate us. It won't be like here, Mama. There it'll be run by Germans, and they will know exactly who we are. Gilberte described all the details . . ."

Amanda closed her eyes for a moment. How could she convince her daughter that she would be safe, that she would grow up far from her, like Viera. Not on an island, but with friendly people, people who would give her more love and protection than she could. She felt a burning sensation deep in her throat, as if a tangle of thorns were traveling down her esophagus and had begun to perforate the lining of her stomach. Her eyes grew moist with tears; her lips started to quiver.

"Somebody escapes every day. They get over the fence, and the French guards don't care. Gilberte says . . ."

"Escaping wouldn't help, Lina," said Amanda firmly. "We will always be hunted. We need to do something more than that."

"What more, Mama? What more . . . to disappear?"

Disheartened, Lina got up and went over to the window. The clouds were even lower than usual; it was impossible to see the moon or stars. No escape there, either.

She walked slowly back to their bed. Amanda was waiting for her, and hugged her tenderly. Frau Meyer was watching them from her bunk, a vacant expression on her face.

"Mama, do you know what the worst part is?" Now Lina's eyes were brimming with tears.

"What is it, my love?" Amanda tried to gather her strength to comfort her. Such a young child talking of all this pain, of trains heading nowhere, of separation and death.

"I no longer remember Papa."

She leaned gently against her mother, as if asking permission to hug her again.

"Your father has not abandoned us," said Amanda. She looked for the suitcase under the bed and carefully took out a photograph.

"But I've forgotten his face, his eyes . . . I no longer remember his voice."

"Papa is here," said Amanda, holding out their family photograph. "And also out there," she whispered, pointing to the window. She kissed her on the brow. "He's watching over you from one of those stars . . ."

"There aren't any stars, Mama," Lina interrupted her, photograph in hand. "There are no stars here."

25

*E*very day, the path from the hut to the kitchen was a dreadful struggle, away from Lina's warm embrace, Bérénice's watchful eyes, Frau Meyer's sleeplessness; past the blank gaze of the guards and the unseasonably frigid morning. Until she reached the kitchen door with its rusty bolts that she had to force open as splinters of wood penetrated beneath her fingernails. She would sit shivering in a corner, her eyes fixed on the window, beyond that on the wire fences, and beyond that the void. On the horizon was what looked like an endless forest where she imagined herself wandering with Lina while shooting stars flashed overhead. It was only when someone else came into the kitchen and started banging a pan full of dirty water that Amanda snapped out of her daydreams.

Tuesday morning Gilberte's mother lay sobbing on the kitchen floor, in the midst of all the garbage. A guard came in, slamming the door behind him. He grabbed her hair and dragged her up like a dead animal. She got to her feet without a word of complaint and stumbled after him as quickly as she could. She straightened her damp, faded dress clumsily, and Amanda saw her raise a shaking hand to her stomach.

Safe in her corner, Amanda suddenly realized that in fact all the women who worked in the kitchen had been chosen by one or sometimes two of the guards. All of them were young, some were still pretty. She had to admit that, to her relief, Bertrand had never treated her cruelly. She preferred to think of him as her guardian, her savior. She had been lucky, she thought, and she ought to feel grateful. She gave a reluctant smile, the corners of her pale lips lifting slightly.

Any outside news that reached them in the camp was fragmentary and out-of-date. It was hard to follow, because it was circulated by word of mouth and inevitably grew distorted until it became almost mythical. One rumor had it that the Germans were falling back; another, even more of a fantasy, that the Resistance had taken Paris. These rumors grew by the day, and every part of the camp could have a different version. One hut said the British had crossed the Channel and reached the Pas de Calais. The other, that France had gotten rid of all its Jews by deporting them to Poland, and now the Germans, having achieved their plan of racial cleansing, were about to begin the retreat, three years after the war began.

Bérénice roamed the camp with her inscrutable smile, keeping an eye on everything. Amanda was intrigued by the way she managed to elude the guards. She stole food from the kitchen every day, and succeeded in forcing the girl who cleaned the officers' quarters to smuggle out whatever newspapers she could, no matter when they were from. The guards often saw her coming out of the kitchen, her pockets stuffed with bread, but turned their backs on her and looked the other way. They didn't want to get involved or show any weakness faced with the wife of one of the prisoners' leaders, someone who could settle scores with them when the war was over, or even in only a few days' time. Some of them had already been threatened, so it was preferable not to run any risk.

They were convinced it was unwise to challenge Bérénice and her husband. They did not give them any obvious preference, but allowed them discreet access to places forbidden to the others. There was a

Resistance network in that region, perhaps in the whole of France, and the guards had to live with the fear that they could be denounced or have their families attacked. On several occasions when they mistreated one of the prisoners, they had been horrified to hear a phrase that made their blood run cold, "An eye for an eye, a tooth for a tooth."

The freedom Bérénice enjoyed to come and go around the huts irritated the other women. She was the only one who could get near the male prisoners, supply them with food, and even give them stale news—which at that time was the most precious contraband of all. She was also the person who conveyed what was going on between the men's and women's huts: a death, an illness, an anniversary remembered. She gave them such precise, elaborate descriptions that Amanda came to suspect that Bérénice invented them all to help the other women survive and keep them from despair.

Amanda considered herself lucky to have the protection and even the complicity of the most powerful woman in the hut. And that closeness allowed her to perceive a restlessness that went far beyond the normal routine in the camp. *Something is in the air, I can sense it, something big.* With Bérénice nothing was left to chance; every movement was calculated, every approach had a purpose; she didn't risk the slightest false move. Amanda trusted her, but couldn't help being worried: even though she was almost sure that Bérénice's plans wouldn't get in the way of hers, the fear that they might kept her constantly on edge.

Once in the middle of the night, when one of the women began to shout, tearing off the rags she was wearing and rolling around naked on the beaten earth floor, Bérénice, who was a light sleeper, was the first to react and get up. Running over to her, she slapped her hard until she calmed down. The other women watched how coldly and determinedly Bérénice acted, whereas they didn't even have the strength to sit up in their bunks.

"If you don't keep quiet, I'll make sure you choke to death if need be," she shouted in her ear, throttling her with her hand. "I'm not going to allow the French guards to come and punish us because of your behavior. Pick up that rag of a dress, calm down, and go back to bed. Right now!"

The woman did as she was told, even though she was still shivering. Covered in dust, eyes downcast and feeling humiliated, she went back to her bed and lay down, her face to the wall. Bérénice dusted off her own dress and quickly surveyed the hut. Those who had been looking on curiously avoided her gaze. In a few seconds, calm had been restored.

What a courageous woman; if only I was as strong as her, Amanda thought. For the first time, she saw the veins standing out in her friend's hands. To her, Bérénice was essentially a kind person, with a still intact soul, a combatant whose sole aim was to defend herself and those dear to her. The most unlikely legends had sprung up around her: that she had killed a German soldier; that she had left her daughter in a Spanish orphanage; that she had taken revenge on more than one collaborator. Some of the women even said she had a hidden pistol and was eager to get her hands on ammunition. The first bullet she fired would be at any guard who dared venture into the women's hut, as she had once threatened. For them it was forbidden territory, and she made it clear she intended to keep it that way. Rather than fear, the women felt respect for her. To the guards, she was untouchable.

Bérénice had decided not to share Amanda's plan with her husband. It was a silent, well-conceived idea, and she was determined to support her to the hilt. It was also her way of staying in control of the possible consequences. Everything would be all right. One little girl more or less would not upset the camp's routine.

Whatever Bérénice is up to, Amanda prayed, *please let it happen after Saturday.*

26

On Tuesday they were awakened by noises outside the hut. They ran to the main yard, where a group of women were clinging to the fence, shouting. Some of them were weeping; others cursing the French guards.

Lina squeezed her mother's hand. Maybe, she thought, the moment to escape had arrived. They could run and hide in the nearest church. She would pray at the foot of the altar the way Father Marcel had taught her. "God will not abandon us," she muttered, and Amanda heard her. Without another word, they crept to the corner where the women's hut joined the men's. There were no guards to be seen. "Now's the moment," said Lina. "There are no guards or Germans. We're free, Mama!"

Lina closed her eyes tightly and began a silent prayer. She allowed herself to be dragged along by her mother as she pushed her way through the frantic crowd. *I promise you, God, that every night I'll say two Our Fathers and four Hail Marys,* she begged.

Amanda suddenly looked away, then hugged her daughter to her, trying to cover her eyes. The bloody body of one of the male prisoners was lying in the middle of the yard.

"There's no point escaping. What for? To end up torn to pieces like him?" said one of the women standing by the body.

The man's face was a mass of bruises and dried blood. His top lip had been torn off. He was barefoot, and the soles of his feet were red raw. Two men came over, lifted him, and took him away to their hut. His arms dangled down, his head brushing against the ground.

Struggling free of her mother, Lina watched all this without so much as blinking.

"He's dead," she said.

"No, Lina, he's alive and he'll recover. In here, we all have to learn how to survive."

At a distance from the crowd she could spot the figure of Bérénice, who was also looking for her, and waved for her to come over. Telling Lina to return to their hut, she followed her friend toward the kitchen. Bérénice whispered to her: "They're going to change the guards. There've been too many escapes in recent days, and they don't want any more problems with the Germans. They've lost control of the camp and want to punish us. You'll have to hurry."

"It's late, I should get to the kitchen," was all Amanda replied. She was grateful for Bérénice's warning, but there was no way she was going to change her plan. Saturday was in three days: they wouldn't change the guards until the following week. Nothing would happen before then. Nothing could happen. She glanced nervously at her friend, and hurried off.

"Amanda!" shouted Bérénice. Amanda came to a halt; for a moment the two women were face-to-face. Silently mouthing the words, Bérénice added, "I'm sorry," and turned back to the yard.

There's no reason to be. Don't feel sorry for me. Nothing's going to happen, Amanda wanted to tell her. She rushed into the kitchen. It was Bérénice who had no way out, she thought. They would all be deported, maybe even before the guards were changed, if that in fact happened. She could hear Bérénice's sad voice as she mouthed those words, and could sense the compassion her only confidant felt for her, this woman hardened by experience who was a true friend. But Amanda couldn't be dissuaded by any compassion, or by feeling sorry for herself, nor could she hasten her plan.

"Everything will work out," she told herself, momentarily blinded by the steam in the kitchen.

She began peeling potatoes, but was so caught up in her thoughts that she stabbed the palm of her left hand with the rusty knife. Rather than react to the pain, she stopped to observe how the blood was gushing from this red fountain in her hand. She smiled: she was still alive. Slipping the rudimentary metal blade with its wooden handle into her apron pocket, she walked calmly over to the sink. Seeing the blood, one of the other women came over, took her hand, and held it under the tap.

"All we need is for you to get ill," she grumbled. "Another two have already caught tetanus in the kitchen. This is a really bad start to the day, really bad."

Amanda stared at the open wound under the stream of cold water, watching how the color changed from red to purple. The knife had cut as far as the muscle, maybe even a nerve. She had lost all sensation in her hand, and was glad. It was a sign: she had become immune to pain; no one could harm her, much less a feeble, rusty knife. A burning sensation shot up her arm and she almost passed out.

"I think you should rinse off your hand with some hot water if you don't want to die of an infection."

She couldn't understand why they were helping her, moving her around the kitchen like a puppet. She let them do it, fascinated, her mind distant but at the same time pleased she could confirm that her body was no more than simple matter, alien to what she in essence was.

Crowding around her, the other women rubbed salt in the wound and began to bandage her hand with a length of greasy cloth.

"Don't worry, you'll recover," the impromptu nurse reassured her, seeing her blank gaze. Amanda smiled: how could she explain that she was prepared to receive whatever blows came her way, that she no longer felt pain, that nothing could make her happier.

Feeling her wound pulsing to the rhythm of her heart, she left the kitchen in search of Bertrand. Spying him in the doorway to one of the guard posts, she approached cautiously. When he saw her, he gave her a threatening glare. Ignoring this, Amanda walked around to the side of the hut.

"I need to see you tonight," she said serenely, when she was only a few steps away from him.

She had dared invade enemy territory; she was no longer afraid. She felt as if she were on a higher level, from where she could control Bertrand, Bérénice, anyone who stood in her way. She had nothing to lose.

Bertrand folded his arms in disbelief. His look seemed to say: "How dare you?" Turning his head toward her, he began to mutter something incomprehensible. Amanda thought he must be cursing her, and interpreted that as a sign of weakness. She realized she was able to get under his skin, to approach him even if he forbade it, even give him an order. If she so wished, she could get him stripped of his rank, make them give him menial tasks. And yet, it suddenly occurred to her, what job could be worse than the one he was condemned to perform now? *Who on earth wants to keep watch on somebody else's enemies?* she wanted to say to him. She felt sorry for this man who had agreed to help her.

She raised her wounded hand to her chest to ease the throbbing, then made her way back to the kitchen, certain that she had the insatiable Bertrand under her control.

❦

On Wednesday night as she made her way to the corner of the shed, she was surprised by a cold shower of rain. She wanted to be sure that Bertrand would be staying in the camp for a few more days at least, and that there wouldn't be any other changes that could endanger her plan. She didn't expect any guarantees, she simply needed to make sure. By now she wouldn't have been able to think of an alternative anyway.

She sought refuge in the corner they had made their own, and closed her eyes to wait, trembling from the cold and remembering every one of their encounters, every caress, every promise. She was roused from her daydreaming by a warm hand wiping her wet brow.

"If you stay here you'll catch pneumonia. What happened to your hand?" said Bérénice, without waiting for her to reply. "I don't think he'll come in this rain. It's very late. Lina has a fever, you need to return to the hut."

Amanda did not react immediately. She had been worried by Bertrand's absence, but was sure it had been due to the rain. She knew that although her rose essence perfume bottle was empty and her hair was less shiny than when she had arrived in the camp, she was still attractive to him. Besides, there were the jewels she had promised him. Jewels that also meant salvation for him.

She hurried off after Bérénice. Entering the hut, she ran over to Lina and placed her cold hands on the back of her neck to bring down the unwelcome fever flushing her daughter's hollow cheeks. She felt her daughter's stomach, which was soft, and like the good doctor's wife she was, listened to her chest. No inflammation, no constriction.

"It must be just a cold, the fever will break," she told Bérénice, who was still standing beside her, looking on. Amanda took her friend's hands in hers. "Thanks for telling me."

"I could see something was wrong, so I came over to see what was going on. She seemed delirious: she was talking about somebody called *Maman* Claire," explained Bérénice.

"She'll be fine, you'll see. Go and get some rest," said Amanda, settling down beside Lina.

27

$\mathcal{O}$n Thursday morning, Amanda hurried to the kitchen, hoping to bump into Bertrand. Only two days now for everything to come together. Frau Meyer offered to look after Lina, as she had done in the past with Viera. If the fever got worse, she would come and tell her. They both smiled sadly, remembering her earlier promise in Hamburg. Amanda saw in this coincidence a desperate token of good luck.

She was about to enter the kitchen when a hand gripped her by the wrist. Bertrand had run the risk of touching her, but this wasn't a caress.

"The rain never stopped," he excused himself tersely. She smiled inwardly, without looking at him. "It'll be Saturday night, as we arranged. Make sure your friends bring what you promised."

He spoke these last words with his back already turned. Amanda stayed motionless in the kitchen doorway for a few seconds. He didn't look back at her, but strode off, as though being there had been nothing more than an involuntary detour.

Almost forty-eight hours to go before her daughter was free again, and this time for good. The goodbyes had begun.

Neither she nor Lina, and especially Lina, belonged in this place. They had been brought here by mistake, the result of a decision Amanda now bitterly regretted. Julius had prepared everything to save his daughters, and she had betrayed him. With the best of intentions, and certain that she was doing the right thing, but still she had betrayed him. It was her duty to correct that mistake.

At dusk she looked for the remaining two pages from the mutilated book to write a last letter to Viera. She was certain her daughter would read it someday. Perhaps in a year, or even a decade, that wasn't so important. The letter would reach its destination, together with the others she had left with Claire. Her daughter would know she had always loved her, and that it was precisely that love which had led her to abandon her. And Viera would come searching for Lina, because in this last letter she intended to include all the information she needed to find her sister once again.

She had already written the heading on one of the sheets of paper. In Claire's house she had only had enough energy to begin with the date, at a time that now seemed far distant. Next to the drawing of the flower she could recognize her own handwriting: "Summer of 1942." She decided to set aside that one, which would be her last goodbye, and use the other sheet.

This was her lucky day. She smiled contentedly when she saw the *Impatiens balsamina*, the small garden balsam with tiny petals, lanceolate leaves, and flexible yet resistant stems. "Keep the soil moist. Don't overwater. Avoid very cold temperatures." She read the instructions very carefully, attempting to memorize every phrase. She tried to remember all the flowers in her previous letters.

"Where the hell did you put that knife!"

The shout startled her so much she jumped off the bed and dropped the sheet of paper onto the floor. She scrabbled on her knees to retrieve it in the darkness. Lina awoke in terror.

Holding it once again, Amanda got to her feet to confront the woman from the kitchen.

"We've been looking for that stupid knife everywhere. You've had us checking every shelf, every corner since early this morning. Do you think we're fools? We're sick and tired of your airs and graces. You deliberately cut yourself so that you could keep the knife."

Silence. Insults couldn't touch her, shouting didn't worry her. The woman lowered her voice, stressing every word.

"Don't try to deny it. Give me back the knife. Right now." She grabbed Amanda's bandaged hand and brought it up close to her eyes to inspect it. "Anyway, from what I can see, you'll end up rotten like those other two."

"Oh, *that* knife! It'll turn up," replied Amanda, in the tone of someone who has completely forgotten the incident. "I think that when I cut myself, the handle came off. I passed out, so somebody must have picked it up . . ."

"We're not all going to suffer on your account, do you hear me? Make sure that whatever's left of the knife reappears," growled the woman, striding out of the hut.

Bérénice came over to Amanda.

"The knife got lost, end of story. Make sure you hide it. One of these days we're going to need it," she whispered in her ear, before returning to her bed.

Lina's hacking cough echoed through the hut once more. Amanda made her more comfortable and sat beside her.

"She didn't want to eat anything all day," Frau Meyer told her. "If the sun shines tomorrow, it would do her good to get out."

Amanda went back to her letter in the darkness. She didn't need any light to shine on what she had already thought of writing to Viera. Her hand didn't shake; there was no time for tears or nostalgia. She couldn't linger over expressions of love or lengthy farewells.

This letter would not have a date or begin like the others: "My little Viera . . ." All she wanted was for the two sisters to find each other again. *When the war is over, you must come to France, to Haute-Vienne, and look for the Duval family . . .*

"You're a very courageous woman," said Frau Meyer, who was still standing beside the bed.

Amanda laughed wryly to herself and patted on the back the woman who had protected both her daughters.

"What else can we do? Our destinies don't belong to us anymore."

"But you're going to save Lina. I know it. She'll get over this fever and go out to play."

"It's not the fever I have to save her from, Frau Meyer. The fever is nothing."

"I know, dear Amanda, I know . . ." she said, stroking her brow gently and kissing her on the cheek. "Your eyes are beautiful and still full of life; but she is hope."

They were close to the window. They both stood in silence looking out at the night. In that brief moment, which for them was endless, they felt free.

28

On Friday evening, Amanda rushed back to the hut. Pulling out the battered suitcase, she took out the two small candles and held them to her chest. Closing her eyes, she began to say a silent prayer. Frau Meyer followed her. It was the Sabbath.

The two of them went to the window and waited for the sun to set. Before darkness fell over the camp, they placed the candles next to each other in the center of windowsill and took each other's hand, sharing the moment. They struggled to light the candles with a match. The quivering amber glow from the flames brought a touch of color to their faces and lit up their timid smiles. Little by little a group of women gathered silently around them. Lina crept out of bed and went over to her mother as the two flames spread a golden glow over the gray of the hut. Amanda could make out the reddish hair of one woman near her, the deep blue of Lina's eyes, the freckles dotting Frau Meyer's wrinkled cheeks. A few minutes later, they raised their hands to their faces and began to move them in circles, palms over their eyes.

Shielding Lina's head, Amanda began a prayer in Hebrew that

only her daughter could hear properly, but which the whole group followed.

"Blessed are You, Lord, our God, King of the universe, who distinguishes between the sacred and the mundane, between light and darkness—"

A woman's indignant voice interrupted her prayer. Amanda paused and kept her eyes shut, listening to the woman's howl.

"It's your fault that France is suffering. We opened the doors to you! And now the Germans are making us pay!"

Bérénice cast around for where the words were coming from. She paused when she discovered who had been speaking, and silenced her with a glare. Then she looked at the dozen women staring at her and glanced back at her friend, still focused on her candlelit prayer. Amanda raised her eyes and smiled at her, then moved away from the others, still concentrating on her rite, her face lit by the flickering light and the intensity of her prayers. She walked across the room praying to God on her behalf and that of her friend.

"I'm sorry . . . I didn't know you were . . ." Even the normally fearless Bérénice was at a loss for words.

"I'm not from Alsace . . . You have no reason to apologize. For what?" said Amanda, taking hold of her hands.

"Now I can understand what you and your daughter must be suffering. Where can you flee that you won't be persecuted?"

"We're all in the same situation, Bérénice. Look what they've turned us into. I don't think I can stand this a day longer."

Bringing her lips close to her friend's face, she said in a heartwarming whisper: "Lina will be safe."

∞

That night Amanda found it hard to sleep. She was watching over her daughter's fever, laying cold hands on the back of her head and crooning lullabies just as she used to in those far-off days when they were still a family. She didn't feel any nostalgia. She saw herself sitting at the table with Julius and the girls, but the image was so distant now that she could scarcely recognize herself.

When she opened her eyes, it was the dawn of the seventh day. She woke with a start because she had fallen into a deep sleep. Turning toward Lina, she saw she was ghostly pale, her skinny arms dangling over the side of the bunk.

"Come on, Lina, we have to wake up. Let's get some sun," she said, stroking her hair.

Lina was drenched in sweat. Amanda tried to settle her in the middle of the bed, raising her head and pulling up her hair. She didn't react. The mattress was wet with urine.

"Lina!"

Frau Meyer came over, lifted her in her arms, and took her over to the window so that she could get some fresh air.

"Lina!" This time Amanda's cry reached the whole hut. The women were observing what was going on, but were reluctant to draw near. Amanda fell to her knees and began to pray. She shook her head from side to side, waiting for a reaction from Frau Meyer, some words of encouragement, but soon realized that the previous night's intensity had been a farewell. She had no more prayers left, no more imploring gestures, no more hopeful smiles. Lina had succumbed on the seventh day.

Just a few more hours, give me a few more hours, she begged, resting her forehead on the wet mattress.

"I promise I'll get you out of here. Just a few more hours, little Lina."

Sighing, Amanda remained on her knees for several minutes in a reverie where only she could take refuge. When she closed her eyes, she could feel her heartbeats and clearly saw Julius holding out his hand to her. He was wearing a white shirt buttoned to the neck, with the sleeves rolled up, and she recognized the brown leather belt he had inherited from his father. What about his smell, Julius's smell? She took a deep breath to inhale it, but her senses failed her. The color had drained from everything around her as well; it had all gone back to a uniform gray.

"It's time to count heartbeats. Come on: One, two . . ." She could hear Julius's voice like a distant echo. The words were repeated time and again, cascading over one another. "Julius! Julius!" she called out to him. Her voice mingled with his. A few seconds united outside time.

"Lina! Lina!"

The two candles had burned down on the windowsill. Against the light, she saw her daughter standing with a steaming cup in her hands. She was drinking and smiling.

"Be careful, drink it slowly, slowly, your stomach's been empty a long time," Frau Meyer said out loud, giving Amanda time to recover from the shock. "Your girl is stronger than all the rest of us put together."

Lina left the mug on the windowsill and went over to hug her mother. "I think I wet the bed, Mama," she said in her ear.

You won't be sleeping in this bed anymore, my child, Amanda thought, but did not dare say it.

"You scared me, Lina . . ." She clasped her gently but firmly, with a quiet, imperceptible anxiety. "This nightmare is coming to an end."

Lina's face contorted, and her eyes filled with tears. She pressed herself fearfully against her mother.

"Don't abandon me, Mama. Don't abandon me. Remember what happened to Viera. We don't have any news of her."

"I'll never abandon you, Lina, my love. And believe it or not, Viera is better off than we are. Your papa and I managed to save her. Now I have to save you."

"Mama!" cried Lina, flinging herself on her neck and hugging her as tightly as she could.

"Trust me," said Amanda. "Please trust me."

29

On Saturday evening, a wave of damp hit the camp. At sunset, Amanda watched as the clouds swirled overhead, waiting anxiously for the three stars to come out—the signal for her meeting with Bertrand.

As usual there was a lot of noise from the men's hut. They would frantically pass around pages from newspapers, throw them to the floor in disgust, and then somebody else would pick them up, read them, and curse the heavens. The guards kept their distance and overlooked the insults some of the men dared shout at them in Spanish. Even though they didn't understand what the prisoners were saying, the meaning was perfectly clear: the moment for them to pay for what they were doing was bound to come someday.

"It's not just the Germans who'll be in the dock!" one of the inmates shouted. "You'll pay the price as well!"

Amanda and Bérénice were listening.

"There's no more room in Drancy," said Bérénice, shaking her head.

In a clean dress and with her coat buttoned to the top, Lina was sitting at the doorway to the hut, apart from the other children.

"She still doesn't feel well," said Amanda, looking over at her, her mind preoccupied by that morning's incident. "When night comes, the fever and cough will return . . . And now it looks as if it's going to rain. That's all we needed."

"But we do need lots of water. Let's see if it can wash away the bitterness of this place," said Bérénice, rubbing her arms furiously.

Amanda went to sit with Lina, observing her every movement and reaction. She had timed all the comings and goings from the kitchen, the changing of the guards in their post, who went most often to the outhouse. On Saturdays the guards were less careful; they ignored what was going on in the huts. This lack of attention worked in her favor. But they also started drinking whole pitchers of wine in full view of the thirsty prisoners, and it wasn't unusual for this shameless display to end in violence. Sometimes they began to sing, and one or other always ended up bawling a strident rendering of "La Marseillaise." The men in the hut responded with the same anthem, then shouted that what the guards should be singing was a German one instead.

At six in the evening the storage shed was usually locked for the night by Bertrand, who was in charge of opening and shutting it each day. But not that night.

The drizzle was persistent. When Amanda arrived there, Bertrand was leaning against the wall opposite the door, in darkness. On the floor were several empty bottles, pieces of wood, wet chunks of coal. They had agreed he would wait for her in the corner closest to the wire fence looking out to the forest.

Amanda had left Lina in the doorway of the women's hut, where she had no protection from the rain and was shivering. When Amanda headed for the shed, she was convinced the deal could be concluded quickly. There was no need for any talk, seductive gestures, or clumsy caresses. The negotiations were complete; all that was left now was the exchange: the handover and the reward. When she drew near, she saw Bertrand raising a half-empty wine bottle to his lips, and noticed how red his eyes were. This didn't worry her. He needed her: she was his future.

"Bertrand," she whispered, cajoling him like a lover. "You'd better not drink anymore tonight."

He smiled and took another long swig, then tossed the empty bottle as far away as he could. He fumbled to undo the buttons of his uniform and extended his arms to receive her.

She approached him cautiously, trying to postpone their embrace.

"My daughter is outside, waiting in the rain." She hurried him as she drew near.

"She's fine where she is. Come here."

"The thing is, she has a fever. She's had it for several days now. It would be best to take her and hand her over. After that I can come back to you," she said, stepping back.

He burst out laughing and eyed her hungrily.

"Come here," he insisted, arms wide and a drunken grin on his face.

When she didn't respond, he pulled her roughly toward him. Amanda lowered her head and repeated his name again.

She tried to free herself, but he grasped her even more tightly. Amanda pushed him off, but in the struggle, he pulled on her dress until violently unclasping her brassiere. Something fell to the ground. Glinting at their feet was the promised treasure: the diamond bracelet and ring, with its spectral turquoise-blue gleam.

Gripping her with one hand, pinioning her by the throat, he flung her against the shed wall. She was cornered, unable to move or breathe.

"So your friends were the ones who were going to bring the bracelet . . . Did you think I'd let you escape with your daughter and the treasure? Who did this society madame, the cardiologist's widow, think I was? Nothing stays a secret in here."

His words flew around her incomprehensibly, striking her like icy gusts. She didn't dare say anything in response.

With one of Bertrand's hands around her throat and the other between her legs, it felt to Amanda as though the rusty barbed-wire fence she was hoping to cross was slicing through her, sinking viciously into her flesh. As he began to move rhythmically inside her, she gave a low moan.

"You're used to it," he said, panting and licking her ear. "Don't tell me it upsets you now."

Struggling to get her breath back, Amanda pretended to briefly pass out, and let him do whatever he wanted.

"My daughter's waiting for me," she repeated.

Bertrand seemed determined to obtain as much pleasure as possible. He didn't want to waste his Saturday night; he would sleep peacefully, relieved and satisfied. From time to time he paused, searched for her eyes and smiled a crazy, drunken smile.

Amanda slowly moved her hand to her coat pocket, feeling for the handle of the rusty blade. Grasping it as cautiously as she could, she closed her eyes and blindly, as though in the grip of an uncontrollable impulse, stabbed at the jugular of the man pushing against her. She struck a second time, and could feel the battered blade slowly cut through the neck muscles. Still inside her, Bertrand stopped moving. Amanda drove the knife in again and again. With all her strength, all her rage.

"And on the seventh day, God ended his work, and rested," she said in Hebrew close to Bertrand's neck, as if about to kiss him. Then she did kiss him. She could feel the blood trickling down her lips, her hand, but only reacted when the warm, sticky liquid seeped through her coat and threatened to stain her dress. She carefully pulled out the knife and dropped it. Coldly, she inserted her fingers in the wound, searching for any remaining sign of life, the last heartbeat. There was still a pulse, as if he was drawing sustenance from her. But when she jerked her fingers out again, Bertrand took his last breath.

Amanda didn't move. She felt a deep calm sweep over her. Now she had absolutely nothing to lose. Her daughter would be free. She would keep the bracelet and diamond ring. Bertrand's death brought her not only a strange sense of peace, but a disconcerting sense of fulfillment. Lina was safe.

Bertrand's corpse was still upright, jammed between her and the wall. He was steady, with eyes staring blankly and a grimace on his lips.

She stepped back, and the lifeless body slid to the muddy floor of the shed.

The rain eased off, and the moon appeared from behind the clouds. A silvery gleam lit the face of the man with the slashed neck. Dazed, Amanda sat beside the body, just as she had on the nights when she gave him her body as her part of the bargain. There was no hurry: this was simply another nocturnal encounter between a hungry officer and a prisoner from the women's hut. No one would wonder where he was until dawn the next day.

Amanda straightened her dress and coat, then walked slowly back to the women's hut. She found Lina asleep in the doorway. She was trembling; her fever had returned, her quiet cough more like a groan. Amanda put the bracelet and ring in the inside pocket of her daughter's coat. In the other she placed the letter with instructions for Viera. Without any greeting or goodbye.

She still had that summer's letter with her, the last letter, which she had never finished. She peered at the sheet from the mutilated book, which was still blank. *No, there's no time for goodbyes,* she was convinced. Shakily, she traced the first letter, then a whole syllable. Yes, she at least had to complete the single word, and yet it took her several minutes to do so. At the bottom of the empty page, she wrote: *Mama.* This was her goodbye, what else could Viera need? She was sure that every night, before going to sleep, her daughter listened to her lullaby. She was delighted by the gleaming white of the faded sheet of paper and its washed-out image of *Anagallis caerulea*. Rejoicing, she finished writing that one, unique, true word, the one that could save them and rescue them all from oblivion. A single word would be enough.

She folded the sheet and placed it in her daughter's coat pocket as well.

"Lina, it's time for us to go."

She shook her daughter tenderly and tried to lift her, but didn't have the strength. Lina gradually woke up and, without asking what they were doing or where they were going, grasped her mother's bloody hand.

30

$\mathcal{A}$manda and Lina carefully separated rows of barbed-wire fence and crossed over. In the distance, the whole forest trembled as Amanda peered into the darkness, her eyes veiled by a feeling of hatred completely new to her. The night's cool air began to dry the dead man's blood, turning it into crystals on her skin.

She turned to look back at the dark camp in the distance. Her daughter was leaving behind a past that should never have existed. She would forget the insults, the fever, the escape, the apathy, the rejection. She would wake up in Claire's arms and forget her name. She would have to forget it: that was the only way she could save herself.

Before first light, Amanda would return to the hut, alone. She would wash off the blood with steaming hot water in the kitchen. No trace would remain of the vile man who had betrayed her, who had turned her into a murderer. She would get another dress from the suitcase, and when she was clean and without guilt, she would say goodbye to Bérénice and Frau Meyer. As she embraced them, she would say, "I did it. My daughter is safe. It's time to forget."

Then she would return to the shed and close Bertrand's eyes. After that, she would go and find one of the guards and take him to the scene of the crime. At dawn, the camp would wake up to a deafening uproar. The French guards would have yet another reason to be afraid. She would confess her guilt and be sentenced yet again. A few days later, she would be deported in a train packed with dying souls, and would end up, as she herself had predicted, in an oven. She was no longer afraid of fire. Or maybe, when she returned to the camp, she would be met with a bullet to the head. That simple, that painless.

The forest was a huge shadow that separated the concentration camp from the nearest village. Amanda and her daughter plunged blindly into it, until far ahead of them they could make out two silhouettes. In the darkness, they could hear footsteps on the fallen leaves. They came to a cautious stop. Amanda knew she shouldn't go too far from the camp: in a couple of hours at most she had to be back there. She could feel Lina's hand squeezing hers, and bent down so that she could hear.

"You're to look up at the treetops, as high as you can, and search for the stars. All I ask is that, whatever happens, don't look back. I'll be here or somewhere else, always keeping watch over you and Viera."

Lina clung to her.

"Now you must promise me something. You're about to start a new life, and must forgive me for having made you suffer so much."

"Mama, don't abandon me . . ."

"How can you think I'm abandoning you, my little Lina? Look who's over there."

Deep in the shadows of the forest, Lina could only see a hand being held out by a man as tall as a silver birch.

"You have the letter you need to send to Viera, the last one I wrote. When the time comes, she'll look for you and you'll get your name back. Our name."

At that moment Lina saw Claire's face beneath the trees. Her body stiffened, as if she was asking: "Why do you want to take me away from

Mama?" She began to tremble uncontrollably. Next to Claire she recognized Father Marcel.

Feeling weaker, her vision blurring, she shut her eyes tight and counted her accelerated heartbeats: *One, two, three, four, five, six* . . .

Opening her eyes again, she cried out as loudly as she could: "*Mama, verlass mich nicht,*" and collapsed to the ground. Father Marcel picked her up; Claire felt her forehead. The fever was raging.

By the time Claire looked up again, Amanda had vanished. Claire bent down to the little girl's face and kissed it.

"From now on, you are Elise. Let's go home, sweet Elise."

Spring of 1942

My little Viera:

I can recall my mother's terrified face on the day when she said goodbye because she knew she was about to die. I can recall my father's anxious look when he gave me away at the altar. I can recall those summer evenings by the lake when we played at being happy. I can recall your father's warm embrace on winter nights when I was trembling, not from fear, but because the silences between us frightened me. I can recall his last letter, word for word. I can recall the smell of the antique books in the Garden of Letters, mixed with the stench from the bonfire in the middle of the square, and the crunch of broken glass everywhere. I can recall those long, peaceful afternoons when we had tea with Hilde, unaware of what our fate might be. I can recall the day you were born and when for the first time I had the dreadful premonition that I would not see you grow up. I can recall the day I discovered I was pregnant with your sister, and again began to tremble with fear. I can recall Frau Meyer's stern gaze when I abandoned you at the foot of the gangway.

And yet I have trouble recalling your eyes and your smile. I know that I once held you in my arms, but I cannot recall when you took your first steps, or said your first word.

Now I struggle every night with my poor memory. I don't have the strength to fight oblivion.

How could I have abandoned you, my little Viera? How could I then have protected myself by forgetting you? That wasn't the fault of the Nazis, the war, or the hatred that now guides my hand across this faded sheet filled with wallflowers. It was the fault of my fear.

Fear led me to oblivion.

This may be the last letter I'll be able to write to you. All I ask is that your sister and you always wear the chains with your names engraved on them. They are the most precious possession you will ever have. That way you will never forget who you are.

The day this inferno is over, come and search for your sister. Protect each other and recover your name. To save herself, she now must forget who she is. But you don't have to.

Mama

FIVE

The Abandonment

Haute-Vienne, 1942–1947

31

*F*or six days and six nights, the little girl's lacerated body lay beneath damp sheets in a room where not even the smallest shaft of light was allowed in. Only the moon's reflection entered to bring a pale glimmer of life to the inert face.

The fever had gradually abated, but she was still breathing with difficulty, as if she had already given up the struggle. Eyes closed, she barely moved her lips, and her body began to shake uncontrollably whenever Claire rubbed her lips with small pieces of ice to try to rehydrate her. She refused to eat, drink water, smile, or cry.

She did respond to caresses, or so Claire, who was always at her side, liked to believe. She reacted to Father Marcel's prayers with sporadic sighs that brought a timid smile to the faces of the two adults, in the hope she would pull through. At night, Danielle sang her songs, searching for a sign that would let her know her friend's soul had not been lost in the dark forest.

After the little girl had been unconscious for a week, Father Marcel decided they had to take her to the hospital in Limoges. They couldn't leave her another day without eating or drinking any water. He picked her up before Claire had time to object. Her arms hung down like broken branches; her head hung lifelessly against his neck.

"She's only seven, and we're all she has," Claire protested. At that moment Father Marcel felt the girl snuggling against his chest.

Claire was still kneeling at the foot of the bed, praying for a miracle. The priest took some ice and dripped a few drops of water onto the girl's brow, violet-tinged face, and cracked lips.

"Claire," he said gently, "she's going to be all right."

When Claire saw the girl had opened her eyes and offered him a wan smile, she came up and touched the priest's arm. At that moment the two of them were again as close, or possibly even closer, as when he had kept vigil over her for a week. Sickness had once again brought them together.

The girl began to stir. Taking her in her arms, Claire held Father Marcel's hand and broke into sobs. The priest wished the embrace could also include him, and immediately asked God's forgiveness for the thought. He didn't want anything to spoil this moment of rejoicing. The girl was saved, and Claire was beside him. Concentrating his mind on the little one, he prayed with all his might that she would thrive, for Claire and for him.

Day dawned with both of them at the bedside of the emaciated girl, who soon began to anxiously devour everything they offered her. For the first time since they had recovered her in the forest, they dared open the windows, hoping that the merciful angel who had restored her to them would remain there the whole time they hid her on the farm.

"My child, my child," Claire said, trembling. "From today I'll be your mother," she repeated as if it was a lullaby. "My little Elise . . ."

Standing in the doorway, Danielle surveyed the scene uneasily. She couldn't recall having been ill, or that her mother had ever devoted herself to her day and night the way she was now doing with Elise. Left to her own devices, she roamed the house, sighing.

By day, Elise learned to live in hiding, passing the time reading the tangled stories in a battered Bible in French that she could barely understand. She learned about the forbidden fruit and snakes, kisses and betrayals, angels, virgins, apostles and saints, crowns and crosses. She could recite whole verses from memory, even though they meant little to her. The rhythm and old-fashioned language fascinated her.

For Elise, the past was nothing more than the moment when she had woken in the arms of Father Marcel; the rest was shadows. Further back than that was only a distant trace in her memory, a heartbeat, the confused taste of fear.

She accepted the command to hide from the sun as if she was sick and the sun's rays could scorch her skin and destroy her. She learned that during the day she was destined to remain in the attic, like a bat relegated to the darkest part of her new home.

After dark, she played outside with Danielle, who protected her with motherly devotion while Claire looked on.

Through that first fall and winter, Elise felt secure, because the others gathered around the warmth of the hearth. But by the following summer she fell prey to dark premonitions. Almost a year had gone by since she had been abandoned in the forest, and she still had to calm her fears, repeating her name over and over: "Elise, Elise, Elise . . . My name is Elise."

She cherished the time she could spend with Danielle. She became the sentinel of the attic, where she tried to entertain herself by telling herself tales of far-off lands where no one would ever take her. She had nightmares of going to live on a forgotten continent, where the sun's rays would weaken until they disappeared completely before they came into contact with the surface of objects; the days would be long and dark, the winters frozen.

It was hard to bear being confined to the windowless dungeon of the attic. She dreamed of having a friend she could protect, be it a wounded soldier, an abandoned dog, a threadbare ball, an insect, even a worm—something she could give a name to and talk to, so that her words did not rebound emptily from the rough walls.

What had started out as a kind of game now became torture. Confined, utterly alone, she spent hours praying in silence while Danielle went to Father Marcel's mass. She began to loathe the searing heat. She had recently turned eight, and felt that time was slipping away. She was growing, and the gloomy attic seemed to her more and more like a cramped prison.

One night she woke up terrified and bathed in sweat. She had had a premonition that led her to cover her ears and sing furiously in an attempt to erase the image that pursued her even now that she was awake. One day they were going to forget her up in the attic, and a hurricane of fire would destroy houses, farms, and even Father Marcel's church.

Life at night had made the colors fade, and tinged the world around her with a uniform silver sheen. She waited anxiously for the leaves to fall, the roses to wither, and the lavender fields to give way to the dry, icy winds of winter.

One morning she discovered next to her a motionless larva, frozen beside what seemed to be a little ball of solid dung. She wondered if this was a trick of her lonely imagination, but when she bent over to examine the tiny, transparent being, she could see that inside it a shadow was slowly stirring. It was alive.

"Who are you?" she asked quietly, worried that the slightest breath might destroy the creature being born in front of her eyes.

Her prayers had been heard: she wasn't alone anymore. She went in search of a piece of bread, a grain of sugar, a drop of water to feed to this minuscule worm. She began to fantasize about what this solitary larva might become. She hoped it would be a wingless insect that would not be able to fly away, one that, like her, would remain on the ground.

Within a few days a dark shell became visible. Two enormous eyes started to appear on its head, and four legs with tiny spines on them. Sitting back, she studied it closely.

"A beetle, it's given birth to a beetle," she said, astonished at her creation. "Jepri, that's what I'll call you, and you'll be my friend."

She recalled the words her father would repeat to her in German, resurfacing from a past she preferred to think she had forgotten. *A child can crush a beetle, but not even a professor could ever create one.*

With Jepri's arrival, the days became short and the nights long. Elise would lie down next to it and observe it from so close up that to her the insect looked like a giant come to rescue her. She watched it eat and scuttle away into the darkness; she studied its routine and tried every day to modify it, testing how far an insect could be trained and become a real pet.

She knew its life would be short but that, like all beetles, it would be resurrected by recreating itself. She did not want to see it die, and preferred that it lead them together into the land of shadows.

"You'll live in my heart, Jepri, my love," she said one night, raising the beetle to her chest, waiting for the mortal bite.

But beetles don't bite, she told herself.

When she woke up, it was to find her friend's lifeless corpse next to her. Jepri the beetle had refused to follow its instincts and let itself die rather than attack her. It had saved her.

Overcome with emotion, she hoped against hope that Jepri would recreate himself. Now that her only friend was dead, she decided she must bury alongside him all the misty images of a past she saw only in dreams. A faceless father, a sister vanishing on the deck of a ship, a mother who abandoned her in a forest. Jepri's death meant the end of her childhood. From now on she would be no one else but Elise.

32

On the morning of June 10, 1944, the sun was beating down on the nearby barns. Thinking that a little bit of light would help her mourn her friend and deciding she didn't care if she was seen, Elise peered out of her living room window and saw her neighbors running scared in the distance.

Seeing this, Danielle pulled her away from the window, then ran outside to find out what the farmers were so afraid of. Without getting too close, she realized that an alarming number of Germans had poured into the village. She was told that a detachment of soldiers was posted at every entrance; they had closed the bridge, and even blocked the railway line. Their uniforms were unmistakable. Danielle got close enough to recognize the dreaded initials SS. She ran back to the house, out of breath.

"The SS?" Claire wondered. "I don't know what they can be looking for here. Why didn't they stay in Limoges?"

She took off her apron and stood for several minutes staring down at the water as she washed her hands. They lived in an insignificant village, whose inhabitants had accepted the German occupation with stoic apathy. Apart from ration books, the war had not changed their daily routines; the Resistance was a fantasy, a myth the men preferred to ignore as they drank coffee on Rue Emile Desourteaux. Claire couldn't explain this disproportionate military presence. Tales of courageous men blowing up a railway line or abducting German officers happened elsewhere, in places like Saint-Junien or Saint-Léonard-de-Noblat, some sixty kilometers from Limoges. Nothing ever happened in their village: they lived at peace, even if this was only an illusion. None of its inhabitants wanted or was willing to defy the occupying forces.

Perhaps the only serious offense they had committed had been to take in refugees from Moselle or Charly who had been evicted from their homes by the SS. There had also been a few German Jews that Cuba had refused entry to several years earlier, although they had been deported shortly afterward in a massive roundup. *Who were they looking for now? A defenseless little girl hidden in an attic?* Claire wondered anxiously.

They're coming for me, they're coming for me, Elise told herself fearfully. *But Jepri's spirit will save me. He is immortal.*

Claire walked up to the road and stopped one of the neighbors.

"I'm really worried," the woman moaned. "Something is going to happen. We all have to go to the main square: it's an order from the Germans."

Claire rushed back to her house. Without explaining anything, she began to pack a suitcase as carefully as possible.

"We'll eat something and then go into the village," she told the girls calmly. "Don't worry, nothing will happen."

Danielle sat at the table, with Elise next to her. Avoiding their curious gaze, Claire went into their bedroom. Elise got up and followed her furtively. She saw her arranging letters in a wooden chest, and then adding a small red box. She shut the suitcase and went over to the window: she needed fresh air.

"Whatever happens, you two will always be together, do you hear me?" During difficult times like this, *Maman* Claire's voice was always heartwarming. The two girls nodded silently.

Claire hugged them and laid her head on top of Elise's. She glanced one last time at the few family photographs in the room: one of her husband in the colonies; Danielle as a baby in her arms; she herself, wrapped in a thick raincoat, smiling with the Eiffel Tower in the background (the only souvenir from her trip to Paris before she was married). With a little sigh, she moved away from the girls. She brushed her hair in front of the mirror, and smiled. They were ready to leave.

"Combi! We have to take Combi with us!' cried Elise, running to fetch the old deflated soccer ball from under the bed.

"There's no need, Elise," Danielle tried to convince her. "We'll be back very soon."

But Elise clung to the ball, which would be her only personal luggage.

As they left the house Claire paused on the threshold, gazing at the lavender fields that would soon be blooming.

They joined the small groups of neighbors hurrying to comply with the occupiers' commands.

Elise was afraid that although she looked like Claire's daughter, some of them—the girls from her old school at least—would recognize her. With Danielle holding her hand tight, she inhaled lungfuls of the morning air. *I'm just one more in a crowd, nobody's going to notice.* When they reached the first village street, she buried her face in Claire's skirt. *Maman* Claire came to a halt and stroked her brow.

"Everything is going to be all right, little one," she said again. "The important thing is that, no matter what happens, you do not leave Danielle's side. She's your sister. Always follow her, okay?"

Claire's instructions echoed in Elise's mind. Far from reassuring her, they seemed like the warning of a change she couldn't quite understand. For her part, once again Danielle felt that her mother was more concerned about Elise than her. She was only twelve years old, but now she had to be responsible for someone else.

I'm only three years older than Elise, Maman. *And I'm your real daughter,* she wanted to say, but couldn't.

As they crossed the village, they smiled at everyone they met. They walked past the train station, where a train had left earlier that morning for Limoges. It was just a normal Saturday like any other. The doors and windows of the empty houses were open to the summer breeze. They reached the main street, where in the corner café a few men were still arguing fiercely.

"These aren't ordinary German soldiers, they're from the second SS Das Reich division," said one of them, wiping his mouth on his forearm, proud of his precise knowledge. "They're the toughest."

The three of them walked on to the main square, where they found the German soldiers deployed in a circle, like a barricade. The church doors were opened, and the women and children went inside to shelter from the heat.

"Where is Father Marcel?" asked Claire, hoping that someone would be able to answer. "Have you seen Father Marcel . . . ?"

The men were herded together and led off toward a farm south of the village. Nobody said goodbye, why should they? This was simply a routine operation, one of those absurd roll calls they had grown used to in the war.

The soldiers were speaking French to one another, and Danielle and Elise studied their uniforms, trying to distinguish the differences between them. Elise recognized an insignia shaped like a wolf trap on one of the soldier's chests. He was smiling at her all the time. A local woman interrupted them to explain to an officer that she had left a cake in the oven. She was unable to hear his reply before she was dragged away by the crowd that the soldiers were forcing into the church.

Maman *Claire is the only one who brought a suitcase,* Elise realized. Just then a huge explosion flung her down onto the cobblestones. Claire threw herself on top of her. Danielle, who had been blown some distance away, could scarcely make them out amid all the turmoil, smoke, and flames coming from the church. Bodies were piled on bodies, with shoes strewn everywhere.

The first explosion deafened Elise. The next one lashed at the soles of her feet. At that moment, she realized that fear was rooted in the body, that it could tear at your skin and hair, smash your teeth. She could feel *Maman* Claire's body protecting her on the cobbles, and closed her eyes. In the distance she heard a lullaby: *In German?* Snatches of sound, disparate words. *Maman?* A child's cries broke the silence until they were suddenly cut short by rifle fire.

Pieces of debris were still falling on her, or rather on *Maman* Claire, who was lying on top of her, her body hot, wet, heavy. The gray dust dissolved in tears that would not dry. The dust turned to stone.

"*Maman,*" whispered Elise, barely audibly. It was no more than a sigh, but when she got no response, she cried out loud: "*Maman* Claire!"

The wail of a siren pierced her ears. She remembered she was in the village square, opposite the mayor's house, near Madame Beauchêne's corner café, outside Father Marcel's blazing church. Its bells rang out crazily, until they were drowned out by the loudspeakers. She couldn't see the cake shop or the cemetery, only the walls of the Hotel Beaubreuil slowly emerging from the clouds of smoke.

She tried to open her mouth, but her parched lips were stuck together by the solid dust.

"*Maman!*" she mumbled again fearfully, but couldn't get any other words out.

The third explosion seemed to go off inside her head. The shock wave freed her; she could no longer feel the weight of the body on top of her. She had lost *Maman* Claire; she had lost her protective shell.

33

She opened her eyes slowly. There was *Maman* Claire, facedown in the dust, with one shoe missing and her silk stockings torn. *Where can the other shoe be?* Without stirring, Elise looked all around for it. She had to find it, but couldn't move, only turn her head.

The paunchy little angel was still standing in the old stone fountain. Water trickled from its mouth into the basin, sending orange and blue glints through the smoke.

When Elise plucked up the courage to move, she felt a stabbing pain in her right shoulder. The square had disappeared: all that remained was dust and a naked angel floating above black waters.

The vision of this inferno took her breath away. She tried to breathe, but felt she was about to choke. She cried out, and immediately was able to inhale once more. She was alive; she had survived yet again.

"Elise, get up!" it was Danielle's voice, calling to her from somewhere she couldn't see. She peered through the clouds of smoke, over the dead bodies. Dumbstruck. Danielle managed to reach her and grabbed her hand. "Wait."

The suitcase was there, next to Claire's body, under a thick layer of dust and stones. Danielle clambered over to it, pulled it out, and came back toward Elise.

"Let's go!" was all she said.

"*Maman* Claire . . ." whispered Elise.

"*Maman* is dead," Danielle said curtly.

They had no time. The soldiers would be back, looking for survivors: they were only waiting for the flames to die down. The two girls were a danger now; they were among the few still living in a village buried beneath a thick, dark cloud.

They paused for a moment, trying to get their bearings amid this emptiness, to find a direction in which to flee. Beyond the smoke pouring from the church they could make out the cemetery. They could cross it, or run along the riverbank in the opposite direction toward the abbey, although that would be a huge risk. It would take them several hours, thought Danielle doubtfully. She didn't understand who they were fleeing from, who exactly the enemy was.

They had lost all sense of time. They couldn't tell how much daylight was left, if night was about to fall. Clinging to each other's hands, they trembled with fear and anguish.

"Let's hide here," said Danielle. "We have to wait for it to grow dark."

Hide? Elise couldn't understand her. There were no nearby trees, street corners, or houses that could shelter them. But Danielle flopped down beside the suitcase and closed her eyes.

Elise's feet were burning; her eyes were full of sand, her throat parched. She didn't dare tell Danielle she was thirsty, that she had to find water before they set off for the abbey, she knew it was far too dangerous to budge from their hiding spot. And who knew whether the Germans had also been there and done the same, shutting the women and children inside the building and blowing it up. But Danielle was asleep, or pretending to be. She had no answers to Elise's questions.

For the first time, Elise shed silent tears, trying not to wake Danielle. She turned her back and sobbed, thinking of how *Maman* Claire had saved her. They had to reach the abbey to get help, at least to make sure all these torn bodies were given a decent burial.

Or perhaps it was best not to think, to close her eyes, try to sleep and forget. That is what she was trying to do when she felt the first raindrops. Looking up, she saw how low and heavy the clouds were. A fine rain began to settle the dust. The air was filled with sinister smells.

The roar of a convoy of trucks bearing the swastika on their sides and packed with soldiers woke Danielle. They were not headed toward the abbey, but in the opposite direction. The two girls looked at each other hopefully before terror struck. Maybe the Germans were on their way back from there after wiping out everyone, including Father Marcel, the only person who could have saved them.

Elise got up and walked a few steps away from Danielle. For a few seconds, the red taillight of the last German truck lit her face up. A soldier saw her, quickly put on his helmet, and sat staring at her. Elise wasn't afraid: she stared back at the youth as his truck sped down the road, growing smaller and smaller in the rain and dust.

The soldiers are fleeing, ashamed of the crime they've committed, Elise dared to hope.

She was sure they wouldn't come back just for her. The German soldier must have thought she was a ghost. Or maybe he didn't see her because she no longer existed. She had died several hours earlier, like all her neighbors in the village. In the church, the square, the barns.

She had also died two years earlier, that night in the forest, before she woke up burning with fever in *Maman* Claire's arms. Now she was living another of her deaths. God only knew how many more deaths she would have to escape.

Even the worst murderers can have an ounce of pity, she thought. By not giving her away, Elise saw something akin to compassion in the young soldier. Even so, she would have preferred to be taken to the nearest village. There she would be given water, maybe even a piece of bread. The soldier had not saved her, she decided, he had abandoned her to her fate. To her death.

"We have to stay away from the main road," Danielle warned her, standing up and starting to walk away without looking at Elise, who followed her silently.

"I don't think I can keep walking without water . . ."

The rain had soon ceased, barely moistening her lips. Danielle walked on without replying; they couldn't go down to the river either, that would be too dangerous. This was no moment to look for water, let alone food.

"When we reach the abbey, let's say as little as possible," Danielle said. "We'll stay together all the time. We don't know if the Germans will be there as well; we'll have to find out before we reach it. Keep going a little while longer, we're almost there. Can you make it?"

Elise said nothing, but followed Danielle as best she could, trying to avoid putting any weight on her right heel. It was difficult not walking on the road: the ground under the trees in the forest gave off a warm vapor that disorientated them. When they came to a clearing surrounded by undergrowth, they decided to stop for a rest. Curled up together, they shared a troubled sleep.

❦

It was late morning by the time they set off again. The closer they got to the abbey, the slower Danielle walked, dragging the suitcase along with one hand, supporting the limping Elise with the other. She was tormented by the image of her mother lying among the rubble in the square. It was only her solemn promise to her that kept her going.

"Look after Elise as if she was your sister," her mother had asked her as she put a Bible in the suitcase, a change of clothes for each of them, and three thick coats. *Why is she doing that,* Danielle had thought, *when we're at the height of summer . . .*

It was a heavy, annoying burden, but she had to carry it with her. She tried to understand why her mother had gone to the village with a suitcase when nobody else had, what had really happened, why they had survived. What did her mother know, what had she foreseen? The suitcase was a reminder, a record of scattered memories. *The suitcase is Maman*, she told herself as she continued walking.

Though they kept on, both of them were convinced they had died in the square together with *Maman* Claire. The path to the abbey was an illusion. They were still there, next to Claire's body, waiting to be buried in a mass grave.

When at last they spied the abbey walls on the horizon, a stab of fear returned. There were no Germans in sight. As the two girls approached it warily, the massive building rose silently in the glow of sunset. Danielle squeezed Elise's hand; they gazed at one another for a few seconds and then prepared to cross the threshold of the rusty, iron-studded oak door.

Perhaps they were safe, for now.

34

The main nave of the abbey was packed with children running, tumbling, crying, laughing. There was a smell of manure, butter, sweat, and rancid cheese, broken pipes, stagnant water. The dim light made their weary faces—the pallid, sunken cheeks—seem like pathetic ochre visions.

Father Marcel was standing in a corner flanked by worn stone pillars, his head soaking wet to calm the stifling heat. The girls didn't recognize him, even though they had last seen him only two weeks earlier at one of their Friday night suppers. He had not shaved for days, and his greasy black hair was plastered to his skull. His cassock was mudstained, with white patches on the chest and under the arms.

Sitting to his right was Father Auguste holding the abbey's heavy baptismal register, writing down the names of the children who were arriving. With his crabbed, elderly hands he was jotting down the details of the new arrivals on separate sheets of paper: who had brought them to the abbey, what village they came from, what school they went to, their parents' professions. If they had brothers and sisters, he also asked their names and dates of birth and added them to each note. A little girl was standing in front of him, replying in low murmurs that exasperated him. He waved her away to sit with the others.

He was about to close the baptismal book when Father Marcel stopped him.

"I've just been told two more girls have arrived. I hope they're the last today."

The priest lifted up a small two-year-old boy who had been crying for hours. Taking a handkerchief from his cassock, he wiped the boy's runny nose. The little one nestled against his chest, flung his arms round him, and gradually began to relax. It seemed as if this was the first physical contact he had enjoyed in a long while.

"Here come the girls," Father Auguste said as he saw them enter the nave. Father Marcel sat the little boy down on a bench to receive the newcomers.

When he saw who they were, he rushed up and embraced them. All three remained silent for a few moments. There was no need for questions; there was nothing to explain. They were safe. Father Marcel closed his eyes and gave thanks: his prayers had been answered.

"Danielle and Elise Duval," he called out to Father Auguste. "They're sisters, I baptized them both."

Danielle clasped Elise's hand as tightly as she could. Elise was breathing heavily. Father Marcel stroked their heads, and led them from the nave into the kitchen.

"Trust me, everything will be all right," he said. "Now you must eat something." Seeing that the girls still seemed lost and afraid, he went on, looking them straight in the eye: "The time for secrets is over. Now we can try to find Claire's brother in America. Your uncle," he turned to Danielle, "will take charge of you. This accursed war will soon be over."

Reassured by his words, the girls ran to get a glass of water while Father Marcel went back to complete their details with Father Auguste. It was important for the children to appear on the register: it was a kind of legal guarantee for the Germans, and would be helpful after the war, when their relatives came looking for them. Father Marcel wanted everything concerning Elise and Danielle to be in order, especially since, so far, they appeared to be the only survivors from their village. He even thought that perhaps he should change the name of their place of birth. His sole mission now was to protect these orphans. To do that, he was capable of anything, even lying. God would forgive him. His eyes were bloodshot from lack of sleep, a sense of anguish, and the frustration that all he could do was wipe noses and bow his head.

He sensed that the crime committed against his parishioners had been a last-gasp act. The Germans were losing the war: the end was drawing closer and closer. Father Marcel saw the fact that he had survived as a punishment: he should have been there with all the others in the village square. He was sure that his presence would have acted as a restraint on the bestiality of the soldiers thirsty for revenge. *What did they expect to find, weapons? There were only defenseless, docile villagers, and yet they unleashed their fury on them. They'll pay soon enough*, he told himself. At moments like these, the Bible wasn't his most reliable ally. He couldn't help feeling hatred; he asked God to allow him to curse so that his wounds might heal. He was convinced they were all guilty for having accepted the German occupation as nothing more than an irksome imposition.

He was tempted to return to his church and amid the ruins to renounce God, the Creator who closed his eyes when faced with the crimes his creatures committed.

◈

Kneeling at the altar that evening, he prayed with all his might for the orphans who were his responsibility. As he did so, he saw a blurred image of Claire's face in a summer dusk some years earlier. Knowing it could be his salvation, he tried to concentrate on the image, but couldn't make out how blue her eyes were, or the tone of her voice, or her pale freckled skin. All he could see were her delicate hands in his as she begged for his understanding: as she explained, if she was putting her family at risk it was because she felt it was her Christian duty. Now it was his duty to protect the girls.

That night, after several sleepless hours, when he finally recalled Claire's sweet, melodious voice Father Marcel fell asleep.

At first light he headed for the dormitory. The nave that had once sheltered pilgrims was now providing refuge for more than twenty children. He checked that Danielle and Elise were there and found them lying in each other's arms, perhaps sharing the nightmare of still being alive. He didn't even want to think about what they had been through.

Claire was no longer able to be there for them, but he was.

35

$\mathscr{E}$lise was the first to wake, surfacing from a deep, untroubled sleep. She had spent the whole night curled up with Danielle, who was still fast asleep despite the sobs of a little boy who, when he saw Elise's eyes open, began to howl. Maybe he thought she should pick him up, give him something to eat, or take him to the bathroom. He obviously didn't realize that she was just another abandoned child.

Elise reflected that she must have slept so peacefully because she felt protected by this fortress and the strong arms of Father Marcel, who like a knight of old was defending the territory of the abbey. No one, not even the evil Germans, could attack her there. Nobody would dare force their way through the centuries-old walls surrounding them. Father Marcel was the hero of her adventure story.

The little boy got out of bed and came teetering over to her, as if he had only recently learned to walk. Sitting next to her, he began touching her hair, which was matted with dust and sweat. He pointed to Elise's eyes.

"Blue," he stuttered, as if playing at identifying colors in a place where everything was in shadow, with blackened walls and dark, damp wooden beams.

Perhaps even though she was only a young girl, she reminded him of his mother. Elise thought she must smell unpleasant, possibly because she had only washed her face and hands. The rest of her body was still covered in dust, sweat, and other people's blood. She had no idea what to do with the little boy, so they sat there waiting for Danielle to wake up and tell them whether they should go out into the courtyard, the kitchen, or attend mass, if there was one.

"What's *she* doing here?" came a shout from the doorway, where an adolescent from the village had recognized her and was pointing at her contemptuously.

Elise stared back at him, then lowered her eyes. The little boy, who was still sitting beside her, took her by the hand.

"The same as you," was Father Marcel's only comment as he appeared at the door. "Come on, into the chapel," he ordered the teenage boy.

The youngster left without complaint, although as he did so he shot Elise a poisonous glance. By now she was accustomed to being rejected or labeled as the enemy, to being seen as different. In the end, she was always the other, the one who didn't belong anywhere, the one who had come to take somebody else's place, the one who was meant to live in darkness. The old story was simply being repeated here in the abbey.

She took the little boy back to his spot and tried to get him to lie down, covering him as best she could, but he only laughed as if wanting to play. She could see a plea in his eyes for her not to leave him on his own, not to forget him.

"I think we'd better go outside," she said. He smiled. "We should take advantage of the summer sun and get some fresh air."

The boy held out his arms to her. Elise lifted him out of bed and walked with him down a gloomy corridor lit at the far end by stained-glass windows that gave onto the garden at the back of the abbey, which had once been a vegetable garden. For the first time in two years, she felt free. She didn't have to live in darkness, hiding from inquisitive stares. She had a new friend. She had slept well.

"What's your name?" she asked him. His only reply was a chuckle. "I'm Elise."

As they approached the inner courtyard, they came across a small passageway leading to the kitchen at the rear. The door was half open, and the sound of voices was added to the news being broadcast on a radio set. Elise couldn't make out what was being said, because the sound wasn't clear. The little boy let go of her hand and ran into the room when he saw Father Marcel seated in front of the radio, trying to tune in a station. Elise ran after him, but came to a halt on the threshold.

"More than six hundred dead," a terse, gruff voice was saying. "Those bastards wiped out the entire village. They left nothing standing. And meanwhile we're here, doing nothing except listening to the news and waiting for them to come and force us out into the yard at gunpoint."

Elise couldn't identify the harsh voice, and motioned to the boy to be quiet. Now on the radio someone had begun a speech, but it was even more difficult to hear. All she could make out were voices shouting, followed by applause and cheering.

"The Allies are already on French soil," said another voice. "The bombing has started. We'll soon be free of the Boches."

"We won't be able to go on taking in children. It's too dangerous," said Father Marcel, standing up and turning off the radio. "If any of them gets ill or dies, we'll have worse problems."

When he saw Elise and the little boy at the door, he smiled and invited them in, opening his arms wide to receive the boy, who ran to him.

Two men were with Father Marcel, whose face was now washed and freshly shaven. He was wearing a clean cassock that was less worn than the one he had on the day before. In his right hand he was holding several leaflets, which he immediately tried to hide in his pockets. One of them fell to the floor, and when Elise bent to pick it up she could smell the fresh ink. One of the other men, a short stocky fellow, stopped her and put it into his jacket pocket. Elise noticed a deep recent wound on his left forearm.

The older man, who was wearing a clean but wrinkled white shirt, went over to the window and lit a cigarette, glancing at Elise warily. The shadows under his eyes, as dark as the stubble on his chin, contrasted with the whiteness of his hair and shirt. Elise looked around the room in astonishment: it did not seem to fit with the rest of the abbey at all. There were no religious images, no benches, no Bibles. In one corner, she could see a white rabbit in a metal cage, a black top hat, and a stick with a golden tip. There was also a rolled-up map on a tall, narrow wooden table. On it stood an empty fishbowl. Elise went over to the rabbit, which didn't move. If it hadn't been for the sudden twitches it gave, she would have thought it was stuffed. She studied the men, wondering which of them the rabbit and the rest of the magician's paraphernalia belonged to.

The little boy paid no attention to the rabbit, perhaps because he didn't even see it. His attention was focused on Father Marcel, who picked him up, tickled him, and started calling him by his name.

"Did you know that Jacques is invisible?" he said. He put him down on the floor and began pretending that he couldn't find him. He stumbled around the room, pretending not to notice the little boy, who stood there without moving, trying hard not to burst out laughing.

Elise smiled when she heard the name of the lively little boy. Now Jacques ran over to the rabbit and rattled the cage, but the animal didn't respond. It was probably waiting for an order or a whistle to perform. There was no grass or carrots at hand, and it was useless for the boy to shake the cage or blow into its nose: it simply refused to react, realizing they were not a real audience.

There was some bread and cheese left on the table. Father Marcel waved to Jacques and Elise to help themselves, and the little boy wolfed down the crumbs and the remaining bits of cheese, except for one piece that he took over to the rabbit, which sniffed at it disdainfully. Watching this scene, Elise laughed out loud, and suddenly realized this was the first time in a long while that she had done so.

36

Outside, Danielle was confronting two boys who were busily bouncing a ball in front of her. "Don't even think of insulting my sister again," she growled, stressing the word "sister" as she stared menacingly at them.

"She has no right to be here. She's a Boche," retorted the taller of the two, dressed in short pants that showed his grazed knees. "She's to blame for everything that's happening to us."

"As Father Marcel told you, she's my sister. She has the same right as me to be here," said Danielle, straightening up as if about to launch at him. "If you're scared, get out of here. This yard is for everyone."

"They should have killed you both," the boy said, spitting on the ground.

Disgusted, Danielle met his gaze, and squared up to him. Taking a step forward, she blew into his face, arms akimbo, daring him to react.

"Just try it," she said without blinking. The boy stood silent and motionless, taken aback by her attitude. "You're a coward. Why don't you go out and fight the Germans? They're the ones you need to show how brave you are to, not us. The war is outside these walls, not inside them."

Seeing Father Marcel approaching with Elise and Jacques, the two boys slunk away to the far end of the yard, leaving Danielle in peace. She stood there, brow furrowed, arms folded, and biting her bottom lip, as she always did when she felt challenged.

"These are difficult times," said Father Marcel, trying to relieve the tension. "We're at war, and have only just realized it. Now it's right in front of our eyes, we can feel it . . ."

"They don't want us here," Danielle interrupted him. "They don't want us anywhere."

"War brings out the worst in us," Father Marcel continued calmly. "It's nothing more than a way to survive. We have to be patient, to understand other people. No one wants to die, and fear can do terrible things to us."

Father Marcel understood it would be too much to suggest to Danielle that she kneel at the altar and pray for those aggressive boys. Praying was not a priority for any of these children who woke each day with one sole idea: how to survive.

"I've got something for you," he said, holding out a small book without a cover. "When was the last time you read?"

Danielle's eyes lit up, and Father Marcel thought he could detect a smile on her face. The last thing she could remember reading were the loose pages from Madame Sternberg's botanical album, but it was best not to mention that. Taking the little book from the priest, she thanked him without speaking, afraid her anger would still be obvious if she said anything.

Cigarette in mouth, the man with the dark shadows under his eyes came panting up to them. He whispered something in Father Marcel's ear, and the two men hurried away.

Danielle didn't pay much attention to this, but Elise glanced at her conspiratorially and told her of her suspicions.

"Father Marcel is in the Resistance."

Danielle remained silent for a few moments, then burst out laughing. Elise's idea seemed to her so ridiculous, the product of her childish fantasies. She recalled how over their Friday night suppers the priest used to praise those who risked their lives to confront the Germans, but couldn't believe he was one of them. Lately, any man who left the village was said to have gone to join the maquis.

"They're up to something, I'm sure of it," said Elise, waiting for Danielle to respond. "And one of them is going to dress up as a magician to fool the Germans. I saw proof," she added. "They were hiding leaflets."

"If they're part of the Resistance, it's better that we don't know about it. What you're saying is very dangerous." Danielle knew she shouldn't add anything to encourage Elise's uncontrollable imagination, but at the same time had to admit her sister had raised a doubt in her own mind.

Jacques was playing happily with other children of his age in the middle of the courtyard, throwing stones at the dry fountain. Taking Danielle by the hand, Elise led her to the supposed plotters' room. They came to a halt outside the closed door. Elise looked around to make sure they hadn't been followed, while Danielle surreptitiously turned the door handle. The door opened a crack, enough for her to see the room was empty. She decided to go in.

"See? There's no one here. No conspirators, no Germans, no magicians," she mocked Elise. She spoke slowly, as if she also wanted to convince herself they really were protected inside the abbey. Although she was worried they could be sharing it with people plotting, she also felt a shiver of satisfaction that somebody close to her was willing to teach the dreadful occupying forces a lesson.

Elise was searching every corner of the room for some evidence that would stop Danielle from thinking she was a spoiled little girl whose imagination ran wild. She was sure of what she had seen and heard. She paused at the window, looking out at the monks' cloister in the distance, and next to it the abandoned cemetery where the remains of friars and abbots had lain since time immemorial.

The rabbit and the cage had disappeared, so had the top hat and the magic wand. All that was left was the smell of tobacco and cigarette ash on the floor.

37

$\mathcal{W}$henever Danielle went off to a corner to read a book she had come across, Elise would roam the abbey with Jacques, who had become her constant companion. She devoted herself to him, putting him to bed, getting him up in the morning, feeding him, taking him out into the sunshine. She talked to him as if she was his mother, and the boy joined in merrily.

She would lie down beside him every night and invent stories about terrifying dragons and tremendous battles. Watching over Jacques's nightmares helped ward off her own. Ever since she had begun to look after him, she was no longer tormented by her nighttime imaginings, or awakened by the fear of what the next day might bring. For her, the future was limited to the games she would play with Jacques when they got up.

When he fell asleep and she went back to the bed she shared with Danielle, her mind would be filled with wild speculation until she herself dozed off. She was convinced no one would come for them after the war. There would be no uncles or absent parents, no cousins lost in lands on the far side of the earth.

In the morning, the pleasure of seeing Jacques so content and happy revived her. The little boy ate slices of butter as if it was cheese, and drank his soup like water. His great fear was that one day a relative would appear to take him away from Elise, to a town in Alsace, where it was said no one felt French because the German border was so near that the sidewalks, houses, and even the rivers became confused and went from one side to the other without asking permission.

The summer days were lengthening. Elise chose to spend the greater part of them in the abbey kitchen, where daylight filtered in through high windows. Every morning, she sat in the half-light with Jacques awaiting the arrival of Marie-Louise, the cook, who came before sunrise. Since Elise didn't sleep much, and Jacques even less, they would slip silently into the kitchen to greet their new friend. Elise didn't much like peeling potatoes or onions, still less being close to the boiling water or the wayward flames of the stove, which blew everywhere. She was no lover of fire, but her visits to the kitchen allowed her to find out everything going on in the abbey: who was ill, if any new child had arrived, if the Germans were pulling out, or the Allies were taking over the nearby villages, whether or not the bishop was a collaborator, and, most important of all, if there was enough food for them to survive another week.

Marie-Louise felt comfortable with her, because Elise spoke very little, whereas she spoke a lot. If he had something to eat, Jacques was quiet, although that could be dangerous because he greedily swallowed anything he found on the kitchen floor.

"During a war people always lose the ability to listen," the cook would say, busily peeling potatoes and throwing them into a giant blackened and dented pot.

Even though she talked a good deal, the cook liked lengthy silences, and Elise had learned not to interrupt them. She sat silently next to her until the words started pouring from the mouth of this kindly, wise woman once more.

"Everybody has their opinion. Everybody thinks they're right, but where does that get them? Nowhere. Nobody does anything," she would say, occasionally raising her arm and trying to wipe her runny nose. "I at least cook potatoes and fill lots of people's stomachs."

Even though she didn't look it, Marie-Louise was a city woman. All that remained of her golden years were her elegant neck and glossy hair. Her breasts were so big and heavy that she tended to lean backward in order to keep her balance. She would tell the children that her eyes had once been green, but that with all the suffering during the war they had turned a sad, yellowish gray. Her skin was still white and firm, although sometimes it turned red round her nose.

Hearing other people's stories helped Elise forget her own suffering, or rather left it somewhere where it couldn't hurt her. One morning, Marie-Louise began to tell her about her past. She had once run a small café in Le Marais, close to Place des Vosges, inherited from a Russian uncle on her husband's side of the family. Until the Germans came, her customers had been the "infidels," as the majority of those who lived in the neighborhood were known.

"I was very young. I'd just arrived in Paris, and I met my husband in the café soon after he'd inherited it. His hair was jet-black. How could I have imagined it would end up as white as snow? When I learned he was an infidel . . ." Marie-Louise saw that Elise didn't understand, and so explained, "I mean, he was Jewish," she added in a low voice, while Elise swallowed hard. "We decided we wouldn't want to bring a child into this world to have it suffer."

After a pause, she added, "A crisis always brings out the worst in Parisians."

This was followed by another long silence. Elise waited calmly for the cook to continue her diatribe against the capital's inhabitants.

Her husband was rounded up one summer's day. The café was destroyed, and so Marie-Louise decided to return to her village, to the house her mother had left her, which she rented to a family from Paris who had left the capital the day of the occupation.

"When he was taken away, everyone slammed the door in my face. Nobody lent a helping hand. A lot of our former clients, whom we sometimes didn't even charge, turned their backs. Garbage, that's what they are. Garbage."

Marie-Louise never saw her husband again. Along with all the other Jews in the neighborhood, he was taken to the Vélodrome d'hiver and from there to who knows where.

"I'll never forget that night, the sixteenth of July, 1942," she said. "I was left all alone. And guess what the people who had been renting the house for so long did? They sold all the furniture. Yes, all my mother's furniture. Why? Because they were hungry, they told me."

Now she had to sleep on a mattress on the floor, but she made it clear that was all she needed.

"You're my family now, you, Father Marcel, and Father Auguste. Garbage into the garbage can." She repeated phrases like this every day, usually adding some new criticism. "We French have lost our dignity. They burn a village, savagely kill six hundred people, and what do we do? Run away."

Marie-Louise had just said this when she noticed Elise's tear-filled eyes and shrunken body.

"Oh, forgive me, my child, forgive me!" she said, her voice choking. She went over to Elise. "I can't imagine what you and your sister must have been through. But now I'm here. For whatever you need."

The cook wrapped her in her arms, and Elise's face was plunged into the folds of her dirty apron. It reeked of onions and sweat, but that didn't stop her from feeling an immense tenderness toward this woman who had taken her in and who she felt was part of her new family. She nestled between her enormous breasts like a puppy protected by its mother, and forgot fear, the Germans, and the older boy who ever since her arrival had done nothing but attack her.

Father Marcel interrupted them, bringing a chunk of butter wrapped in greaseproof paper.

"Here you are, almost four pounds of it," he said, laying the lump of butter on the table. "I don't think we're going to get any more for some time. My contact has disappeared."

"The altar's soon going to be bare," said the cook. "A ruby for a piece of butter. My God, what are things coming to?"

Elise pictured the saints and virgins stripped bare, the chalice without rubies, and no more silver cruets or candlesticks. The mass would soon be reduced to the sign of the cross.

"I've been promised some meat for this evening," added the priest.

"So this evening we'll have a good supper, but what about tomorrow?" Marie-Louise wondered aloud. She was troubled that Father Marcel found it necessary to sacrifice the altarware, the only treasures the abbey still possessed.

"I'd rather barter things for food than let the Germans come and plunder everything," he said, without ill-feeling.

"All you need are dark glasses and an umbrella and you'd look just like a young man in the city, one of those protesting against the occupation. If it weren't for the cassock, you'd be the image of a *zazou,* a provocateur, strolling round Place du Trocadéro," said the cook, gesticulating at him.

"You'll soon see him on his knees praying Our Fathers," she went on, whispering in Elise's ear so the priest wouldn't hear, although he was casting glances at her and smiling. "He thinks he has to atone for all his sins. Why? The war has led a decent, kindhearted man like him to steal from his own church. Because, whichever way you look at it, what he's doing is stealing."

Elise was increasingly convinced that Marie-Louise was a saintly woman who would one day be beatified, like the figures in white gowns who appeared, eyes turned up to heaven, on the cards *Maman* Claire kept in the chest of drawers in her bedroom. The cook was as compassionate as Father Marcel; it gave Elise a warm feeling to know they were both protecting her. And to know they were also protecting Danielle and little Jacques.

"Ever since the war started, the vegetable gardens have withered away," complained Marie-Louise. "Nothing is fertile in the abbey."

One morning, Elise was surprised that Jacques had not run over to her bed to wake her up. Disturbed, she asked Danielle if she had seen him, but her sister was still asleep and simply muttered an unintelligible reply. Elise rushed to the kitchen, where she found Marie-Louise already busy with her morning chores. The cook only had to glance at her to see what a state she was in; there was no need to ask why. She paused by the kitchen table and eyed her tenderly, feeling very sorry for her. Such a young girl didn't deserve so much loss.

"You know we're all only passing through here, don't you? This isn't our home, is it?" She was carefully weighing every word, but Elise couldn't understand what she meant. "There are too many mouths to feed here, and I've no idea how many candlesticks are left to barter for food. In a few months, I don't know how we're going to survive. How much longer will we be able to shelter so many small children in the abbey?"

When her explanations still didn't seem to have any effect on Elise, she decided to come out with her news directly.

"At first light this morning, Father Marcel took Jacques away," she said, immediately turning her back on Elise. She didn't want to see her angry face, and didn't know how she would cope if she burst into tears. She herself had woken up that morning feeling completely exhausted.

She said nothing else, and Elise didn't want to break the rule tacitly established between them about her silences. She was aware that Marie-Louise told her stories in her own time, and this was a very important one for her to hear: Elise needed to know what had happened to Jacques. Until now, no one had shown the slightest interest in him, and so she had somehow felt that the boy belonged to her. She had looked after him, fed him, was teaching him things: What more could be expected of her? She knew he was too young, that the children taken in by the abbey had to learn to fend for themselves, but she was there to help, and so far no one had complained.

"Father Marcel found a cousin of his. A man from Bordeaux. Can you imagine? Jacques is going to Bordeaux," said the cook, laughing to relieve the tension. "They left in a car for the train station. Somebody is waiting for him there."

Elise flinched when she heard that word "somebody." So it wasn't Jacques's cousin! They had sent a stranger to pick up the boy. But so what, the cousin was a stranger as well.

"He'll have a better life there, Elise. You can be sure of that. I think you should be happy for him," added Marie-Louise.

Elise was surprised no tears came to her eyes, that she didn't have the slightest inclination to cry. It was more like a feeling of emptiness: Jacques's departure had left a hole, and yet she was lighter somehow. She would no longer have to worry so much about him, to keep him amused, look after him. It was better this way: if when the war was over she and Danielle managed to get to Paris, they wouldn't be able to cope with another mouth to feed. Marie-Louise was right about that. Thinking over all the advantages of not having Jacques constantly at her side, she felt relieved. Another one who had gone to the land of shadows.

"At least they didn't take him to Alsace, and starting tomorrow I'll be able to sleep in," she said, trying to sound ironic. But no sooner had she said it than she burst into tears. Oh, she should have kept quiet: she didn't want anyone feeling sorry for her.

Marie-Louise looked up at the ceiling, shook her head, and smiled.

"This weekend you're to sleep at my house. Father Marcel already knows. I need your help on Sunday morning."

Her words worked like magic. Elise quickly calmed down: her face lit up, and she ran off to tell Danielle, who like always was caught up in her tattered books. Marie-Louise was able to return to her chores: she scarcely had time to console a little girl who had lost her friend.

38

$\mathcal{H}$alfway along the road, a few meters from the first houses, Elise saw that Marie-Louise was out of breath and sweating profusely. It didn't seem as if it was any cooler now that the sun had set; the cobbles were scorching, and unpleasant waves of heat radiated off the stone walls. The streets, windows, shops, and cafés were deserted. It was as though most of the villagers had fled to the south, and the few who remained had taken shelter indoors. A village emptied even before the curfew.

When they reached Marie-Louise's two-story house, Elise noted that all the buildings in the street were different, despite the fact that they formed an untidy line, as if each house needed its neighbor to stay upright. Helped by the light of a streetlamp, Marie-Louise was just putting the key into her front door, when she was blinded by the headlights of a slowly approaching car.

She and Elise paused to examine the dusty black car that eventually pulled up two houses farther on. When the car door opened, Elise caught a glimpse of a woman's leg in a silk stocking and high-heeled shoes. The lights immediately went on in the house opposite and a woman emerged.

"That's the baker's wife," said Marie-Louise. "She doesn't miss a beat when it comes to what's going on in the neighborhood."

The car engine was still running. It was obvious the driver had no intention of spending the night in this out-of-the-way village.

The young woman with the silk stockings took her time saying goodbye. As she finally emerged from the vehicle, she smiled at the neighbor across the way, whose only reply was to spit on the sidewalk. Ashamed, the young woman lowered her eyes and rummaged in her bag for her house keys. The car had moved off and she felt vulnerable. Marie-Louise folded her arms and stared at the baker's wife, then smiled at the young woman.

"That filthy slut Viviane," the baker's wife complained, loud enough for Marie-Louise to hear. "The village slut. Who can wear silk stockings with no holes these days? Only her. And she even has the nerve to hang out of her window chewing on a bar of chocolate. Who can get chocolate these days? Only her."

Elise gazed at the perfect seams on the shimmery silk stockings in the dim glow from the streetlamp. Then the young woman disappeared inside, slamming the door behind her. The cook inhaled deep lungfuls of warm air. She was exhausted.

"Tomorrow is ration card day. Let's see what we can get."

Inside the house, Elise followed Marie-Louise up a worn staircase with peeling walls. Green damp showed through the original pale pink, while in some corners bare stone and seemingly indestructible wooden beams poked through.

"Since my mother died, we haven't been able to rent out the store down below. Nobody wants to buy cloth or upholster furniture," explained Marie-Louise as they climbed the stairs.

Elise was anxious to know more about the young lady in the car, and to get to know the home of the woman who cooked for them every day, but Marie-Louise didn't switch on any lights, simply picking up a pair of candles like those in the abbey.

"Every Friday night I burn a candle in memory of my husband.

That's all I can do for him," she said. "Tomorrow morning you'll see how the house is filled with light."

Elise uneasily pulled away from the candles, following the flickering light and the cook as they walked through the upstairs rooms. She noticed there were very few pieces of furniture, along with some photographs and ornaments.

"It's true that Viviane makes us Frenchwomen look very bad. I wonder what's brought her back to the village?" Marie-Louise was not a great conversationalist, more of a specialist in soliloquies. "But who am I to judge a woman they want to spit on?"

She placed one of the candles on the bedside table and tucked Elise in among the feather pillows. Snuggling in the white, freshly washed sheets, the little girl thought she was in paradise.

"In the end, I feel sorry for Viviane. She's a victim too," Marie-Louise continued in a weary voice. "When I came back to the village on my own and she heard my husband was an 'infidel' and had been arrested, she was the only one who felt sorry for me. All the other neighbors looked down on me."

Marie-Louise wasn't expecting any reply, but all Elise wanted to do was close her eyes, sink into her fantasies about Paris, and forget about the shameful young woman.

"We're all victims of this war," the cook went on. "Time is against us. One morning, Viviane and the baker's wife will wake up, and one of them will no longer have the car to get her home safely. She'll have to take the train, and from our windows we'll see her arrive, dragging her feet along, with no silk stockings to wear or any sad chocolate to eat. And the other will have lost that vile *milicien* son of hers who does dirty work for the Germans and makes her feel so high and mighty. By then it'll be too late to ask for forgiveness," she said, snuffing out the candle between her fingers. "There'll be no forgiving, not for those two, or for anyone."

She paused in the doorway, glancing back at the already sleeping Elise. *And you, where were you brought here from?* she said to herself.

She went and filled the bathtub with steaming hot water and poured in what was left of the salts in their purple jar. A perfumed vapor hung over the surface of the water. Marie-Louise got in, careful not to splash any water on the immaculate black-and-white bathroom floor tiles.

39

As usual, Elise was the first to wake up. She walked into the living room and opened all the shutters. Light flooded in. She was surrounded by books. A heavy green-upholstered armchair and a standard lamp were the only furniture that had survived the tenants' greed.

The books were piled up in different sizes, thickness, and colors. Some had red or golden leather or paper covers; others were very tattered. When she saw this enormous quantity of books, Elise shivered, and crept over to the bookcases. Fascinated, she read the authors' names: Racine, Balzac, Flaubert, Dumas. This was a new side to Marie-Louise, although in fact beyond the sad story of her life in Paris, Elise didn't know who this cook with her answer to everything really was.

"My books are the only thing I brought with me from Paris," Elise heard behind her. "But there's no point reading these days. That's a thing of the past. Besides, I don't have the time. My husband and I used to spend hours on end in the bookstore on Rue de l'Odéon . . ."

Elise went with her into the kitchen. In the hallway she discovered a collection of family photographs. A baby covered in lace and ribbons, a man in a bowler hat, a woman in black behind a counter stacked with rolls of cloth who must have been Marie-Louise's mother. To Elise it seemed as if her stern gaze was following and judging them. Marie-Louise told her that the portrait had been with her for her entire life, shooting out its invisible threads. Her mother had been convinced her daughter had chosen an unsuitable husband, and never stopped repeating that the marriage would come to a sorry end.

The smell of hot chocolate took Elise back to the happy days with *Maman* Claire; she smiled at the comfort the memory gave her. Other treats were awaiting her: an omelet, cheese, and a slice of buttered bread. What more could she ask? She was the cook's friend, and was in heaven.

"One day I'll live in Paris too," she said contentedly. "And I'll go to the Rue de l'Odéon bookstore as well. When there are no soldiers in Paris," she went on, savoring the chocolate.

Marie-Louise was watching the dreamy child, unable to avoid the thought that there would be no future for her either in Paris or anywhere else in France, but she said nothing: it would have been unfair to shatter her illusions. Father Marcel spent every evening writing letters to find the children's close or distant relatives. He also had hopes that strangers would take pity on them and adopt some of the older ones, who could help in the fields or with housework. A few days earlier, he had written to the archdiocese of New York to try to find Danielle and Elise's uncle, Roger Duval, who had left France a few years earlier, but Marie-Louise didn't want to worry the girl with that news just yet. Who could be sure if some bored priest in New York would take the trouble to track down a Frenchman who possibly didn't want to be found? And even if they did, he had every right in the world to argue that he couldn't take on the responsibility of two young girls. But Father Marcel, who remembered him as a youngster in the village, assured her that Roger Duval was someone with a kind soul, a staunch believer who would reply as soon as he heard his sister had left behind children.

But Paris? No, she couldn't see Elise in Paris, that was for sure.

"Paris isn't what it used to be, and it never will be again," she declared, a piece of bread in her mouth. "The day the swastika flew over Place de la Concorde and the French chose self-preservation, the spirit of the city vanished, and its magic ended up in the gutter," she said, with one of her mordant cackles. "They thought that by letting the Nazi flag fly, or by allowing the German choir to sing on the steps of l'Opéra, they would leave us in peace, with our newspapers on the table and a madeleine dipped in our coffee cup. Elise, Paris is no more than a fantasy."

Marie-Louise asked her to tidy the kitchen while she ran an errand for Father Marcel, and as the young girl washed up the breakfast things she gave her imagination free rein. She was now certain that Marie-Louise, whom everyone thought was no more than a simple cook, was in reality a sophisticated woman, a rebel intellectual, a fighter in the heroic Resistance led by the priest and those two mysterious magicians.

Elise saw her leave with several enormous rolls of cloth under her arm. From the window, she was able to watch her until she saw her go unannounced into the house where the girl with the silk stockings lived. In broad daylight! But Marie-Louise had nothing to fear. After having lost her husband and her beloved café, she would lose no sleep over being rejected again in the village, thought Elise. In her imagination, Viviane was not the slut everyone thought she was, but had been forced to create that facade to disguise the fact that she transmitted messages from the Paris Resistance to the group of men hiding behind the walls of the run-down abbey. It was also possible that Viviane's mission was to poison her lover, a forbidding German officer responsible for the deaths of more than one French hero who had courageously confronted the enemy . . .

A few hours later, Marie-Louise returned out of breath, laden with three heavy bags. Leaving them on the table without any explanation, she withdrew to have a nap.

❧

On Sunday morning, just before sunup, Marie-Louise and Elise set off for the abbey. Elise had to carry a huge bag, but didn't dare complain.

Before they left the house, the cook took a piece of chocolate wrapped in foil out of her pocket, broke it in half, and shared it with her.

"We're all entitled to a delicacy like this," was all she said of her visit to Viviane. Elise happily devoured this kind of dark communion host that dissolved in her mouth like a sigh.

"Don't you miss anything about Paris?" Elise insisted.

"Of course I do. But do you know what I miss most? The poplars lining the Seine."

40

*E*lise felt restored, and returned to the abbey keen to tell Danielle all about her adventures in the village. She was convinced that the harmless cook was a brave Resistance fighter who, rather than hide out in the woods, had turned the abbey into her secret operations center from where she would drive the Germans not only from France but the entire continent.

Before reaching the dormitory she heard an uproar. Some of the children were shouting so loudly they seemed to be making the stone walls shake. In the distance she could see Father Marcel running toward her, and stepped warily into the darkened room. Danielle was sitting astride the boy who had never stopped insulting Elise, throttling him with both hands and cursing him angrily with words the others couldn't make out. The boy was struggling to breathe, and his eyes were popping out of their sockets just as Father Marcel arrived and pulled Danielle off him. In a corner of the bed the two girls shared, *Maman* Claire's suitcase lay open. The clothes were strewn across the floor, the ebony box had been tossed aside, the photograph and letters were everywhere, and a gold chain lay at the far end of the bed. Elise began to weep as she picked up her belongings, *Maman* Claire's treasured heirlooms. A tall, thin boy came over to defend her and shot a challenging look at the aggressor, who was still sobbing fearfully.

"Don't even think of attacking them again, do you hear me?" the tall boy threatened him. "Or you'll have me to deal with."

"Boche," the attacker whispered slyly at Elise, so quietly that no one else could hear. He crawled over to a corner, where he writhed silently for a few seconds before lying down cowering in pain, trying to avoid the other children's gaze.

"I'm Henri," the girls' new defender introduced himself. Wiping away Elise's tears with the back of his hand, he helped her put the coats, a photograph, and letters back into the suitcase. "Trust me, that bully won't bother you again."

"We'd better keep that case in my room," said Father Marcel, who had observed the scene without intervening. He laid his arm on Danielle's shoulder as Elise closed the suitcase. Then he went over to the boy who was still sniveling by the wall, and hauled him up by the ear. "Into the sacristy. Right now! Get a move on!"

When Danielle recovered the case, she saw that the small purple box was still lying under the bed. Henri saw it too, and kneeled down to pick it up and return it to her. Her hands still shaking, Danielle took it and thanked him with a look. Her chest was still heaving with rage. She could have killed that wretch and got him off their backs once and for all. She should have escaped much farther away with Elise, to another village where no one knew them or would recognize them. She didn't understand why they still had to put up with this kind of insult. *Father Marcel's cell won't be enough. Why not shut him in the cloister, where only monks are allowed to enter? The Germans would never dare cross the threshold into a place where people devote themselves to prayer*, she thought, desperate to find a solution.

She left the dormitory, suitcase in hand, accompanied by Elise and the lanky boy with the name of a Resistance hero. To Elise, Henri was another warrior who had come to defend them, a valiant member of the maquis, ready for anything. In her eyes, he looked much taller than he really was, with muscular arms and wearing the scruffy uniform of a fighter from the hills. In fact, Henri was simply a skinny young man, not even fifteen, whose khaki shorts revealed a pair of socks with holes in them, a short-sleeved shirt with three missing buttons, and a pocket about to come off.

At the entrance to Father Marcel's cell, Henri stopped them solemnly.

"We're going to win. We are winning," he said, pausing for effect. "We won't be here much longer."

Danielle and Elise said nothing, but glanced at each other. There was no one else they could trust.

From that moment on, Henri became the girls' inseparable ally. His gentle expression contrasted with a badly healed wound on his forehead, his sad, ragged clothes, his shoes full of holes, and a slight limp that he tried to hide.

⊂∽⊃

A few days later, the three of them were sitting out in the courtyard with nothing to do.

"We ought to head for the mountains down by the Spanish border," said Henri, breaking the silence. His voice sounded more and more like that of an adult. "We'll have to walk for days and nights, crossing bridges and sometimes swimming across rivers, but we'll get there. We can't stay here a day longer. The Germans are desperate because they know they're about to lose the war, and the first thing they'll do when they think they've been defeated is to come and finish us off."

"Count me in," said Danielle, in all seriousness. She was determined once and for all to leave behind the role of a victim that the Nazis had imposed on her. An orphan with no home or family to claim her, waiting for an uncle on the far side of the Atlantic to appear as her savior.

It would be safer if she left the suitcase with Father Marcel. She would come back for it once they were free.

"If we get far enough south, we won't meet any filthy Boches for kilometers," Henri went on, absolutely determined. "The danger there is the *milices*, those damned French traitors who collaborate with the Germans. A *milicien* is a thousand times worse than a Boche. But don't worry, the farmers will lend us a hand, you'll see. We'll find shelter from village to village until we reach our destination."

"But what is our destination?" Elise asked hesitantly, not wanting to dampen her sister or her new friend's rebel spirit.

"To be part of those who face the Germans day and night. That's our destination," said Henri grandiloquently, imagining a crowd listening to him with expectant fervor. "The bombing of Paris will begin very soon. The English, Americans, and Russians are determined to wipe the Nazis from the face of the earth. Not a single one will be left alive." At this he fell silent for a long while, before adding somberly, "And soon perhaps we'll also see a bomb fall here. The abbey would be left in ruins and we'd all be buried in oblivion. Who knows?"

The three of them remained quiet, gazing at the stones of the abbey walls that now seemed to them as fragile as the straw and mud shelters that the seasonal workers built on the nearby farms. But only a few seconds had gone by before Elise leaped to her feet.

"Follow me!" she ordered. She had adopted her most conspiratorial air. Danielle and Henri hesitated.

"Follow me, it's important!" Elise insisted, heading for the kitchen. Curious, the other two stood up and reluctantly obeyed.

She led them to the mysterious room where she had once seen the rabbit, the top hat, and the magic wand. The room where—and this was what was important—she had discovered the telltale leaflets that Father Marcel had quickly tried to hide.

"Not your story about the magician again!" Danielle mocked her.

Henri, on the other hand, was alert and excited. This was the first time he felt he might find an escape from the boring life in the abbey.

He knew that Father Marcel had already been in contact with his older brother, the son of his father's first marriage, who lived in Alsace, a man who had married a Frenchwoman who regarded herself as German. The two men must be organizing his departure—that was why he wanted to put his plan into action as soon as possible, to set off down unknown roads, to escape. He preferred to die of hunger and thirst than to live with a brother he considered a collaborator. He refused to be sent to one of those border villages where they spoke French in an abnormal German accent that drove him mad.

He went into the room and began examining every corner, like a forensic expert searching for clues. It was the start of a fascinating game. Though she was skeptical, Danielle realized she didn't want to be left behind, and so allowed herself to be swept along by Elise's curiosity and Henri's enthusiasm.

After making sure nobody had followed them, Elise pushed aside the oak table in the center of the room. Henri and Danielle glanced at one another, trying to guess what would come next. The table sat on a big dark, frayed carpet. Elise tried to roll it back, and Henri went to help her. Under the heavy carpet was a hidden trapdoor. Elise beamed at them triumphantly.

"Go lock the door," she ordered Danielle, who rushed to do as she was told. Elise was in control now, and nothing could have made her happier than to see the impact her discovery had made on Henri. Between the two of them, they began to raise the door.

"How did you know there was a secret passage?" Danielle asked fearfully.

"Simple," said Elise, pausing as if to stress how obvious the answer to her sister's question was. "There's no other explanation for an oak table that's up against the wall when Father Marcel is plotting with his friends and then returns to the middle of the room once the room is empty again," she said, with childish pride at her powers of deduction.

Eventually they succeeded in pulling up the trapdoor. Henri was the first to venture down into the hiding place, followed by Elise. Danielle, who was far more cautious, came last. The only light in the stinking hole came from the windows in the room above; thanks to it, they could see that the steps down ended at a beaten earth floor.

Henri covered his nose; Elise felt sick at the stench of excrement and urine. As Elise's eyes adapted to the darkness, the first thing she made out was the top hat. Next to it, leaning against the wall, was the magic wand. And from its cage, alive but still motionless, the emaciated rabbit stared at them.

"Now do you believe me?" Elise asked Danielle, without turning around.

"*Combat!* These are copies of *Combat*!" exclaimed Henri, stuffing one of them into his pocket. He continued groping his way forward, trying to work out how big and deep the basement was.

Neither Elise nor Danielle could understand his enthusiasm for these old pamphlets, since you could find heaps of out-of-date pamphlets anywhere.

"It's the magazine of the Resistance!" Henri said proudly. "If we're found with them, we could all be sent to jail!"

Up above, the summer heat meant the abbey garden was parched, but down in the basement the air was icy. The three of them clustered together, holding hands. They took a few more steps to try to reach the end of this secret hiding place, when suddenly they heard something hurriedly dragging itself along.

"There must be hundreds of rats down here. This hole doesn't lead anywhere. It would only be a safe hiding place if we were being bombed. Of course, that's it!" exclaimed Danielle, anxious to get back to the room above. "It's the air-raid shelter!"

Henri and Elise both shushed her. They thought they had seen a reflection on the earthen floor, next to a bucket overflowing with filth. There was a pale white patch they couldn't distinguish properly. It came and went in the blink of an eye. All of a sudden, a low moan rooted them to the spot.

"*Wasser . . . Wasser . . .*" came a whispered voice that seemed to echo from the abbey's foundations. *"Wasser . . ."* they heard again, then the white patch disappeared.

The three of them stood quaking. Henri was the first to react, and approach the place where the sound came from, measuring every step.

"It's a Boche, a Boche . . ." he stammered, his voice cracking over the final words.

"What's a German doing down in the basement? Let's get out of here!" shouted Danielle, still unable to move. She looked around desperately for the steps out.

"Wasser!" they heard a third time.

Without realizing it, they had crept close enough to make out the eyes and gray-green hue of the man's face. He was propped against the wall in the darkest corner of the basement. His eyes had a crazed look, his lips were bloody, and his skin was flaking off, with dried scabs all over his skull.

"We have to get him some water," said Elise, approaching the dying man and trying not to let the nauseous smell overcome her.

"Wait! Can't you see?" Henri ordered them, in a calm voice that took them by surprise. "Take a good look."

The two girls went so close they could almost feel the faint breaths coming from the cracked mouth. They examined the shattered body. Danielle squeezed Elise's hand and groaned. This wasn't just any Boche. Even in the darkness, they could spot his military insignia. He was a German officer!

"Let's get out of here now! The game's over," said Danielle, trying to drag the immobile Elise away. "Elise! That's an order!"

Henri looked at her as calmly as before, and folded his arms defiantly.

"What are you afraid of, Danielle? Can't you see this German swine is at death's door?"

The officer begged again for water, his voice no more than a murmur. He couldn't move his head or body: it looked as if he had spent days surrounded by this mess of excrement, rotten food, and dried blood. Per-

haps weeks. From a wound on his ear close to his skull, some white mag-
gots had emerged and were slowly crawling around, piling up blindly.

Danielle's face was a picture of terror. She was trembling all over,
and had no idea which way to turn. She was certain the Germans, or still
worse, the *miliciens* would be waiting outside for them. They were bound
to have arrested Father Marcel and Father Auguste already, and shot
the two men pretending to be magicians in a traveling circus. When the
three of them emerged, all the children would be lined up in the sacristy,
and the Germans would throw a grenade, a bomb, or flames to reduce
them all to dust and ashes on the spot. *One calamity leads to another*,
she thought. She was convinced this German was condemning not only
the three of them to death, but everyone seeking refuge in the abbey, the
entire village, and possibly even the whole of France.

"The German is dead." Danielle sobbed.

"The dead aren't delirious, and this one is begging for a drop of
water. Can't you see him?" Henri argued impatiently. "Let's get out of
here."

He took the lead again and they retreated hastily, recoiling from the
horror of what they had just seen. They left the German officer gasping
for what they thought must be his last dying breaths. As they climbed
the steps, their fear gave way to a troubling sense of guilt.

Like Danielle, Elise thought they should have given the officer
water, something to eat, and tried to ease the pain of his wounds. If
nobody came to rescue him at once, the worms would end up devouring
him. They had descended into a sepulcher, an abandoned torture chamber, an inferno that was directly beneath the house of God.

"Why should we take pity on a murderer?" asked Henri, trying to
reassure himself and the girls, to assuage the weight of guilt pressing on
them, and yet at the same time annoyed at himself.

Once they were safely up in the room again, they replaced the carpet
and table exactly as they had found them. Elise stopped to make sure
that the table was lined up with the windows as it had been before.

Heading back to the dormitory, they skirted the chapel, from where they could hear the dull monotone of the rosary being recited. The three of them desperately wanted to believe that when they woke up the next morning they would find all this had been a dream, or rather a dreadful nightmare. All of a sudden Henri remembered he was still carrying proof of the crime on him: the copy of *Combat* was sticking out of his pocket, and he had no idea how to get rid of it. Even if he tore it to pieces or found a way to burn it, a trace of the pamphlet would always remain: even its ashes could give him away.

They crept to their beds without saying goodnight to each other. Henri was so exhausted he collapsed at once, convinced he would be tormented by a host of nightmares. Maybe it would be better to wait for the answer from his brother the collaborator. He was wracked with guilt.

Every muscle in Danielle's body ached. She felt as weary as when she had walked dragging the suitcase from the burned-out square to the abbey on the day of the massacre. She knew nothing good would come of their adventure. She had witnessed a crime, and that made her as guilty as the criminal or more, because she had said nothing. Closing her eyes as soon as she felt Elise get into bed beside her, she slipped away into a pleasant fantasy that saved her from the nightmare she had just experienced.

She was on the prow of a giant ocean liner, from where she could already spy the skyscrapers of New York. They had left behind the shimmering Statue of Liberty. Below her, at the dockside, she could see her Uncle Roger waving to her. She smiled back at him. She was the first to disembark and when her uncle saw her, he threw his arms round her, stared at her, and kissed her on the cheek.

"You look just like your mother," he said warmly. "You may not have her blue eyes—they came from your grandmother—but you have the same look, the same smile."

Danielle was overjoyed, and left with her uncle in a car perfumed with the essence of jasmine. They sped through a city full of vehicles, elegant women wearing hats strolling on the arms of men in suits. There were no soldiers or other signs of a military presence, no sirens could be heard, only the cheerful music from the passing cars and the laughter of the children playing without fear on the sidewalks.

They came to a house with a garden blooming with violets. Someone led her to her room. From the window she could see a park filled with trees and tulips.

The peaceful images of her fantasy soothed her and she managed to fall asleep.

The next morning, she woke with a start. In the dream, her sister didn't exist.

41

*R*ather than lessen the heat, the rain seemed to have intensified it. Searching for Danielle, Elise found her on her own in the chapel, kneeling in front of the Virgin in her blue-and-white robes who was gazing up at heaven as if deaf to everyone's prayers. Elise knelt down beside her. She stared at her clasped hands, closed eyes, the lips moving to the rhythm of her prayers. She was at peace. Danielle smiled, afraid she wouldn't be able to stay calm or silent now that she had refused to fetch water or food for a man who also had the right to be redeemed.

"They've already killed us once, Danielle," said Elise with resignation, shrugging. "They can't kill us twice."

Danielle looked up, trying to understand how Elise could be so serene. She was speaking to her just as *Maman* Claire might have done. She smiled in her turn, as if that were enough to stop the tears that had already welled up and were about to roll down her cheeks.

"I need to stay here alone for a while longer, Elise. Go and play, but stay away from the basement. And Henri has to get rid of that pamphlet."

"Do you think God listens to you?" asked Elise.

"God may not, but *Maman* does," she replied, even though she didn't think this wise girl she called her sister would really understand. Closing her eyes again, she dropped her chin onto her hands and continued with her prayers. Thoughts were swirling around her brain, and Elise's presence only made things worse.

On her knees, Elise also raised her eyes to the Virgin. She prayed that the Germans would be driven as far away as possible from the village, that the war would finally end, that the dying German officer would survive.

She got to her feet, still praying, and left the chapel without turning her back on the Virgin, begging for some compassion. Before she crossed the threshold, she came to a halt.

"You know what you are doing," she said, addressing the Virgin once more. "All I ask is that you give Danielle strength."

She contemplated her sister, who was still on her knees, focused on a plea that seemed pointless to Elise. She decided to wait for her. A few minutes later, the two of them left the chapel, eyes downcast, heading for the kitchen. As before, Danielle let her sister lead the way. Henri was waiting for them on the threshold, and through the half-open door they could see Marie-Louise busy preparing an herbal tea for Father Auguste. The tea was so fragrant it was as if the hillsides themselves had come down into the kitchen.

Henri approached Father Auguste and greeted him.

"I think time is running out for me," said the emaciated old man. Hands trembling, he settled on one of the wooden chairs. Henri looked on sadly.

"This Sunday, Father Marcel will say mass. I'm having problems with my voice," said the priest with a forlorn smile.

"Come on, make yourselves useful," said the perspiring cook when she saw them standing there idly. She began dragging a sack of potatoes toward the table. Henri helped her, and she smiled with relief.

On the table was a leg of lamb covered in flies, a couple of bruised onions, and what was left of the butter, soft and melting in the heat.

"Today we'll have a banquet," said Father Auguste. Spoken with emphasis, this last word brought on a fit of coughing. He raised a white handkerchief to his mouth, which soon became stained pink. He shuffled out of the room without saying goodbye, clutching his steaming mug.

Still busy with her chores, Marie-Louise observed the children out of the corner of her eye, wondering what she could offer them.

She was a woman who lived on her own and came to the abbey each day to give her life some meaning. She didn't expect anything from anyone: for her, the war was already lost. She had learned to survive, and had no fear of the Germans arriving, taking over the village, and setting fire to her house and the abbey. Pain and the defeat of reason, which was what she called the German occupation, had made her immune to tragedy. What more could she suffer?

This was why she refused to become emotionally involved with the children, who did have a future. She was aware that, just as they had appeared, they would one day disappear. But at least, for now, she had someone to talk to. Since they'd been around, her words no longer echoed off the kitchen's bare walls.

"All three of you are coming to my house with me. I need you," she said eventually. "Henri, you can help me a lot. I need a strong man."

The children still stood there in an awkward silence, without showing any great enthusiasm for her proposal. The weight of their secret made them tense and anxious. Perhaps they did need to get away from the abbey to let off some steam.

"The Germans will soon pull out of France. The war will come to an end, and the bombing of Paris will cease. And yet the damage has already been done, and the scars will take time to heal, if they ever do," said Marie-Louise. "Don't expect any great revelation. Life in this village, and especially in this abbey, will go on as before."

Elise was ready for the next adventure. Henri kept furtively glancing around, as if making sure they weren't being followed. Danielle's eyes still looked blank.

"By the time we get back on Sunday, they'll have removed the German, or what's left of him," Henri whispered to Danielle to comfort her.

But Henri's remark didn't have the desired effect. Danielle thought that someone had to report (although she hated the word) that a German officer was dying in a corner of the basement. She was sure he would die if he was left there another day.

They glanced at one another as they prepared to leave with Marie-Louise. They fell in with her, imitating her short steps and observing everything around them along the way.

The cook led the small procession into the village, paying no attention to the neighbors who poked their heads out of their windows from gloomy interiors. She didn't care about being seen, and didn't want to exchange any polite conversation. Elise quietly followed, careful not to accelerate her pace to avoid getting ahead. None of them spoke as they walked along. Marie-Louise could tell something was wrong with the children and that there was tension among them, but she put it down to them having had a silly argument.

Elise recognized the house of the indecent woman and admired the window boxes overflowing with tiny white flowers that added a splash of life to the village's dull facades. They entered Marie-Louise's house still silent. Henri felt that if no one said something soon, he was going to explode. His darting eyes betrayed his anxiety. As usual, Marie-Louise lit her candles; the girls went to their bedroom, and she put Henri on a mattress with a bedside lamp in the room with all the books.

Staring up at the beams in the ceiling, Henri went over and over a decision that had been troubling him for weeks: he couldn't wait another day before he joined the Resistance. This dramatic choice soon left him fast asleep.

Meanwhile, relaxing between clean white sheets, feeling more at peace with herself, Danielle hugged her sister.

"I'm sure Father Marcel won't let that officer die," she whispered to Elise, whose eyelids were already growing heavy. "Father Marcel is kindhearted. He knows that, even if he's a Nazi, the German is also a human being. Don't you agree?"

But Elise was already asleep, and Danielle decided her calm, even breathing was a good answer.

❧

The next morning, they were woken by the smell of hot chocolate with cinnamon. The girls went silently into the kitchen where an embarrassed Henri was trying to calm the rumbling of his stomach. When she heard the noise, Elise burst out laughing and her laughter infected Danielle as well.

It wasn't a mirage, and they weren't dreaming. Henri jumped for joy when he saw the small banquet awaiting them: slices of bread covered with cream and cinnamon, cheese, butter, and hot chocolate.

"Good morning, my dears," said the cook, greeting them with a smile. "Who says that because there's a war on we have to eat like beggars?"

Their hunger sated, for a few hours at least they forgot about the dying German officer. After breakfast, they went downstairs to the shop to help Marie-Louise with the rolls of cloth. Behind the counter, covered in at least a decade's worth of dust, the cook showed them a trapdoor leading down to the basement. They all immediately felt guilty again.

We're not going to come across any wounded man down there, Danielle told herself as Henri and Marie-Louise swept aside thick cobwebs and ventured into this dark cave that stank of neglect.

A few minutes later, the two girls saw the cook returning with a heavy roll of cloth on her shoulder. Behind her came the lanky, hungry-looking figure of Henri, dragging another smaller roll. His face was bright red from the effort. Elise's eyes lit up when she saw the brocade with its silver filigree and glints of magenta. She had never seen anything so beautiful: it was a treasure worthy of a princess in some far-off frozen land, a princess guarded by an army of faithful, brave soldiers whom the Germans wouldn't dare confront even in dreams.

Marie-Louise gave one of her usual cackles when she saw Elise's fascinated expression, before the girl slowly returned to the reality of this desolate room that had once no doubt been a bustling store.

After hibernating for heaven knows how many years, more than ten rolls of different textures and colors were brought up into the light. Out of breath and exhausted, Henri collapsed in a corner, but his eyes still had their unquenchable gleam.

Elise thought that these rolls would turn like magic into pounds of butter, lamb joints, bread, eggs, and cheese. She gave thanks to God for having been so lucky as to find such a noble, generous woman to protect her. What need was there for them to disappoint her or worse still, alarm her, with their tangled story of Resistance fighters and dying German officers, plotting priests, magicians, and rabbits?

The cook carefully chose a small roll of yellow silk and went down the street to meet Viviane. The children ran upstairs to watch her from the window and let their imaginations run wild.

The baker's wife came out of her shop, ready to gossip about this neighbor who had once made the huge mistake of marrying an infidel. Marie-Louise, who at that moment appeared empty-handed out of Viviane's house, confronted her. She didn't say a word, merely glared straight at her for several intense moments, until the baker's wife slunk back into her shop, eyes downcast. Openmouthed, they watched all this from the window, proud at seeing the woman who had taken them in and given them hot chocolate defy the village gossip in this way.

Marie-Louise did not come back to the house at once. First she had to go in search of what she could get with her ration book: that week, it was only tobacco and coffee. In the back room of the store, she caught sight of the baker's wife's son. He was wearing his blue jacket unbuttoned, with a brown shirt underneath, and a beret on his knee. He seemed immersed in a copy of *Je suis partout*, the appalling publication that gave his sympathies away. His mother, a scrawny, bad-tempered woman, was going to find it increasingly hard to hide the fact that her son was a collaborator, a disgrace to all the French people.

"He's a *milicien*," Marie-Louise confirmed to Henri when she finally returned home, out of breath. "He's a damned *milicien*! How on earth does that vixen dare look down on Viviane? And accuse her of *collaboration horizontale*? In wartime it's easy to lose your way in the shadows. Some won't be able to emerge, and will have to live the rest of their lives like a weak flame, always about to go out," she said. Falling silent for a few moments, she added, "Because the end is near."

She shot them a solemn look and then collapsed into the armchair, near her beloved books. Elise went into the kitchen and came back with a glass of water, spilling some as she crossed the room.

"Thank you, my love," said Marie-Louise, fanning herself with her hand. "We're falling apart. It'll be hard to survive when all this is over. What's to become of the French?"

She could hear a whispered conversation between Danielle and Henri. She peered at them, trying to make out what they were saying.

"What are those two up to now . . . ?"

Elise noticed how Henri looked at Danielle with appreciative eyes, how closely he listened to her. She yearned for him to look at her that way and not like a little girl.

They all came and sat down on the floor in front of her, as if waiting for another of her monologues. But Henri couldn't contain himself any longer:

"They need us, Marie-Louise!" His way of thinking might be more adult, but his childish voice betrayed him.

They waited for Henri to explain. When he saw they hadn't understood, he launched into one of his diatribes, like a frustrated combatant.

"Between the Nazis and the communists I don't know what we'll do . . ." Marie-Louise interrupted him.

"But Marie-Louise, what we have to do is to get the Boches out of our country!" he said, the frustration straining his voice.

Henri's convictions made Elise's heart race, but Marie-Louise's eyes gleamed tenderly. Listening to him, her pessimism, her disappointment with the French and the rest of humanity evaporated. There was hope, she told herself, and suddenly she turned to remove some of the books from the nearest bookcase.

"So you'd risk your life for all those crappy French, would you?" she said, pinching Henri on the cheek. Then, immediately changing her tone, she told the children to close the shutters. When they'd done so, from behind the books she was still holding they saw an old black radio emerge, with two buttons on each side and a golden grille in its center.

She told them that after she had married an infidel, she and her family were forbidden to listen to the radio or to buy any newspaper. All news was banned for them. But by this stage of the war, and with her husband missing, what did she care? The armchair with the standard lamp beside it were not placed like that to help her reading. Instead, it was a ruse, a piece of domestic theater. In this corner of the room, thanks to the BBC, Marie-Louise kept up-to-date with what was happening in her country.

When the radio was switched on, there was no need to move the dial. The French general in exile in London was speaking to his country-men, urging them to take to the streets.

"You see? Our time has arrived!" crowed Henri, but the other three told him to be quiet.

Judging from what the general was saying, Germany had already lost the war. The Allies were advancing, and the French army was about to take Paris and raise the French flag on Place de la Concorde. The war, which for a long while had seemed like a hallucination, and which many Parisians had at first called "the phony war" had become all too real.

"What French army?" the cook asked sarcastically.

Elise was listening closely, but was confused by rapid-fire messages she couldn't fully grasp: "The hour of hope," "The Resistance," "Atro-cious spectacle," "Numerous flotillas," "This year the fields are greener than ever," "Your children wish you a happy birthday," "Nothing is lost for France."

When she heard one of the presenters announce that the German tanks were pulling out of Paris, the color drained from Elise's lips and cheeks. A cold shiver ran down her spine. She buried her face in her moist hands and burst into tears.

"But the Germans still haven't surrendered. They haven't said the Germans have surrendered," Marie-Louise said to herself.

"Let's go to Paris!" shouted Henri. He stood up, waving his arms above his head. "What are we doing here? Our brothers need us! Let's go and cleanse the streets of the Nazi hordes!"

Henri had the spirit of a rebel and a saintly hero; a soldier without an army, a saver of lost souls. Still tearful, Elise was only waiting for the order to get up and go from Marie-Louise, who couldn't believe what she was hearing on the radio. Their nightmare was coming to an end.

That night, none of them could sleep. Marie-Louise was trying to keep a cool head to analyze the possible implications of this longed-for end to hostilities. She could go back to the apartment in Le Marais, salvage her café, find out where her husband was, if by the grace of God he was alive and safe in one of those terrible, distant German concentration camps, and then live her remaining years between the capital and the village, trying to forget, free of sorrow and remorse. And yet she wasn't entirely convinced by this scenario. She couldn't understand why Henri was increasingly sure that his place was on the streets of Paris with his Resistance brothers-in-arms, on the bridges and rooftops, brandishing the French flag.

Danielle and Elise were curled up together. They shared their dreams of walking hand in hand at dusk on the banks of the Seine, then resting at the foot of the Eiffel Tower, just like *Maman* Claire in the photograph taken before her marriage. Always together; and with that thought they fell asleep, comforted by an illusory peace.

42

At sunrise the next morning they met the baker's wife and her son, who this time wasn't wearing his *milicien* uniform. Marie-Louise hurried on ahead of them; most of the village knew that Father Marcel was saying mass that day, and none of them wanted to miss it.

Before the service, the murmur of the congregation echoed through the abbey church. Viviane was seated in the front row. The baker's wife and her son came in and tried to hide at the back. The children and Marie-Louise were seated on the side where the priest would enter from the sacristy.

The quiet was disturbed by the cries of a baby. His mother was trying to whisper in his ear to soothe him, but the howls went on and on, so that in the end she had to leave, with the entire nervous congregation staring after her. She sat outside in the sun by one of the windows, the baby on her lap.

Father Auguste made his way painfully from one side of the altar to the main aisle, and went to sit in the only place still free, next to Viviane. Once he had done so, Father Marcel appeared and walked wearily toward the altar. Coming to a halt beneath the austere crucifix, he closed his eyes and slowly recovered his breath. There were to be no customary rituals that day.

"We live in a time of darkest night," he began, then fell silent. Elise felt she was being observed; so did Danielle and the others. "To emerge from the shadows will be a difficult task, but we must find the necessary strength, even if it's all that we have left. I know we will succeed. We will not perish, drowning in darkness.

"Who among us has not at some time or other been assailed by the darkest thoughts? Believe me, I myself am no exception. I confess I have doubted God. I have doubted his mercy, his compassion."

A ripple of sound spread through the abbey. Some nodded, others protested angrily; still others crossed themselves at what they considered blasphemy.

"Have none of you been in my situation? I don't think there is anyone courageous enough to tell me, here in the house of God, in our house, that they have never doubted his mercy. When I arise every morning, after praying and sometimes even during my prayers, I wonder how many more sins we will have to pay for, and for how long?"

By now the silence was overwhelming. One woman was weeping. An old man nodded shamefully.

"God has abandoned us. He has placed all human beings on this earth as meek lambs for the slaughter, and we've ended up like wild beasts thirsting for blood. We go from city to city conquering and killing, dominating all those who are not like us, as if we were the chosen people. And we think we have the divine right to decide who is to live and who is to die. It's time we rose up. No longer will we let ourselves be struck down, allowing others to steal our lands, burn our temples. We can no longer stand by and see our people erased from the face of the earth. It's time to say no, even if this means we have to stain our hands with blood."

Another pause. Henri's chest swelled with patriotic fervor, as if the priest were talking directly to him. The priest's last words echoed in an anguished silence. He was staring blindly at the stained-glass window above the abbey's main door. Father Marcel was no longer looking at anyone, as if his soul was somewhere far away. So distant that the empty husk of his body began to tremble in that sacred place.

"I pray for all of you, I pray for myself. I beg God to have mercy on us all." His deep voice fell to a murmur. "To doubt is human. And if one morning we wake up having lost our faith, let us close our eyes and not open them again until we can see clearly. Better for us to stay asleep if we cannot act lucidly. With you here, in front of me, recognizing all our sorrows and sharing our common pain, I can see the light. I see in you the light of the world! Let us not lose faith, my beloved children, let us not lose it, because in such difficult times is there anything worse that could happen to us? I can see God in each and every one of you. God is within us all."

Enveloped in the solitude of the sermon, Father Marcel let out a deep sigh and withdrew from the altar. He left, slamming the sacristy door and abandoning the horrified congregation without granting them the final "Amen."

43

A dust storm swirled through the village streets, up over roofs and around corners, sweeping away everything it encountered. The villagers began to close their windows, trying to avoid the dust filtering inside and weakening their already frail lungs. The abbey's heavy oak doors had been pulled shut, but the gusts blew into the middle of the courtyard in search of whatever they could take with them. They couldn't lift the dust-colored rocks, or uproot the only tree that stood stoically in the sun. The unforgiving north winds reached the abbey when least expected. And with the storm came the Germans.

When Elise heard the Germans were approaching, accompanied by the *miliciens*, her heart seemed to stop. Perhaps it had grown weary, or perhaps fear was no longer an option for her. Taking Danielle's cold hands in hers, she stood motionless again with her sister, watching the other children running this way and that like a river flooding the abbey's narrow corridors.

"Into the courtyard! Everyone into the courtyard at once!" they heard somebody shout.

"Wasn't the war supposed to be coming to an end? What happened to the Allies, the French army?" moaned Elise. "We should have escaped as far as we could to the south, as far away as possible rather than seek shelter in the abbey. But I was very thirsty, do you remember?" She turned to Danielle. "What more can they take from us? We've already lost *Maman* Claire, and now they'll separate us from Marie-Louise, Henri, and Father Marcel. And we'll never get to see Paris."

"We have to go into the yard with the others. They're going to show us a magic trick. Let's run," said Henri. The girls fell in behind him, matching his every step, as though they were all in sync and nothing could force them apart.

When all the children were in the main courtyard, silence descended. Elise's breathing became shorter. The faces of the scrawny man and the one with dark shadows under his eyes were covered with cracked white paste. Their eyes had been outlined in black, and their mouths were a red line that ran from the corners of the lips to the tips of their chins in an expression of disgust or disdain. They were pretending that an imaginary glass screen separated them from the audience that was eagerly following their movements. With the palms of their hands they fixed the limits of this reinforced space that no one, thought Elise, not even the Germans, could penetrate. But the gestures of the two mimes only made the children feel even sadder. *Aren't they supposed to make us laugh?* Elise wondered.

There was the sound of marching footsteps so loud they seemed to shake the foundations of a building that had withstood many past invasions. The audience looked around for a way out, but the mimes demanded their full attention, and they got it.

Sitting in a battered armchair next to Marie-Louise, Father Auguste was the only one laughing at the antics of these improvised actors. Catching the children's eyes, he winked at them with boyish enthusiasm, then turned back to the mimes, who had now become magicians and were producing an endless stream of colored handkerchiefs out of an enormous black top hat. When one of them tapped the hat with the golden wand, a trembling white rabbit appeared. This was the only trick it had been trained for.

For the first time, everyone applauded. All the same, Elise, who was sitting in the front with Danielle and Henri, thought she could detect a look of terror on the mimes' faces.

"Don't turn around. They're here," Henri whispered to her. "They can't do anything to us. They must be lost; the best thing is to ignore them."

Henri's words sounded like a distant murmur to Elise. Yet again they were heading for the cliff like docile sheep, one behind the other. Yet again, the whole village was gathered to await the explosions. *I ought to run, I ought to confront them. Let's all join together and walk out toward the village. Then we'll see if they're brave enough to shoot us in the back, not locked in a church or an enclosed courtyard.* Her face twitched with each of these thoughts, so clearly that both Danielle and Henri noticed. Seated nearby, Marie-Louise was afraid one of them might react foolishly.

Escorted by two *miliciens*, a German officer stood in the center of the courtyard, on the same spot where only moments before the mimes had been performing.

"We are looking for weapons," said the officer with icy calm, in perfect French.

The same as always, thought Elise, her face taut.

"And for one of our men," added the officer.

Henri jumped in his seat. Danielle closed her eyes. Elise gulped. Marie-Louise observed their reactions from afar.

"Can anyone help us? Have you seen anything suspicious in recent days?"

Silence.

"Very well. Then we will talk to the children one by one. They always tell the truth." Smiling, the German officer stressed every word. He looked straight at Danielle: "Shall we start with you?"

Why did we sit in the front row? Why didn't we run away? Why didn't we hide in the cloister? Be strong, nothing's going to happen, trust me, think of Maman. Elise wanted to convey all this to Danielle by repeatedly squeezing her hand. But Danielle couldn't feel anything: she was weightless, floating over the courtyard, high above them all.

The two *miliciens* took Danielle into the sacristy, where the German officer was waiting for her. Elise didn't react as she watched her disappear, but at that moment into her memory floated the first traces of the stench of death that had always pursued her.

A few minutes later, the door opened and Danielle ran into Elise's arms. Now it was Henri's turn. He rushed inside, slamming the door in the face of the *miliciens*.

All alone with the German! If I was as strong as him! thought Elise, and began staring intently at the sacristy. Marie-Louise came over to Danielle, wondering how she could protect them. But what could she do: she was only a cook, who had been unable even to save her husband.

"Be strong," she told Elise. "This morning Father Marcel told me Henri's brother is coming for him tomorrow."

"Where is Father Marcel?" Danielle asked. Marie-Louise lowered her eyes and remained silent.

Before Henri reappeared, the *miliciens* had already led Elise to the sacristy entrance. The two of them glanced at each other as they passed in the doorway.

"They'll soon be gone and leave us in peace," Elise said. As she suppressed her fury, a tear rolled down her cheek.

Shortly afterward, Henri came out of the sacristy red-eyed. He hurried to rejoin Danielle, looking to her like a scared boy. The German officer followed him, marching across the courtyard before coming to a halt in front of Father Auguste and the two mimes. Elise remained motionless at the threshold of the sacristy, alone.

"Where are you keeping the officer?" the German said to the old man, who said nothing. He ordered the *miliciens* to start the search. Turning to the two mimes, he forced them toward the kitchen at gunpoint.

Danielle began to shake and murmur inaudible phrases. Reading her lips, Henri understood she was praying a silent Our Father.

"Stay calm," he told her.

"The suitcase," Danielle said faintly. "The suitcase is in Father Marcel's cell."

The men searching the abbey entered the room next to the kitchen and switched on the radio. They turned up the volume and the sound of a speech in French drifted out into the courtyard, only to be brusquely cut short. It was followed by piano music, then the sound of a trumpet accompanying a woman's voice.

"It's a broadcast by the Allies," explained Henri, trying to contain his excitement. "It must be an American song!"

The words reached them through the crackle of static like a distant lament. *"I'll be seeing you, in all the old familiar places . . ."*

The German officer took the two mimes into the room. Out in the courtyard all they heard was the deep voice of a woman singing on the radio, abruptly interrupted by the sound of blows, shouts, and furniture being moved, chairs toppling over.

Elise fixed her eyes on Henri and Danielle.

Then the first shot rang out and everything remained in complete silence. After the second shot, cries of panic broke out all over the courtyard. The third produced an overwhelming emptiness.

The German officer opened the door and came defiantly out into the courtyard, his lips a taut line. Casting a disdainful glance at them all, he strode out of the abbey. Behind him, the *miliciens* hurried to the exit, carrying the bloody body of another German officer.

Now there'll be explosions, flames. They'll burn us alive and throw us all into the same grave. Elise was convinced.

Running into the room, Marie-Louise smacked the radio to the floor, but it kept playing. *"I'll find you in the morning sun, and when the night is new, I'll be looking at the moon, but I'll be seeing you . . ."* Making a supreme effort, Father Auguste shuffled inside, followed by Elise. Danielle and Henri remained in the courtyard, where time had stood still.

Clutching the open trapdoor, Marie-Louise started down the steps. From up above, Elise and Father Auguste could glimpse the two mimes.

They had both been shot in the forehead; the cracked layer of white on their faces was stained red. At the far end of the basement lay the body of Father Marcel, a bullet hole through one eye. Blood streamed from his head. Marie-Louise's anguished cries drowned out the voice of the woman singing on the radio.

"How long until the song is over?" murmured Elise, her lips trembling.

Nobody answered.

44

The winds swept out of the village, leaving only dust and traces of blood on the walls of the abbey basement. Elise was on her own in the dormitory; her face was wet, but she wasn't sure whether it was from tears or sweat. She didn't know when she had closed her eyes, or how she had reached her bed, if she had slept with Danielle.

She got out of bed and went to the kitchen. Danielle and Marie-Louise were there. When they saw her they fell silent, and she knew they were trying to hide something. But she didn't need protection anymore. What else could happen to her, when she had already lost so much? Paris, the uncle in New York—it all meant nothing to her now. They were condemned to stay in this windswept village. Her last and only hope was Henri.

"Good morning, Elise. How'd you sleep?" said Marie-Louise. When Elise didn't answer, she added, "Everything is going to be all right."

Elise was weary of hearing that stupid, senseless phrase. *All right? How can someone still tell me that everything is going to be all right?*

"Henri is gone," Danielle blurted. "His brother came to fetch him, but he'd already vanished. No one saw him go."

Elise's stomach sank.

"Couldn't he be hiding? Or maybe he was arrested. They might have found that pamphlet hidden under his mattress . . ."

"Henri ran away, Elise," said Danielle. "It was his fault they killed Father Marcel."

"Danielle, you don't know what you're saying. You can't blame Henri."

"After he came out from talking to the German officer, they went straight to the basement. What more proof do we need?" Danielle spat out the words contemptuously.

"We can't be sure," Marie-Louise interceded. "I told him his brother was coming the next day. Perhaps he was scared; he didn't want to go and live with him. You two both knew that."

"It's not Henri's fault!' cried Elise, her voice cracking. She ran to a corner of the kitchen and stood trembling. "It's not his fault; it isn't!" she shouted through her sobs.

"Well, we're not to blame either!" Marie-Louise burst out. "Nobody's to blame. This is a war," she added, tired of trying to comfort other people. "It's good you can still weep. I have no tears left."

The radio had ended up in the kitchen, beneath the window, in full view. They no longer had to hide to listen to it.

That morning, the light was streaked with violet rays, and the beams of dust shone in the air like extinct stars. Elise stared at them one by one, her eyes cloudy with tears. She thought of Henri and all the miles he would have to walk in the hot sun to reach the south, where the Germans couldn't reach him. She once fancied herself all grown-up, almost as tall as Henri. She even dreamed that Henry looked at her differently and together they walked hand in hand without Germans or *miliciens* to fear. It was only a dream.

On the radio, she heard the first four notes of Beethoven's Fifth Symphony. It was Henri who had told her they represented *V* for victory in Morse code. Henri knew everything, and now, yet again, she had lost her friend. How many more would abandon her? There would be no more verbal jousts with him. No one would be able to tell her their plans for defeating the Nazis or for raising the French flag over Place de la Concorde.

"*Ici Londres! Les français parlent aux français* . . ." Elise heard on the radio. This was not a coded message, but someone speaking directly to them. All three of them went closer to the speaker, and the irritating German interference fell silent. "Today, August twenty-third, 1944, the French Forces of the Interior have liberated Paris." "An American army unit has occupied Grenoble." "Allied forces advance on the Robots bases."

"Is the war over?" asked Elise.

The other two didn't know what to say. Marie-Louise switched off the radio.

"Let's go home, quickly. Don't say anything: it could be a false alarm or a fake message to scare the Germans," she said, removing her apron. They left the kitchen.

The struggle against the Germans might have ended, but the abbey was still shrouded in silence. Father Auguste had shut himself in his cell; a group of children was playing in the dust of the courtyard, and the room next to the kitchen had been locked. Elise didn't have the courage to ask what had happened to the bodies of the two mimes and Father Marcel, if they had been tossed into abandoned graves in the monks' cemetery, or been given the Christian burial they deserved.

Danielle ran to retrieve the suitcase, then joined Elise and Marie-Louise.

"It'll be safer in your house," she told Marie-Louise, holding on tight to her treasure.

The village streets were deserted, although behind the shut doors and windows they could hear shouts, applause, isolated words they couldn't make out.

In the distance they saw a group of men kicking something crawling along the ground. At first, Danielle though they must have caught a deer.

A Boche. They've caught Father Marcel's murderer. I hope he suffers; he deserves to, Elise said to herself, with contained rage.

They came across a red high-heeled shoe in the dust of the road. A few steps farther on they saw some long, chestnut-colored locks of hair that couldn't be a German soldier's. As they drew closer, they could hear the moans, and finally made out the badly beaten face of a woman with a shaved head. A bare-chested man tore her dress off and she collapsed naked onto the cobblestones. Blood was coming from between her legs; she was desperately clutching her belly to protect herself.

"She's pregnant," Marie-Louise confirmed in a whisper. "You animals!" she shouted, and the mob began to disperse.

It was Viviane. Marie-Louise approached her and held out her hand. Viviane refused to take it, waving for her to go away and leave her alone.

"Let them finish, let them finish what they started . . ." Her voice was deep and firm; her eyes flashed. "I've got nothing more to lose."

Marie-Louise stared defiantly at the attackers, then helped Viviane up out of the dust and traces of spit. She dragged her to her house. Elise ran to help, while Danielle opened the front door.

Viviane had cuts on her skull. A few strands of hair still hung down the back of her neck; there was a purple bruise around her right eye, and she had lost some of her upper front teeth. Her breasts were smeared with blood and dirt.

Marie-Louise shut herself in the bathroom with her. The girls heard the sound of running water, which drowned out Viviane's muffled sobs.

"One war has finished," said Elise. "Now another one begins. What about us? What's going to happen to us?"

They went into the living room and switched on the radio. The Germans had begun their retreat. The general was on his way to Paris. The swastika had finally been uprooted from Place de la Concorde.

They spent the evening gathered round the darkened kitchen table, quietly sipping herbal tea. Viviane was wearing a white bathrobe. With her shaven head, as she leaned over her drink, she looked even younger.

"Let's go to Paris," said Elise, risking breaking the silence. The others simply smiled.

Elise didn't know what it meant to live at peace. Ever since she could remember, there had been enemies lying in wait. Ever since she could remember, her only thought had been to survive. What would Paris be like without swastikas? Paris was the photograph of *Maman* Claire smiling in front of the Eiffel Tower. The Germans might be retreating, the Allies might be advancing, the French army might have liberated Paris, but none of that would bring *Maman* back.

"We're going to be living days, weeks, and maybe even months and years of real chaos," said Marie-Louise. "France is a country without a government. God knows how many Germans are still hidden here and there. And how many others, like the son of the baker's wife, who won't know what to do with their shame and fear. Desperate people are capable of anything."

Danielle couldn't take her eyes off Viviane. She felt overwhelming pity toward her. She saw her as a victim of the Germans, not as the collaborator that the villagers loathed.

Viviane sipped her tea, trying to avoid the cuts in her mouth. Her eyes were still filled with tears, but she was no longer sobbing. When she realized she was being looked at, she lowered her head still further.

"Tomorrow is another day," she murmured, and closed her eyes.

She no longer felt ashamed; she didn't care what else they did to her, if they beat her to death or sent her to jail. She had thought she was already dead, until she felt the intermittent movements in her belly that at first she confused with the shuddering of her whole body. She was bearing another life inside her: a child of shame, as they had shouted at her, but her child all the same. Another kick from the baby made her forget her pain, and she tried to smile, or at least that was what she thought: the others did not detect it. All they saw was her bruised and battered face, still bearing traces of blood.

"I may have made a mistake," she went on in a dull monotone voice. "But my child is not a mistake. We are at war, and the father of my child is the enemy, but we won't be at war forever. I've no intention of running away for the rest of my life, or of hiding my child. What is my baby guilty of?"

⤜⤛

The following day they avoided listening to the radio, not wanting to risk any disappointment. Maybe the Germans had counterattacked, or the reinforcements meant to bolster the weak French army had somehow vanished on the outskirts of Paris. Perhaps, as many people suspected, that army itself was a chimera.

They leaned out of the window and could feel how the summer was beginning its retreat as well. Marie-Louise could sense it would be a harsh winter.

At dusk they returned to the abbey, while Viviane remained at the cook's house. She needed to rest, to sleep as much as she could for several days. Elise had heard her talking to herself and pacing round the room, eyes downcast and burdened by the guilt her child would be born with. Whenever the pains in her legs and back grew too much for her, she sat on the windowsill, and then a few seconds later, she stood up again and repeated the same routine.

At the abbey, Father Marcel's absence could be felt everywhere: in the corridors, at the altar, in the courtyard, in the grieving faces and sad eyes of the children who had not yet found anyone to adopt them. Marie-Louise plunged into the darkened kitchen, where Elise silently observed her pained face.

"Once, pilgrims used to come here," Marie-Louise said softly, not realizing anyone was listening. "Now no one comes to study. What has become of these walls, that in the past gave shelter to so much ancient wisdom, produced such images of splendor, what became of the smell of incense, the chants . . . ?"

Hearing this, Elise no longer saw the cook as someone capable of confronting the most menacing German soldier, of saving Viviane from being stoned, of giving refuge to two abandoned little girls. Now she was no more than a frail old woman lost in the labyrinth of her memories.

Meanwhile, Danielle wandered aimlessly among the pillars of the church, avoiding any children she encountered. For her too, the end of the war meant nothing. She was as lost as Marie-Louise. Perhaps it was better to live life stealthily like this, in a constant flight that gave purpose to waking up each morning, rather than to sleep peacefully after losing her mother. What would she do, what could she do, from now on? Weep?

45

$\mathcal{L}$ittle by little, smells were returning to the village, as if everyone had decided at the same time to light their ovens or to bring their remaining stores out of the larder. The war was over; it made no sense to continue hoarding. The time had come to have a proper feast. From out in the street dinner-table conversations and music could be heard, as well as family arguments that only a few days earlier would have been carried on in silence.

Marie-Louise's house was the only one in darkness. All the windows in the village were lit up, except for hers. With the two girls, she climbed the wooden stairs she knew from memory: this one creaked, that one was firmer, that other one had a crack in it. She avoided the noisiest ones so as not to wake Viviane, who seemed to have finally managed to fall asleep after nights of insomnia.

Marie-Louise stood at the top of the stairs without switching on the light. She turned to Elise, who saw a look of terror flash across her face. The cook had a premonition. She dragged her feet ever more slowly along the passageway. Seeing that the only closed door was to the bathroom, she drew back from it in horror.

You have to be able to anticipate sorrow, thought Danielle. *So that when it catches you by surprise, you're ready for it.*

In the half-light, Marie-Louise's face had become a straight line plunging down from forehead to mouth. Chin drawn back, cheeks sunken, her expression haggard. Elise could see that her lips were trembling. Marie-Louise seemed to already have seen what she was about to face. She was anticipating sorrow.

She switched on the bathroom light from outside. The door was still shut, but a shaft of light shone through the cracks in the frame. Like a perfect wound, this luminous slash turned the three of them into silhouettes. Marie-Louise leaned her head against the door, gathering strength and trying in vain to consider all the different possibilities, although she was sure none of them made sense. If only she had stayed home, if she had devoted more time to her, listened to her. A tiny part of Marie-Louise thought there might still be some hope, and so she called out in a low voice as she banged on the door.

"Viviane . . ." she called several times, wishing for a miracle.

She slowly turned the doorknob, sure by now that the woman she had protected was another distant memory. Her face ashen, she opened the door.

The bathroom window was open; beyond it the night sky was a deep purple, studded with stars.

"Where has the moon gone?" Elise sighed.

The cold air blowing in from the street sent a shiver down her spine, then Marie-Louise's howl made her jump. When the cook fell to her knees on the cracked floor tiles, Elise saw what had so horrified the woman. Viviane's naked body was floating in the bathtub, covered by a thick veil of dark blood. The wounds had disappeared from her pale, innocent face; her lips were pink once more; her eyes seemed to be staring out at the stars. There was a fixed smile on her mouth; a smile without a future. At the base of her throat, between her collarbones, was the open wound. It was as if her head had wanted to detach itself and follow its own destiny. Her left arm was dangling from the side of the bath, and close to the bloodstained hand shone an open razor with an immaculate mother-of-pearl handle.

Marie-Louise's screams tore the deep silence. She was staring at the razor, which had once been her husband's. A long time ago she had put it away on the towel shelf together with a small bag of lavender. In her mind she could see Viviane going into the bathroom and opening the cupboard. There, nestling among the perfumed towels, was her only salvation. Marie-Louise couldn't help feeling certain that she was the one who had brought death within poor Viviane's grasp.

When she reached for a towel, the razor must have fallen to the floor. Opening it, Viviane had seen it was still sharp enough to help her on her journey. Naked, weightless, and free from all contact with the hostile world, liberated from a guilt she had never properly understood, she promised herself that her child would never be called a child of shame. She opened the window and let the stars' distant glow illuminate her: stars that kindly hid all traces of the blows and wounds. She settled as best she could in the cold porcelain bathtub, at peace. The time for explanations had passed. She would no longer have to protect herself from anyone.

She picked up the open razor. The metal edge was like a caress on her throat. No shouting, no tears, no death throes. With her right hand, she stroked her belly.

That night, as she listened to Marie-Louise's horrified sobs, Elise realized the cook would never go back to work at the abbey. She saw herself living with her and Danielle, and this brought her a fleeting moment of comfort.

The girls accepted that they now were the cook's family. Everything was different. Now they had a real home.

46

In times of peace, the nights seemed endless. Elise was constantly wary of the setting sun. She waited for the night to speed by, desperate to see the last star fade. Since Viviane's death, she was terrified of closing her eyes for fear that she would see images of the future. She didn't feel ready to see what would come next. Sleep was no longer a refuge. Elise spent the whole day stumbling along, struggling against the weight of her eyelids.

For her part, Danielle began to show Marie-Louise she was ready to become an independent young woman who would be no burden to her. She gave orders to the daydreaming Elise. "Clear up the kitchen." "The towels should be folded in four." "Make sure you close the windows onto the street." "Don't waste water from the faucet . . ." She gave all these instructions out loud, to reassure Marie-Louise. Danielle had begun to take control of her life. And as the elder sister, she was also responsible for Elise.

They spent that winter clearing the store of dust, and polishing the counter and shopwindows. They told any villagers who wanted to know that Atelier Plumes, which still had its faded sign outside, would reopen its doors and offer its services once more with the arrival of spring. Marie-Louise rescued the remaining rolls of cloth from the basement and took it upon herself to initiate the girls into the mysteries of brocades, velvet, silk, and lace. Some materials were ideal for decoration, others to keep out the light, still others to upholster couches, and yet more to help embellish drab, neglected corners.

"Fabrics are our great allies," she would tell them. "We have to choose their fates carefully; to be loyal to them, without going too far or asking them for something they can't give."

Still daydreaming, Elise learned the difference between cretonne, chenille, damask, linen, and jacquard. She talked like an expert about plain weave bleached taffeta, or which fabrics were more permeable, hard-wearing, or able to resist the ravages of time with dignity. Danielle would fetch the rolls and lay them out on the counter while Elise made sure that their clients, mainly women who could not allow themselves the luxury of reupholstering their sofas, were nonetheless enchanted by the girl who spoke of raw cottons as if they were abandoned orphans, or of moiré as an exotic princess held prisoner in a tower. Marie-Louise listened to her admiringly, and whenever the conversation languished, she would take a sample of the most expensive material and spread it out on an armchair so that a ray of sunshine brought out the magic of its texture, the work of an eminent craftsman.

By now, the Germans and the war were a distant nebula. The radio had been consigned to an empty shelf in the kitchen, because the news brought only sadness. Marie-Louise decided that from this moment on, there would nothing but music in her house and shop. She rescued a battered old gramophone from the basement, cleaned the needle carefully, oiled the arm, and set it up in the back room.

Their days now began and ended with tangos sung by Tino Rossi, once the favorite singer of Marie-Louise's husband.

"At night, when we closed the café, Albert used to dance with me, his hair slicked back like Tino Rossi," she said with a smile. "But my Albert was better looking."

The music brought to the surface the name that until then she had avoided mentioning. To the beat of *"Je voudrais un joli bâteau,"* Marie-Louise would stretch her arms out to Danielle, whom she was teaching the complicated steps of a dance Elise knew she would never be able to grasp.

"If I have to learn to dance tango to get married, I think I'll stay single all my life," Elise would say. With each passing day, she sounded more and more like an old woman in a young girl's body.

Marie-Louise was still hoping her husband would return one day when they were least expecting it. Every time Elise heard his name, she would open her eyes wide as she tried to erase the image assailing her: Monsieur Albert would never come back; he was lost at the bottom of a well; his soul had been drowned, his body burned.

Overwhelmed by this proof that her powers had returned, Elise cursed the misfortune of being able to foresee the future time and again. She had no idea where this gift came from. With the arrival of summer, she started to look for silver linings. Atelier Plumes was prospering; they had more and more clients. Now it was not only indecisive old ladies from their own village, but people from other surrounding places that had heard they offered an exquisite selection of fabrics from a bygone era of a quality not even to be found in the best Paris boutiques.

Now that misfortune had been swept away and the windows could be left wide open without the covering of dust that had veiled them for so long, Marie-Louise felt it was time that Elise began to enjoy herself once more. It upset her to see the young girl still not sleeping well, wandering about with her head in the clouds, trying to interpret meaningless dreams.

"We can't spend our whole lives daydreaming. And if we can't avoid it, we have to remember that dreams are just that: dreams, and nothing more," Marie-Louise insisted one night as she was brushing Elise's hair. "It's the present that matters, the plate of food we have to put on the table in order to survive. If tomorrow takes us somewhere else, so be it, my girl. Neither you nor I are able to change what's coming. So it's better for you not to expect anything: let everything arrive in its own time."

"When are we going to go to Paris?" replied Elise, as if she had not heard a single word.

"Goodness me, there you go again with Paris! There's nothing for us there. First of all, we have to make a success of Atelier Plumes. Besides, Albert knows this is where I'll be waiting for him. That was our agreement before he was taken away."

Elise didn't dare tell her that her husband wasn't coming back, that he had ended up in a dark hole he could never climb out of, that from the day the French police had arrested him he was condemned to death. Marie-Louise had already wept over him. There was no point doing so again. Her husband was dead: Elise had seen it.

She looked for the old Columbia Records album, and Marie-Louise let herself be carried away by the intoxicating voice of her Corsican idol: *"Le plus beau de tous les tangos du monde, C'est celui que j'ai dansé dans vos bras."* She took hold of Elise's hands and they began to dance the tango as if it was a Viennese waltz.

47

A year after the liberation, Marie-Louise decided that to successfully revive the Atelier, she needed to take on someone who could help them lay out the rolls of cloth on the counter, fill the seat cushions, and fit the springs in the heavy armchairs with their carved legs.

Danielle and Elise both hoped this meant there would be another young boy around: that would make the tango lessons much more fun. They were enthusiastic about teaching him to upholster, to show him this world that now fascinated them. But one afternoon, while they were busy sweeping up scraps of material, threads, and tacks, Marie-Louise, who had been to Limoges to buy fabrics, appeared in the doorway carrying two enormous bags, several rolls of cloth, accompanied by a stooped, elderly man who seemed unable to carry even himself.

"Help Señor Soto," said Marie-Louise, dumping her purchases on the counter.

"Does he speak French?" Elise asked in a whisper.

"Señor Soto speaks French as well as we do. Leave your cheeky questions for later. You'll have more than enough time to find out whatever you like, because as well as helping in the Atelier, he's going to be living here for the time being, in the back room."

Señor Soto was a scrawny man with leathery skin and not an ounce of fat anywhere on his body. Elise thought there wasn't a single muscle left on his bones, from which hung clothes that may once have been the right size for him. His pants were done up with a length of rope to stop them from falling down, and his shirtsleeves were rolled up to the elbow. He also wore a black vest, possibly to give some kind of shape to his decrepit figure. His body was as light as the breeze.

He was completely bald, although over time the girls realized that in fact he shaved his head. A sparse white beard covered his sunken cheeks, and in the depths of his pronounced eye sockets shone a pair of gray eyes. He was constantly blinking, as if he was trying to bring every-thing around him into focus. *Poor Señor Soto can't see very well. How is he going to be able to help us?* thought Danielle. When they first saw him, he was so dirty it was impossible to tell the color of his skin, although Elise was amazed that he did not give off the usual smell of death that the itinerant workers of the postwar period seemed to carry around with them. Señor Soto had no smell: What could he stink of, when it seemed as if he hadn't eaten or perspired in years?

That evening they had to wait a long time before they could have supper together, as he spent hours in the bathroom. The water ran end-lessly, but Marie-Louise didn't seem to mind.

"He's a friend of my husband. He lost all his family in the war. He needs us as much as we need him. He'll be staying here temporarily, until he finds out if there are any survivors from his father's side of the family. If Señor Soto can come back, so can my husband."

"Is he sick?" Elise asked, but Marie-Louise ignored her. In fact, she didn't know the answer, and so instead told them what little she had gleaned about him.

Señor Soto, a Spaniard who had fled to France, ended up in an internment camp together with his wife and young daughter, all of them considered *étrangers indésirables*. It was there that he had met

Marie-Louise's husband. According to him, Albert was immediately transferred to a camp at Drancy, and from there to another one in Poland. Despite the fact that both he and Señor Soto shared the same libertarian ideas, to the French and Germans, her husband was above all a despicable Jew.

Elise listened closely to Marie-Louise's account, but instead of concentrating on the past, her eyes were turned toward the future. She could foresee that Señor Soto would not live with them for long. One day he would abandon them. Closing her eyes, she could see him leave the way he had come, empty-handed.

"His wife and daughter died of typhus soon after they arrived in the camp," Marie-Louise went on. "When they were liberated, Señor Soto returned to the only village he could recall, but his house no longer existed, and the neighbors didn't recognize him, and slammed their doors in his face."

It was difficult to accept that in a war someone could die of typhus. That was mere bad luck. In a war you die in a bombardment, are hit by a stray bullet, or are shot through the head as Father Marcel had been. *But typhus . . . that's a death for peacetime*, Elise told herself.

When Señor Soto finally appeared from the bathroom and came to the table, he was a different man. His forehead had recovered a pink glow that gave his lined face a friendly appearance. He was wearing a white, short-sleeved shirt and a loose, well-pressed pair of pants that had once been Albert's. He seemed to be floating inside his clothes.

As he came to sit next to her, Elise discovered a huge scar on his left arm. When he saw her looking, Señor Soto withdrew his arm and kept it under the table throughout the supper.

Danielle would have liked to ask him what life had been like in that prison, how he had managed to survive, how he crossed countries and cities to reach this hidden village where now he would be devoting himself to upholstering furniture for capricious clients, but a stern glance from Marie-Louise prevented her from doing so. They had to leave Señor Soto in peace; he had already been through enough.

His hair will grow back, Elise wished for him as she studied all his movements while he drank his thick potato soup.

After a good bath, a hearty soup, and several hours' sleep, Señor Soto was able not only to carry the rolls of cloth but to move chairs, armchairs, couches, and even sofas with ease.

∞

Over the next few weeks, from hearing Tino Rossi so often, Señor Soto learned the words of the songs, and they discovered that this man who had seemed so wretched when he arrived had a powerful baritone voice. One day he started singing songs that they didn't recognize in a language none of them knew. "*Bésame, bésame mucho, cómo si fuera esta noche la última vez . . .*" By the third verse, both their idol and Señor Soto went back to singing in French. The girls and Marie-Louise applauded.

One evening Elise was on her own with him. She went over, removed a few feathers stuck to his vest, and told him straight out that he was a lucky man.

Soto took a deep breath before replying. She was only a little girl, and so he didn't feel he had the right to disappoint or bewilder her with philosophical comments that would get them nowhere. In the end, he wasn't sure if Elise was referring to him having survived the death camp or for having met such a kindhearted person as Marie-Louise. He smiled a painful smile.

"It's you who are a lucky girl. You have your family."

"You're right. Yes, I think I'm a very lucky girl," said Elise, her eyes lighting up at the idea that someone who had only just met her should see her as part of Marie-Louise's family.

48

*S*eñor Soto soon became an expert upholsterer. It was Christmas, and now without Nazis controlling the world, Elise thought they should celebrate with open windows, lots of music, and a rich dessert. For both her and Danielle, the war was becoming a distant memory.

One evening, Marie-Louise returned from Limoges in a very good mood. Not only had she bought herself a new Tino Rossi record but she had had her hair cut, found a splendid pheasant, and brought home the cake Elise had been dreaming of: a *bûche de Noël*.

Before they sat down to eat, they brought the gramophone close to the table. Marie-Louise went to fetch the new record and, each with a glass of red wine, they enjoyed the moment as they had never done before. *"Petit Papa Noël, Quand tu descendras du ciel, Avec des jouets par milliers, N'oublie pas mon petit soulier . . ."*

From that moment on, *Petit Papa Noël* became Elise's favorite song, and she forced Marie-Louise to play it until she was sick of it. Although Elise felt fortunate, she had an ominous feeling that she tried at all costs to avoid. It wasn't so much at night that she was obsessed by it, because then she collapsed exhausted, but during the day when she grew drowsy, her eyelids drooped, and she began to see things. On New Year's Eve, Elise saw herself all alone on a ship in the middle of the ocean; at that moment, she knew that her days of happiness were about to end.

In the spring of 1947, Señor Soto left them. He had located a brother in a small town on the other side of the Pyrenees. He wasn't too keen on the idea, but his brother needed him to help keep the farm going. Losing an employee for the Atelier wasn't such a problem, because they all knew that another one would appear soon enough: the streets were full of young people looking for work. What saddened them was that no one, however hardworking they might be, would have a baritone voice like Señor Soto's. To Marie-Louise it was like losing Tino Rossi himself.

The same evening that Señor Soto left as empty-handed as he had arrived, but weighing a few pounds more, and with a flourishing head of hair, they got a message from the abbey. Father Auguste was expecting them urgently. He had received a letter from New York, from the girls' uncle.

The news startled Danielle. Trembling, she went to fetch the suitcase, and the three of them set out for the abbey. None of them spoke. Holding tight to Danielle's hand, Elise cautiously followed Marie-Louise. She didn't want to predict the future. She couldn't.

When they reached the ancient building, Father Auguste, leaning on his cane, led them into the sacristy and then went to sit behind the weighty mahogany desk strewn with papers. He picked up a letter, unfolded it, and paused to look at them.

"Claire's brother, Roger Duval, has been in touch with us," he said hesitantly.

Marie-Louise's face lit up. She was expecting to see the same joy in the girls' eyes, but they didn't seem to react.

"When is he coming for us? Do we have to go live in New York? Can't we stay here?" Breathless, Danielle poured out every possible question. Elise stood motionless, trying to keep her eyes wide open.

Looking toward Marie-Louise for support, Father Auguste handed her the letter. As she started to read it, her smile froze.

Elise's heart began to pound as it used to in the past, racing so fast it made her face flush. Yet with the heartbeats, her sense of fear evaporated. She had seen the future.

"Your uncle Roger can only take one of you," the abbot explained.

"I won't go to New York without Elise. I promised my mother," Danielle declared firmly. She took her sister's hand and dropped the suitcase.

"Danielle . . ." Father Auguste's voice cracked. "Your uncle can only adopt one of you, and he wants the younger sister."

Elise could hear her heartbeats. *I have to count them for the first time since I was abandoned in the forest,* she told herself. *Yes, come on, Elise: one, two, three, four, five, six . . . What happened to the silences? Count again, don't give up,* she told herself.

Distracted, concentrating above all on trying to find the silences between her heartbeats, she didn't understand the rest of what Father Auguste was saying. She was busy calculating the speed the blood was coursing through her veins. She could feel it going up, down, back to the head. A cool breeze blew in through the only window open in the sacristy, bringing with it the smell of rain.

"So Elise will go to Paris tomorrow with Marie-Louise."

"We're finally going to Paris?" Elise said, looking joyfully toward her sister.

"May I go now?" was Danielle's only response, said in a disturbingly unruffled voice.

"Tonight you'll both be sleeping at the abbey," said Father Auguste. He stood up and shuffled out of the sacristy.

Marie-Louise tried to understand why Monsieur Duval had chosen only one of them. Maybe he saw Elise as the more vulnerable one, whereas Danielle was ready to fend for herself. The Duvals were immigrants and perhaps too poor to care for them both, she thought.

By nightfall, Danielle had already gone to lie down in what had once been her bed. She took up only a small part of it, leaving more room for Elise, just like when they used to sleep together. She slid the suitcase back under the bed once more.

Danielle felt as if she had been living someone else's life in Marie-Louise's house, in the abbey, in this bed that really belonged to her sister. She was the other, the one her uncle was rejecting, when all she had done was to obey the instructions given by her mother, who it turned out was now Elise's mother. She herself was a dim, nameless phantom, whom nobody wanted. Perhaps even the uncle's final choice—"Just one of you"—had been *Maman* Claire's intention from the start.

She sensed Elise slipping into bed beside her, but avoided the slightest movement and hoped she would fall asleep at once. She couldn't find any prayers or pleas to help her, because she had just realized that the decision had likely been made by her own mother.

When Elise crawled into bed, she recognized the small purple jewel case that Danielle had put on her pillow. *She's forgiven me*, she thought, slipping it into her coat pocket. What did she want a bracelet and a diamond ring for now. She sighed.

Convinced *Maman* Claire had never ceased watching over them, Elise slept soundly.

Danielle meanwhile was struggling with dreadful nightmares. A voice was telling her that it was not for her to absolve nor pardon anyone. There were no guilty or innocent people. Elise would grow up as her mother's daughter, her sister. She would protect her until her dying day, wherever she might be. It was "her Christian duty," she heard *Maman* Claire's soft voice say.

The years would go by and Elise would write to her, but Danielle vowed never to open the letters or respond to her calls. Her sister had become her punishment; since she had appeared in her life, Danielle's world had come tumbling down. Her mother had died protecting this other one. Not her.

She decided that her one final offering would be to keep the box of letters sent back from Cuba and dispatch them again to Viera. She owed that much to her mother and to Frau Amanda.

Elise woke at midnight, safe in Danielle's arms. She tried to turn around gently so as not to wake her or slip out of her embrace. When she was face-to-face with her, she kissed her.

In the first light of dawn, Danielle saw Elise leave the dormitory hand in hand with Marie-Louise. Before stepping out, Elise turned and could see Danielle lying there motionless, her face contorted with pain and anger. She saw her weeping, and knew they were tears of rage. Closing her eyes, Elise realized this was the last time she would ever see her sister.

It was still dark as they walked to the station, but by the time the train drew in, Elise could see that Marie-Louise had put on a blue silk dress and a brown coat. She had never seen her look so elegant.

They boarded the train in silence and sat opposite one another, in their own worlds. As they sped past newly planted wheat fields, Elise was lost in inconsequential thoughts. She ought to try to sleep, this was going to be a long journey.

This wasn't the first family she was abandoning, and it wouldn't be the last. It no longer interested her to see what could be happening in the future. Whatever it might be, she was prepared for it: What more did she have to lose?

Marie-Louise was already dozing. Seeing herself reflected in the train's dusty window, Elise stared blankly into the beyond as the train began to push forward.

49

$\mathcal{P}$aris was cold rain, dark puddles of water, unlit streetlamps, a muddy river. Displaced bodies running around with nowhere to hide. Bewildered, Marie-Louise stopped to get her bearings. Shadows hurtled past her, and she kept turning around as if an enemy were at her heels.

The city was nothing more than a mass of old, dark buildings. Elise wanted to capture every image, to keep them all in her memory: discarded pieces of furniture, battered lamps, drunkards slumped on street corners. A woman in a hat and high heels bent over a pile of rubble. When they saw her, two children ran to join her. In an attic window, someone had forgotten a red and white flag with the black swastika in the center. Nobody cared. There were no stars in Paris either.

In the taxi, Elise stuck her head out of the window. The Paris drizzle soaked her face. The neighborhood they were heading for was a labyrinth of narrow streets, grim facades, lopsided windows. Marie-Louise was busy steeling herself for the return to the street where she used to live. Raising her chin as high as she could and stretching her neck out proudly, she took Elise's hand as they left the cab. Weary from their journey, they entered a small hotel. Elise looked on as Marie-Louise talked to an old woman behind the desk. Soon afterward, Marie-Louise turned back to her, frowning, took her hand again, and they went up to their room.

Standing at the window, Marie-Louise looked out on the continuous line of buildings with their big carriage entrances; a district that had once been hers. The sight was too painful, and nostalgia made her take a step back. The movement stirred the room's quiet light.

They slept in beds separated by a small night table. Elise collapsed onto her mattress with her eyes so wide open they shone like a light in the darkness. She began to foresee a future of clouded happiness. *That's the sacrifice the guilty have to make,* she dreamed. Because she had survived, because she hadn't been able to save *Maman* Claire, because she allowed Jacques and Henri to leave, because she didn't hold out her hand to Viviane, because she abandoned Father Marcel. And the next day she was going to be leaving behind the only remaining people she cared for in the world.

They were woken by a hostile brightness. It was time to face the truth, and their anxiety, by now mixed with a distaste for the French capital, only increased. There were no good mornings, no friendly looks. Marie-Louise went out into the street, yet another phantom from the war that the locals glanced at without curiosity. She lacked the patience to stop outside the building where she had once lived, or on the corner of what had once been her café. With one fell stroke she erased the past, hoping that this would make it hurt less. Watching her gave Elise a more precise vision of what was to come.

Walking well away from Marie-Louise's old neighborhood, they sat on the terrace of an empty restaurant with coffee and a cream tart.

"Stay where you are," Marie-Louise ordered Elise, before leaving without any explanation.

Elise stayed out on the terrace surrounded by phantoms who ignored her as they passed by. This was Paris, a city she would never remember.

When she returned an hour later, Marie-Louise seemed to have shriveled. Looking her in the eye, Elise could see she had been crying.

"Albert is not coming back," said Marie-Louise, slumping into her chair with infinite weariness. "He's dead. They killed him," she explained, raising the cup of cold coffee to her lips.

"You'll be all right. You're going to escape from this nightmare once and for all," she went on. Her face was now as harsh as her voice. "Get away, Elise, get out of this sewer as quickly as you can. Paris: What's left of Paris? Parisians? Luckily you'll be far away."

Elise wanted to tell her that she already knew, that her husband had died in a dark, windowless hole, where they robbed him of even the right to breathe, and yet she knew it would have been pointless.

This was her last day with Marie-Louise. She wanted to fling herself on her, hug her, beg her not to abandon her, but she didn't have the courage. That image was still in the future. For now, they crossed the city to find the building where rescued orphans were gathered. Elise pretended to be resigned to her fate, to accept it calmly, although neither was true.

Best to stay quiet, to follow Marie-Louise without thinking, even when what she really wanted to do was shout at her, drop to her knees in the middle of the street, stop the Paris traffic, and beg her to show some pity. This was her last chance to flee far from everything, from the unknown uncle, from the fate awaiting her.

If Monsieur Albert had survived, perhaps he and Marie-Louise would have adopted Danielle and me. We could have celebrated my twelfth birthday together. No one has ever celebrated my birthday, thought Elise.

She was shuttled around a room packed with howling children. She allowed herself to be led to one corner for her photograph to be taken, to another to be bombarded with questions that she refused to answer. Marie-Louise was her voice, her conscience, her executioner. Documents, letters, forms with signatures and letterheads, a ticket for a ship, a stamp for New York. Her body was in the room, but Elise's soul had already left and was floating through the air.

It was only when Marie-Louise embraced her that she returned to this desperate corner filled with victims about to embark on a new life.

"Don't leave me, Marie-Louise. I shouldn't be here. I'm not like them, I have you," Elise begged her in one last desperate effort.

"You have an uncle who's calling for you, my child. I can't go against that, even if I wished to. How can you want to live with a widow who's only waiting for the moment when she can join the man taken from her?" She didn't want Elise to see her weep again. The only person who now deserved to shed tears, whether of pain or hatred, was Elise.

"*Maman*, don't abandon me!" exclaimed Elise, in a trance. Moved and frightened, Marie-Louise stepped away from her.

It was then that Elise lost her last shred of innocence. Her childhood was at an end. *I'm not the one who should be going on this boat! It should be Danielle!* She wanted to shout, but couldn't.

She saw Marie-Louise moving away among the crowd packing the quayside. She had been abandoned yet again. Not in a forest, as she had dreamed, but adrift on an ocean liner. This was yet another death for her, and with it another of her lives was starting, the one she had already glimpsed in her dreams.

She closed her eyes. When she opened them once more, she saw herself, nameless, on the bow of a ship. In the open sea.

When the war is over, you are to travel to France, to Haute-Vienne. There you must search for the Duval family. Ask for Claire, Danielle, or Father Marcel. Tell them who you are and they will understand.

Your sister may well be an adult, have gotten married and had children. She may not even remember you.

She will no longer be called Lina, but Elise. It's possible she may reject you at first. Why did it take so long to discover the truth? she'll ask you. You must insist and show her our letters, all of them, because by then you'll have received them.

She'll tell you she has another family and believes in another God. That won't matter. God is God, and you are her flesh and blood. Promise me you'll go and look for her.

You are to tell her I loved her with all my life, and that I did everything I could to save her, even though that meant I had to forget who I was, and to make her forget who she was, where she came from.

One day you'll both go back to Berlin and show your children where our home used to be, our Garden of Letters. Then I'll be able to rest in peace. And so will your papa, because both of us will always be watching over you.

Promise me that, even if it is only for a moment, you will both wear the gold chains Papa bought for you, with the Star of David. On one star is written your sister's true name: Lina Sternberg.

SIX

The Farewell

New York, April 2015

50

"*M*om." Adele went over to the bed.

Yes, she was a mother, a grandmother, an old woman. She wasn't on the deck of an ocean liner, or in the middle of a forest begging not to be abandoned.

The first twelve years of my life meant more than all the rest.

My life since has been a sham.

You are the only real thing left, Adele.

The only good thing I've done in this country.

She didn't say all this aloud, or did she? She was almost certain she could still speak.

Can you hear me, Adele?

She gazed around the hospital room. *Maman* Claire, Father Marcel, and Danielle were all there. This was the encounter she had always been waiting for, the last one, when each of them would appear before her and judge her. Was she dreaming?

"We're in the hospital, Mom," Adele replied, reading the question in her mother's gaze.

Hers was the gentle voice of a daughter who would not condemn her. But Elise needed the opposite: the moment had come to confess, and she wanted neither forgiveness nor forgetting.

In the end, we're always guilty, she told herself. *After all, what is memory but a means of survival?* In her one-sided dialogue, Elise shook her head and began to slowly move her lips. Her daughter was there, ready to hold her. To bid her farewell.

"I am guilty of so many things," she said. Her voice was like an echo.

"You were a child, Mom. You shouldn't blame yourself." Adele tried to console her.

Elise smiled. Her daughter's act of compassion moved her; she was relieved she could hear her.

"You don't have to worry, Mom. We'll soon be going home," Adele continued.

But Elise could sense that time was not in her favor, so hurriedly and with great effort, she spoke: "My arrival in New York on that boat, my life with an uncle and aunt who were unaware there was no blood link between us . . . meeting the love of my life, your birth, and my grandson's. They were all derived from a fate that wasn't mine. A life that Danielle should have had. She was the real niece, the French girl, not me, the impostor."

Adele smiled, but then immediately pursed her lips. Elise was reminded of her mother, who used to tilt her head and purse her lips whenever she wanted to avoid showing she was frightened. This was the first time she had recognized her real mother in her daughter, and this glimpse sent a shiver down her spine.

"You know something, Adele? I've lived so many lives, I don't know which of them is coming to an end now."

"They're all yours, Mom. You can be sure of that. Now you must rest, you need it. I'm sure that tomorrow we'll be able to go home."

"Wait, Adele," said Elise, taking slow breaths and grasping her daughter's hand. "Please. I still have too many secrets on my conscience." She paused painfully, then began to speak again. "I betrayed the man who saved me in the middle of that forest. The man who led me to trust in God, and also to doubt him. The one who comforted me when I most needed it, and gave me hope when everything seemed lost."

"You were a child. All you said was that there was a dying soldier in the basement. How could you foresee what the Nazis would do? We've already talked about this, don't you remember? Just before I got married, you told me all about what happened in France."

She stared at Adele, trying to recall her husband's face. The man with whom she had created a real family when they met in New York, soon after graduating from college.

"Your father was very patient with me," she said, a silence between each word. "He didn't want to know anything about my past. In fact, I didn't have one; I had erased it completely."

Another needle pierced the thin skin of her arm. *What will they be able to find in that thick blood? Every drop they take will show I don't exist, that I'm a phantom without a name, a shadow. And my soul: where did I leave my soul . . . ?*

I abandoned my soul close to seventy years ago, on the far side of the Atlantic, Elise concluded, not looking at the nurse who was struggling to find at least one vein that had not collapsed.

Thoughts flitted in and out of her mind as they slid her body into the scanner where they would discover who she really was. All her lies would come to light.

"Try to relax, and don't move," the nurse told her as she monitored her thoughts.

That evening, when Adele came into the room with a bunch of tulips, Elise had collected her things and was sitting by the window, ready to leave the room where they had connected her body to all those cables that tried to read what no one can decipher. Elise stroked the bruises on her left arm. To her they looked like one of the species from the botanical album, the mallows . . . A nurse holding documents, and a male paramedic, were waiting in the doorway with a wheelchair.

Elise kept her eyes fixed on Adele. She needed all the answers.

"And Mama? What happened to Mama?"

"After the war, Aunt Danielle sent the letters to Viera in Cuba with a note saying that they belonged to her, and that Amanda and Lina ended up in Auschwitz. No further explanation. Adele paused between each phrase. "Viera always thought the two of you had died there together. That's why she never looked for you."

"Yet again, Danielle saved me." Elise's eyes brimmed with tears. "I should have gone to Cuba on the *Saint Louis*. With Viera. Just think: everything would have been so different."

"Viera had a son, Mom: Louis. And Anna is his daughter."

"You don't need to tell me: I understood that as soon as I saw her eyes . . ."

Elise struggled to sit up, engulfed by images that kept dissolving.

"You need to stop thinking so much," said Adele. She was standing erect, as though guarding the room. "You're not well."

"What about Viera?" Elise cut in fearfully.

"Viera died many years ago. Her son Louis is no longer with us either, but before he died he had Anna with Ida, the lady you met, the one who brought us the letters."

"The pages from the botanical album . . ." Elise was suddenly troubled by a raging thirst.

"Ida and Anna recovered the letters in Cuba. They immediately got in touch with the town in France," Adele explained. "That's how they found you. The abbey still had the records from the war: the day you arrived and the day you were sent to your uncle Duval. They saved a lot of children in that abbey." Adele saw her mother shudder.

"By the time the letters reached Cuba, I was someone else. At least Danielle managed to prevent Viera from dying without knowing. When she read the letters, she must have realized she was never forgotten."

"Ida did all she could to find you," Adele concluded. "She didn't give up until she discovered your name in the abbey. We owe her a great debt."

"And Danielle sacrificed herself to save me, to fulfill *Maman* Claire's last wish." Elise's voice was a low murmur. "My sister Danielle . . . It's to her I owe the most."

☙❧

A week later, when she was being wheeled home, Elise came to a halt on the sidewalk where she had walked for the past decades. She gazed at the trees in the park. *They're still green*, she said to herself. She climbed the steps unaided behind Adele, who had already opened the front door for her. Elise leaned on the doorframe. Her home was a cell, buried in a bunker made of concrete and reddish bricks. Outside was an unreal garden.

The hallway was an endless bridge she had to cross to face the letters again. A wedding photograph was hanging on the wall. She couldn't recognize herself in a veil that covered half her face. At the far end was another photograph, of her aunt and uncle with a little girl. The girl's face wasn't hers: it was Danielle's.

In the living room, the letters were awaiting her. Carefully folded inside the ebony box, as if they had never fallen on the floor, as if no one had read them, as if they were still waiting to be sent to the far side of the ocean.

Elise's gentle voice broke the silence. She read all six, five of them addressed to Viera. All except one, the last, corresponded to seasons of the year. The undated letter was an order, a decree. And at that moment she realized it was meant for her. That was why her mother had not headed it with the usual "My little Viera."

Adele looked at her, intrigued. Her mother was reading in German, and repeated phrases out loud, as though trying to decipher them. The words were intertwined with drawings of plants and flowers.

"These letters have crossed the Atlantic several times. And look, now they're with us."

Raising her hand to her chest, Elise couldn't detect her heartbeats:

they were too weak. She wanted to count them one by one, as her father had taught her.

"I can't recall Papa's face; all I can make out is a very tall man. Mama saw the world through his eyes; she told us he was an angel, and yet she didn't follow his instructions for us all to travel together on the *Saint Louis*." Elise paused, smiling sadly. "So you see, one should never go against an angel's orders . . ."

She felt so dizzy she was unable to finish the sentence. The sun began to set, and the light in the room faded. With great effort, she went into the kitchen and came back with two candles. She placed them on the dining-room table, and lit them.

"'Blessed are You, Lord, our God, King of the universe, who has sanctified us with His commandments and commanded us to light the Shabbat candles,'" she said in German, then stared at the face of her beloved daughter and added, "'I will lift up mine eyes unto the mountains: from where shall my help come?'"

Adele watched her, uncomprehending. Elise raised her hands to her eyes, then came close to her daughter and pressed them softly against her face.

Elise went into her bedroom and returned clutching a small purple jewel case. She stopped in front of the picture window that looked out over the park. She sank into her favorite armchair and watched as the sun slowly sank below the horizon. As she stroked the damask upholstery, she recalled her beloved Marie-Louise's Atelier Plumes. She felt faint, and the jewel case fell at her feet.

"Mom!" cried Adele, rushing to help her. "We need to call the doctor!"

"I'm fine, Adele, fine. I need time, a little more time, to order my thoughts—alone. There's no doctor who can help me now. Pass me the case, will you?"

Inside were the ring and the diamond bracelet. Whereas once they had seemed so big and heavy, now they looked tiny, fragile.

"These are yours, Adele," she murmured, slipping them into her daughter's hand.

In the open box, Elise suddenly noticed a small compartment. When she groped in it with her index finger, she felt a sharp prick. Taken aback, she withdrew her hand, then tried a second time to discover what was hidden in this secret corner. Feeling more cautiously, she closed her eyes.

She carefully pulled a gold chain out of its hiding place. On it was a Star of David. She realized then that her father's gift had come back to her. She had no need to look for her glasses to read the inscription engraved on the tiny six-pointed star.

"All these years the truth was within my reach, but I preferred to stay blind." She sighed. "Papa, now I know you were always with me."

She took off the crucifix that had been with her since she had crossed the Atlantic and gestured to Adele for her to replace it with the chain with the Star of David. Then she said farewell to her with a long embrace.

"I want to be alone," she insisted, her voice faint.

Gazing at her tenderly, Adele left without another word.

In her armchair, Elise slid back into the shadows. It felt as if time was expanding; that her already fading body was slowly shriveling.

In her delirium, she sees herself thrown into a boat crammed with children. After more than a week on the high seas, an island filled with skyscrapers appears on the horizon. They've reached their destination. Other people's destination. In the distance, the Statue of Liberty stands proud and solitary. Finally, the boat reaches the port.

She runs to a customs official who is blocking her path. He is a wall, the frontier between today and yesterday. The uncle waiting at the quayside for her comes up and asks who she is. *My name is . . . I'm not who I am.* Maman *Claire isn't my mother. My mother . . .*

The official takes her back to the boat. She is alone, nobody else is sailing on the drifting liner. The uncle says goodbye, the definitive goodbye, the goodbye she deserves. On her return, Danielle is waiting for her; they embrace. This time, Danielle doesn't look at her resentfully; she smiles and wants to play with her, but there's no time, the ship is about to sail. It's her last chance. *Come on, Danielle! This is your place. Your uncle is there, waiting for you with open arms.* That's how it should have been.

In the same port she sees her mother with a suitcase. Viera is standing beside her. Elise runs toward them and all three walk away together. Viera is no longer a child, she's as tall as her mother. They cross a bridge, then a river, and stop to rest at the foot of a mountain. They're safe: there are no soldiers, nobody is wearing swastika armbands, nobody is pursuing them, rejecting them. The mother smiles happily. *And Papa?* Papa is waiting for us.

The mother takes grandfather's botanical album out of the suitcase. It's intact. There are no letters, there never were any. No prayers or pleas or lit candles.

They climb the mountain up to the eternal snows. On the summit everything is white, and the white is impeccable, spotless, pure. At the point closest to the sky, where snow and clouds mingle, they open a door and step into the Garden of Letters that no one else can see.

∽◦∽

Elise took her mother's sixth letter, her farewell, and pressed it to her chest. Closing her eyes, she stroked the gold chain, feeling the six points of the small star, her father's gift. With all her remaining strength she silently counted for the last time: *One, two, three, four, five, six . . .*

A faint voice in the darkened room:

"My name is Lina, Lina Sternberg."

Summer of 1942

Shalom

Mama

Author's Note

Oradour-sur-Glane

On the morning of Saturday, June 10, 1944, members of the Third Company of the Führer regiment, the feared paramilitary division of the Third Reich's Waffen-SS, surrounded the small village of Oradour-sur-Glane in the department of Haute-Vienne, in the Limoges region. They ordered the villagers to gather in the main square and locked the women and children in the church.

Most of the men were taken to nearby barns and machine-gunned. The women and children were burned alive in the church. Altogether, 642 people were massacred, including 207 children.

The 1,500 inhabitants of the village included some Jews and Spanish refugees from the Franco regime. The Nazis, in whose ranks were recruits from Alsace, burned the village houses and shops in an attempt to erase all traces of the crime. A few children who survived the massacre sought refuge in a nearby abbey, and were saved by the monks.

A few days earlier, an SS officer had been executed by partisans in the area.

After the end of the war, Charles de Gaulle's government decided to keep the ruins of Oradour-sur-Glane as a monument to the martyrs, a memorial of the Nazi atrocities committed on French soil.

MS *St. Louis*

On the evening of May 13, 1939, the transatlantic ocean liner *St. Louis* of the Hamburg-Amerika Linie (HAPAG) set sail from the port of Hamburg bound for Havana, Cuba. Some nine hundred passengers were on board, the majority German Jewish refugees.

The refugees had permits to disembark in Havana issued by Manuel Benítez, the general director of Cuba's Immigration Department. These were obtained through the HAPAG company.

A week before the liner sailed from Hamburg, the president of Cuba, Federico Laredo Brú, issued Decree 937 (named after the number of passengers due to be on board the *St. Louis*). This decree rendered invalid the landing permits signed by Benítez.

When the ship arrived in the port of Havana on Saturday, May 27, the Cuban authorities would not allow it to moor in the zone assigned to the HAPAG company. Instead, it had to anchor in the middle of the bay.

Only four Cubans and two non-Jewish Spaniards were allowed to disembark, as well as twenty-two refugees who had obtained permits from the Cuban State Department prior to the ones issued by Benítez, who could count on the support of the army commander, Fulgencio Batista.

The *St. Louis* sailed for Miami on June 2. When it was close to the US coast, Franklin D. Roosevelt's government refused entry into the United States. The Mackenzie King government in Canada also refused the ship entry.

So the *St. Louis* was forced to head back across the Atlantic toward Hamburg. A few days before it docked, the Joint Distribution Committee (JDC) negotiated an agreement for several countries to receive the refugees.

Great Britain accepted 287; France 224; Belgium 241; and the Netherlands 181. In September 1939, Germany declared war and the countries of continental Europe were soon occupied by Hitler's forces.

Only the 287 taken in by Great Britain remained safe. The majority of the other passengers from the *St. Louis* suffered the havoc of the war, or were killed in Nazi concentration camps.

March 5, 2018